DISHONORED
THE RETURN OF DAUD

DISHONORED
THE RETURN OF DAUD

ADAM CHRISTOPHER

TITAN BOOKS

PSF
Christop

DISHONORED: THE RETURN OF DAUD
Print edition ISBN: 9781783293056
E-book edition ISBN: 9781783293087

Published by Titan Books
A division of Titan Publishing Group Ltd
144 Southwark Street, London SE1 0UP

First edition: March 2018
10 9 8 7 6 5 4 3 2 1

Editorial Consultants:
Harvey Smith
Paris Nourmohammadi

Special thanks to Harvey Smith, Hazel Monforton,
Brittany Quinn, and everyone at Arkane Studios.

A CIP catalogue record for this title is available from the British Library.

Printed and bound in the United States.

DISHONORED

THE RETURN OF DAUD

PROLOGUE

THE VOID
4,000 years ago

"It is a common story: A person has stopped breathing, pinned under carriage wheels or some other tragic happenstance, and is thought to be dead. But when the weight is removed—they make a quick recovery! But nonetheless, for a moment or two, this person was lost to us, lost to the world itself.

And what did they experience while in this temporary death? Darkness? Nothingness? No, indeed not! They tell us, as so many before have, that they were in a particular place, and can describe it vividly. And who among us does not know this place?

Have we not all seen it in our dreams? This place we share, in the farthest reaches of our minds. The realm where nothing makes sense, where one is at once both lost and at home. The Void."

—WHISPERS FROM THE VOID, by Barnoli Mulani
Treatise on the Physical Existence of that Foreign Realm
[Excerpt]

The place is made of nothing but stone and ash, and is filled with nothing but the cold dark, and it smells of nothing but rust and corrosion, and it tastes of nothing but the sharp and sour tang of fear.

The boy stares up into the sky—although that's not what it is. There is no sky, just a blank curve of curling gray smoke, heavy and foreboding, that stretches from here to the end of the world. This and the two curling arms of shattered stone, twisting like the twin trunks of a petrified tree over the head of the stone slab on which he lies, are all the boy can see. The hands that grip the sides of his head are as solid as the altar beneath him and just as cold, and when he tries to turn his head, the hands just press harder, the fingertips squeezing his temples until he thinks his skull will cave in.

So the boy stares up into infinite nothing above, the not-sky that stretches above this forsaken place, this nowhere.

The *Void*.

The altar beneath him is cold, the stone so ancient it is more like metal, like it was carved out of a single lump of black iron, like the iron found in the hearts of fallen stars, the cold of it spreading through his flesh, soaking his very bones with a chill so deep it feels like he is lying on ice.

He tries to move his arms, but they are tied. His legs are also bound by rope, so tight and so rough that with every movement of his body the fibers carve into his skin, the burning pain as unbearable as the cold of the altar. He flexes his fingers, but there is nothing to hold, nothing to grip. The many golden rings that adorn each digit click hard against the stone.

But he did fight at first, struggling with all his strength as the cultists, their faces hidden in the deep folds of their lead-colored cloaks, carried him up the shallow stones and placed him on the altar. It was no use. There were so many of them, so many hands holding him, and while the boy was strong and while he writhed and screamed and screamed they held him with iron grips. He fought again as they tied him down on the slab, but all this did was exhaust what little energy he had left.

With their victim secured, the cultists had moved away. The boy had looked up, watching the congregation as they gathered on either side of the stone steps, their heads bowed, hands hidden in long, drooping sleeves. The boy began to scream again, his chest heaving as he drew in deep lungfuls of icy metallic air, but the men just watched in silence. When the boy was spent, his head fell back against the altar and two hands grabbed at him, pushing his skull down.

Now the boy blinks. If time passes here then he cannot count it, his mind fogged by the sickly sweet potions they made him drink and the colored sour smokes they made him breathe before bringing him to this awful nowhere. With the fight gone, his energy leeched by the desperate cold, the boy's head begins to spin, so it feels like the Void itself is orbiting around him.

He tries to remember his name. It is no use. He tries to remember his age—he is young, he knows that, even if he has lost count of the years of his life. Is he fifteen? Twenty? Maybe more. He doesn't remember, and the more he tries, the more he forgets.

Now he sees there is a man looming over him, standing at the head of the altar. The man turns and now the boy cannot see him, but he can hear him—the rustle of his cloak, the pad of his feet.

And then another sound, the *shrik* of metal on metal. The man returns, a black shadow filling his vision. The shadow moves and something flashes in the boy's vision, something held by the man high above his head. It is bright and bronze. The sudden blaze of unexpected color terrifies the boy.

It is a knife with two long, parallel blades that shine, reflecting a light that seems to be from elsewhere. A light that is bright and white and then orange and red, as though the knife is being turned slowly in front of a great fire even as it is held perfectly still by the cloaked man.

The others gathered around the altar and down the steps remain silent, their cowled heads turned up toward the sacrifice.

The man with the Twin-bladed Knife murmurs something but the boy cannot hear it, his head now filled with the sound of a keening wind. The fear that fills him suddenly expands, and he feels like he has been dropped down a deep, dark well. His stomach rolls, his throat is filled with bitter bile, and he finds the strength to pull at the ropes again, one last time, as though it would make any difference at all.

It does not. The ropes hold firm, as do the hands that grasp his head, forcing his chin up, his face now tilted back so he can see the face of the man holding the knife.

The face of his executioner.

There is a flash like lightning, although it is accompanied

by no thunder, and when the boy blinks the tears from his eyes the flashing continues, and the boy doesn't know if it is the Void or his mind or the impossible light shining from the knife.

The boy screams.

The blade sweeps to the side, held high in the air, and the man murmurs again.

The blade sweeps across, low, opening the boy's neck. His scream is cut short, replaced by a whistling gurgle. His limbs twitch, his fingernails scraping the hard surface of the altar, as it quickly becomes slick with blood.

And then the boy is still. He stares at the nothingness above him as his life slips away.

He dies.

And something terrible is born.

CHAPEL OF THE SISTERS OF THE ORACULAR ORDER, BALETON, GRISTOL
14th Day, Month of Songs, 1851

"Much has been said about the blind Sisters of the Oracular Order. In truth, their eyes function just as well as yours or mine. However, they do endeavor to become blind to distractions and frivolities. They will, if necessity bids them, walk among us, wearing richly hued blindfolds or otherwise covering their eyes. In this way they remain 'at all times ready to see things clearly.'"

—ON THE ORACULAR ORDER
Douglas Hardwick, Historian

The Cloister of Prophecy was a large, circular chamber situated in the very center of the Chapel of the Sisters of the Oracular Order, the hub from which the seven wings of the chapel proper radiated. The bright white stone from which it was built had been expertly shaped to form a mathematically perfect room, and the high vaulted ceiling gave the illusion that the Cloister was somehow open to the air.

Arranged around a central dais were six rectangular slabs of black marble, each curved to match the arc of the Cloister wall. In front of five of the slabs five Sisters knelt on black cushions, their high-collared, silver-and-white tunics immaculate. Although their eyes were hidden behind red ceremonial blindfolds, the thin veils were merely a traditional, symbolic part of their uniform, rather than serving the purpose for which they were, perhaps historically, designed. As such, each Sister was able to focus their attention, unimpeded, on the member of their order who knelt on a red cushion on the central dais.

By the sixth slab knelt a Sister unlike the others, dressed in a long black-and-red tunic. This was the High Oracle herself, Pelagia Themis, and for her to be attending the Ceremony of Prophecy in person was a rare event indeed. But she was here for a specific purpose—the Sisters had been in position for hours now, the Ceremony well underway and proceeding exactly as the High Oracle had planned.

Which was... *badly*.

Sister Kara frowned as she knelt on the central red cushion. She swayed on her knees, her lips moving soundlessly, as though she was reading something inside her head.

"Sister Kara."

She jerked back at the interruption, nearly sliding off her cushion, and turned toward the voice of the High Oracle. Then she adjusted herself on the cushion, her knees burning in agony after so many hours trying—and failing—to read the Prophecy.

"Yes, High Oracle?"

"The gift of the Prophecy of the Sisters of the Oracular Order is a precious one, Kara," said Pelagia. "We bear the Prophecy not just as a power, but as a responsibility, a gift that cannot be wasted. Much rides on the information we report to our brother, the High Overseer."

Sister Kara bowed her head. "Yes, High Oracle."

Pelagia nodded, then glanced to her left. "Ready again, Sister Beatris?"

Beatris lifted herself off her cushion and leaned over the device on the floor next to her; a small, compact contraption of metal and wood, a long copper listening horn, pointed toward the dais and Sister Kara—an audiograph recorder. She tore the last section of punch card out of the slot on the side, then pulled a fresh section carefully out from the roll inside the machine and aligned the edge with the recording pins. Satisfied, she sat back down on the cushion, her hand hovering over the audiograph controls.

"Recording ready, High Oracle."

Pelagia turned back to the dais. "Now, we'll try again, Sister Kara. And we will keep trying until the complete prophecy is read."

Kara's blindfolded face tilted toward the floor in front of her. "I'm sorry, High Oracle. The prophecy is… difficult."

Pelagia pursed her lips. What Kara said was perfectly true—the Ritual of Prophecy *was* difficult, a skill that required years of practice and a lifetime of dedication. Not only that, Sister Kara was a novice, having joined the Chapel at Baleton only a year before. To be part of the Ritual for one so inexperienced was unheard of, but that was exactly why Pelagia was using her.

What she hadn't told Kara—or any of the others, for that matter—was the *real* reason for her visit. Because she wasn't here to personally supervise a novice attempting her first prophecy. No. She was here to gather more evidence, data she hoped would confirm a theory—one that had occupied virtually all her thoughts these last few weeks.

The Prophecies were being… well, *interfered* with. That was the only way she could describe it. Somehow, what the Sisters were seeing was *not* coming to pass—Pelagia had spent several months reviewing the prophecies sent to the High Overseer in Dunwall, even going back and listening to the original audiographs to ensure there had been no errors in their transcription, or manipulation of their content.

But the facts spoke for themselves. Something was wrong—something that would have profound repercussions not just for the Oracular Order but for the Empire *itself*, if the root cause could not be identified and eliminated. The prophecies of the Sisterhood were used for a multitude of purposes and helped to steer great decisions of state. They could be used to declare war and peace alike, to aid in negotiations between the nation-states of the Empire of the Isles, down to planning crop rotations, fighting natural disasters and even predicting the weather. The fate of the world—the course of history itself—pivoted on the reports they fed to the High Overseer of the Abbey of the Everyman, Yul Khulan, who in turn reviewed the prophecies and disseminated the important information they contained to the relevant parties across the Isles.

The Sisters of the Oracular Order were the most powerful group in the whole Empire.

And interference in their work could not be tolerated.

Which was why the High Oracle herself was here, in Baleton. The Chapel in the small city on the western coast of Gristol had never hosted the Order's leader in its entire history. And that was why she had chosen Kara, the young novice, to read the Prophecy. Her lack of experience and training would, Pelagia hoped, reveal more about the *mechanism* of the interference, the novice's unshielded, naked mind more open to see and read what the other Sisters—trained, experienced, disciplined—had long since learned to disregard, to tune out.

So went Pelagia's theory, anyway.

"Yes," she said. "The Ritual of the Prophecy is difficult. But, Sister Kara, did you expect anything else?"

"I'm… I'm sorry, High Oracle."

Pelagia sighed. Around the circle, the five other Sisters knelt in silence, their own bodies, Pelagia had no doubt, screaming for a rest. But the five other Sisters were among the most senior of the Baleton Chapel. They were used to the discomfort. They were warriors and athletes as much as they were prophets, their bodies trained as much as their minds. Discomfort was a central part of their lives.

"You have nothing to apologize for, Sister," said Pelagia.

"But if you wish to truly embrace our Order, if you wish to give yourself to it, wholly, then you must learn the Ritual of Prophecy. You must learn to reach out with your mind, dream about the Void, to see through it in order to read what the future will be. Remember, we are here to help. The seven Sisters are all part of the ritual, together. So concentrate, and reach out to us, draw on our strength to fuel your own." Pelagia paused. "I am the High Oracle. I am here as your guide. Draw on *my* strength and read the future."

Sister Kara bowed her head, then lifted it toward the ceiling. "Yes, High Oracle. I am ready."

"Good," said Pelagia. "Then we begin again. Sister Beatris, resume the recording."

Beatris nodded and depressed the activation lever on the audiograph recorder. The machine whirred into life, the gentle clicking of the recording pins sounding like distant rainfall as it bounced around the circular walls of the chamber, the punch card slowly crawling out of the slot on the side of the device.

On the dais, Kara lifted herself up, then settled back on her haunches, resting her hands on her thighs. She rolled her neck and closed her eyes behind the red veil.

"The High Oracle guides you, Sister," whispered Pelagia. "You have nothing to fear. Let the future show itself."

The Sisters remained silent. The audiograph recorder chattered. Kara began to sway slightly as she drew short, sharp breaths between clenched teeth.

"Relax, Sister, relax," said Pelagia. "Open your mind and let the Ritual of the Prophecy steer you toward the light. Relax, relax, relax."

Kara rolled her neck again, then curled her fingers into fists. She stretched her neck back, her veiled eyes screwed shut, her face twisting into a grimace.

The audiograph recorder whirred, and the Sisters—and their High Oracle—waited for Kara's vision of the future.

Day passed into night, and the Cloister of Prophecy grew dark. As the seven Sisters knelt in position, another member of the order slipped in and lit the four old-fashioned whale-tallow lamps that stood at the compass points in the circular room then retreated, leaving the others to their work.

The High Oracle and her Sisters waited. They would have no rest, no food, no water, until the Ritual of Prophecy was complete.

Another hour.

And then Sister Kara gasped, taking a huge, gulping breath as though surfacing from a deep, cold pool of water.

On the High Oracle's left, Sister Hathena jumped, startled. She glanced at the High Oracle, her eyes wide and afraid behind the see-through veil.

Yes, thought Pelagia. *She can sense it too.*

Interference.

The High Oracle watched Sister Kara, the young novice rising and falling, rising and falling on her knees. Pelagia felt Sister Hathena's veiled eyes on her, and suspected that any fear she had sensed earlier was now gone. In its place, she thought she could feel a growing anger as Hathena realized Pelagia's plan.

Yes, she knew she had broken all protocol and tradition by selecting Kara to read the prophecy. And yes, she also knew there were reasons why such traditions existed. The Ritual of Prophecy was not just difficult; it was potentially dangerous for the untrained. Without such training—*years* of it—the naked mind could wander far into the labyrinth of the Void, following visions and songs that came not from the depths of the future, but from the depths of the prophet's own subconscious.

Without such training, a mind could get lost forever.

Pelagia knew it was a risk. So did the others. But what the others didn't know was that the risk was worth it. The future of the Order was at stake. And Pelagia Themis was the High Oracle, and the High Oracle's word was the law.

She pushed the guilt away, ignored Sister Hathena's stare, and focused on the disciplines of the Oracular Order, reciting the Seven Strictures to herself to clear her senses. Then, her emotions back under control, Pelagia lifted her chin and spoke, the first sounds recorded on Sister Beatris's audiograph in many, many hours.

"Tell us, Sister," said Pelagia quietly. "Tell us, child. Tell us what you see. Let the Prophecy speak through you. Let the future become clear in the eye of your mind."

Kara opened her eyes. Pelagia could see the girl's eyes through her red veil—they were glazed, unfocused. Kara had done it, finally.

Kara shuddered. "I see… I see…"

Kara gasped. Two other Sisters in the circle jumped, but Pelagia ignored them. Hathena hadn't taken her eyes off the High Oracle.

"Tell us, Sister," said Pelagia. "Divine the prophecy and let it be known to us all."

"I see…"

"Speak, Kara, speak."

Kara gasped again, rising up on her knees. Now Sister Beatris exchanged a glance with Sister Hathena, Beatris's thumb hovering over the audiograph lever. Pelagia didn't take her eyes from the dais, but she waved at the Sister.

"Let the recording continue, Beatris. We are close. We are very close."

"Oracle," said Hathena, turning on her cushion. "Oracle, this is not right. We must stop."

Pelagia hissed, ignoring her. She rose up onto her knees to address the novice on the dais.

"Kara, speak! Tell us what you read, Sister."

Kara gasped a third time, then dropped onto her cushion, her legs folded awkwardly under her. She turned her head, twisting it sideways like a hound listening for its master's voice. Pelagia watched as the muscles at the back of Kara's jaw bunched as the young novice ground her teeth. Kara began to pound her fists into her legs, blood trickling from between her clenched fingers as her nails dug deep into her palms.

"Focus, Kara. *Focus!*"

Hathena shook her head and stood up, clearly unconcerned with breaking protocol. "High Oracle— Pelagia—stop this! Stop this. *Now.*"

Pelagia stood. "Kara, hear me—"

That was when Kara screamed. Then she stood, and…

And she laughed.

"I see it!" Kara lifted her arms up, her face split by a wide grin. "I can *see* it!"

By now the other four Sisters, until then as still and as silent as the black marble slabs behind them, became restless, first looking at each other, then at the High Oracle, then back at their Sister on the dais.

"Tell us, Sister!" said Pelagia. "Read the prophecy."

"I…" Kara lowered her arms and bent her head again. She leaned forward, craning her back, twisting her neck around. "I see… I see…"

"Tell us."

"I see shadows," Kara said, her voice now a harsh, sibilant whisper. "Many shadows, blue and dark. I see light, blue and bright. I see… there is a path, a way forward, but it is blocked. There is a curtain. A veil. A veil of blue. The veil… it moves. I can see… hands? I can see hands. There are many hands. They move behind the veil. Pushing. *Clawing*. Pulling at the veil, reaching out, reaching out…"

"Yes, Kara," said Pelagia. "Reaching out. Reaching for you! Go to them, Kara. Go to them!"

"Oracle!" Hathena broke the circle, walking over to Pelagia and looking down at her. "Pelagia, there is heresy at work. I felt it! Stop this, before Kara is lost."

Pelagia paid no heed. On the dais, Kara twisted on her cushion, rising and falling, her breathing becoming faster, shallower. She clenched and unclenched her hands, smearing the white of her tunic with blood.

"I see a veil… I see a veil… I see a veil. The hands that reach… The hands that reach…"

A thin line of blood spilled from Kara's nose. She didn't appear to notice as the blood ran down, around her mouth, staining her top teeth.

Hathena spun around. Before Pelagia could stop her, the Sister had stepped up onto the dais in front of Kara. The novice didn't seem to notice she was there, she just kept bobbing and weaving.

"I see a veil… I see a veil. The many hands!"

Hathena knelt down so she was on the same level as Kara and grabbed the novice's wrists. She pulled Kara's hands toward her, but Kara fought against her, the two women locked together in what looked to be an equal struggle. Finally Hathena let go and fell back down the dais steps, landing in front of Beatris, knocking the horn of the audiograph recorder. She pushed herself up on her hands.

"Kara, listen to me! Find the path and come back to us! There is no prophecy. Come back and rejoin your Sisters."

"The many hands… The many hands… The blue light that is blue…"

Hathena stood and, tearing the red veil from her face, she turned, looking around the circle.

"What's the matter with you all? Will nobody help me?"

The others exchanged glances but didn't move. Hathena moved back to the High Oracle, standing directly in front of her.

"High Oracle, please. Stop this!"

Pelagia looked over Hathena's shoulder at Sister Kara writhing on the dais, whispering heresies as blood continued to run from her nose—and now her mouth, her ears, even her eyes.

She had found out what she wanted. Her fears were confirmed. And now the Ritual of Prophecy was killing Kara.

Pelagia's hand dropped to her belt, her fingers playing over the pommel of the ceremonial mace carried by all of the Sisters of the Oracular Order.

Hathena glanced down, then backed away, shaking her head. "No. Pelagia, no, you can't—"

The High Oracle stepped forward, lifting her mace from her belt. With her other hand she pointed at Beatris. "Enough! Stop the recording."

Beatris operated the recording lever. The machine stopped with a heavy clunk.

Hathena opened her mouth to speak, but Pelagia pushed past her, her shove sending the Sister careening to the floor. The High Oracle mounted the dais. The mace in her hand felt suddenly very, very heavy.

Kara didn't even know she was there. She had calmed, and was now kneeling, her head upturned, her lips moving, although she didn't speak.

The other Sisters stood. Hathena was shouting, but

Pelagia blotted the sound out, reciting the Seven Strictures inside her head, over and over and over again.

The prophecy was being interfered with. Someone had found a way, *somehow*, to influence the visions, to despoil the power of the Sisters of the Oracular Order.

It had to be some kind of witchcraft. There was no other explanation.

Heresy.

Then the High Oracle swung her arm back, raising the mace. Behind her, the others in the circle called out—Hathena included. She pushed herself up from the floor and dived toward Pelagia, grabbing the High Oracle's arm, yanking it back with enough force to send both of them falling to the floor. Pelagia's mace clattered away across the stones; she struggled to rise, but Hathena was faster, shoving the High Oracle away as she scrambled back to where Kara had collapsed onto the embroidered cushion, her curled body wracked with sobs.

Pelagia stood and pulled the veil off her face. "Hathena, you dare to interfere!"

Hathena wrapped her arms around Kara. She regarded Pelagia over the top of Kara's shaking head. "You were going too far, High Oracle."

Pelagia paused, the silence in the Cloister of Prophecy disturbed only by Kara's weeping. As Pelagia stepped up onto the dais and looked down at the novice, Hathena pulled her even closer.

Nobody spoke, nobody moved. Then Pelagia turned and pointed at Beatris. "Destroy the audiograph recording, immediately. *Burn it!*"

Beatris, shaking, began pulling the punch card reel from the machine. The High Oracle turned back to Hathena, the two women looking at each other as time seemed to stretch out to eternity.

Then Pelagia said, "We had to know, Sister."

Hathena stared at her. "There had to be another way."

"The future of the Sisters of the Oracular Order hangs in the balance," said Pelagia. "We cannot allow the Ritual of Prophecy to be interfered with." She looked at the other Sisters, cowering from their leader. "There is heresy at work," she said. "And we must work to fight it."

She turned back to Hathena, then took a deep breath. "But I must thank you, Sister. Perhaps I allowed myself to be overcome. Look after Kara. You may suspend your duties until she has recovered. I must meditate on my actions and consider a better way forward."

Hathena held her gaze for a moment, then she nodded. Pelagia turned and marched out of the chamber without another word.

After she was gone, Hathena glanced over to the corner of the Cloister of Prophecy, where the High Oracle's mace lay. As Kara's weeping began to subside, Hathena shifted her position, only now uncurling her fingers from the grip of her own mace on her belt.

PART ONE
THE KNIFE OF DUNWALL

1

GREAVES AUXILIARY WHALE SLAUGHTERHOUSE 5, SLAUGHTERHOUSE ROW, DUNWALL
18th Day, Month of Earth, 1852

"He'd looked into Jessamine Kaldwin's eyes at the moment her life slipped away. And in that moment a thought occurred to him: he'd made a mistake. He'd been misled. That kind of thinking was useless. She was just as dead, whether he regretted it or not. But he'd seen his true face reflected in her eyes; seen himself for what he really was. Not a renowned assassin, not some great shaper of history. Just another playing piece in an unknowable game."

—THE KNIFE OF DUNWALL
Excerpt from a penny novel, Chapter 3

He knelt on the hard, wet floor of the ruined slaughterhouse, glanced around at the neatly ordered piles of rubble, and sighed. He pushed the top of his deep hood back a little and tugged absentmindedly on the bottom of his jerkin, wet from the night rain. He pulled at his beard with a gloved hand.

Daud considered his situation, and he sighed.

So, this was it. Weeks—*months*—of traveling, of crisscrossing the Empire. Months of following rumors and whispers, of listening to stories with no endings, of seeking out strange cults, chasing leads that led nowhere. Months of searching, scrambling for what little information there was, grasping at the threads, pulling them gently, as though they would break in his grasp. *This* was it: a pile of rubble in the cavernous, burned-out shell of a whale oil factory in an unsavory quarter of the wettest bloody city in all the Isles.

It was the right place; he was just far too late. The stories were true—something had happened in the factory. Something vital to his mission. But whatever calamity had reduced the Greaves Auxiliary Slaughterhouse 5 to a broken shell, it had happened months ago.

All that time and effort wasted. The factory had been important, but now it was a dead end.

Daud stood, planted his hands on his hips, and tilted his head as he regarded the nearest rubble pile, as though viewing it from a different angle would somehow make any kind of difference at all.

No. It was *not* a wasted effort. This was *not* a dead end. He told himself that, over and over. Yes, he was visiting the scene months after the event, but even he couldn't bend time that far. That was out of his control.

What *was* in his control was what he did now. He was here, he had made it. So now he could search for clues. Yes, the trail was cold—but he would find something.

He had to.

And true enough, the broken mix of ironwork, brick, and blocks of stone was interesting. Altogether, it occupied half of what was left of the factory floor, on the street side of the building's shell, the half that was still mostly intact. On the other side, the river side, the entire side of the building was missing, the gaping maw open to the elements, with fingers of surviving superstructure reaching up into the dark sky and out over the dark river. Most of that side must have collapsed into the water, and while Daud could see the river was mostly clear, there was foamy wash close to the riverbank as the Wrenhaven tumbled over a fair amount of building wreckage lurking just below the surface. The river was a vital working waterway for Dunwall and clearly a great deal of effort had been made to dredge it. The recovered material had first been piled back into the factory, and then the real work had begun.

Whatever had happened, it had been big—big enough to investigate, big enough for officials to spend time moving, sorting, and cataloguing the rubble, which was neatly arranged, by material and by size, each piece daubed with a number in white paint that shone luminously in the night, reflecting back what little moonlight there was with surprising brightness.

An explosion was the official story. On the last leg of his journey, traveling east from Potterstead after landing back in Gristol, Daud had poured over every newspaper report he had managed to collect since he had linked rumor to fact, identifying the event in Dunwall as the pivot point on which his mission would succeed or fail.

The official story was straightforward enough, although it had taken some time to piece together something that felt closer to the whole picture from the myriad of different reports, each one sensationalized or editorialized depending on the newspaper, the personal whims of the journalist in question, and their targeted reading audience. But what he had managed to learn was this:

On the fifteenth day of the Month of Darkness, 1851— a full eight months ago now—there had been an industrial accident at the Greaves Auxiliary Slaughterhouse 5, situated on the banks of the Wrenhaven River, at the far eastern corner of Slaughterhouse Row. Although the specific reason had never been disclosed, there had been an explosion, big enough to not only destroy most of the factory itself, but damage several other buildings in the district, forcing the authorities to put up a cordon—for the public's own safety—manned by the City Watch, effectively sealing off an area of several blocks, with the ruined factory at the center.

A cordon that today, eight months later, was still in place.

Daud found that interesting. He had easily avoided the lazy patrols of the City Watch and slipped into the restricted zone to find no damage at all to any of the other buildings in the block. Which meant the barriers had nothing to do with public safety. The authorities didn't want people seeing what they were doing.

But that was it. Nothing further was reported, save for an editorial a day later on the dangers of whale oil. The *Dunwall Courier* reminded readers that the extraction and refining process was difficult and not without risk. It concluded by noting that the Empress of the Isles herself, Emily Kaldwin, had called in representatives of the Greaves Lightning Oil Company to Dunwall to provide her with a full report on the incident.

He hadn't believed it when he had first read it and, bringing it to mind again, he still didn't. He knew two things. Firstly, that this was no whale oil explosion—the substance *was* unstable, true, but even a storage tank rupture couldn't cause this much damage. And secondly, an official investigation into a simple industrial accident didn't take eight months, no matter how inefficient Dunwall bureaucracy was.

He was in the right place. *It* had been here.

He straightened up and looked around, noting the newer struts and props that had been installed to support the remaining three walls of the factory, the largest segments of which still rose to a prodigious height. The ruin was being preserved, at least for the moment, until the official work was finished.

This was fine. In fact, this was better than fine. Because it had been eight months, and they were *still* going through the rubble, which meant they hadn't found it. Not yet.

He still had a chance. The trail was perhaps not as cold as he had thought.

But was the factory itself a dead end? He turned and walked slowly along the rows of rubble, scanning the pieces and their numbers, willing some clue, some piece of evidence that had somehow escaped the notice of the official investigator to leap up at him. As he walked he lifted the edge of his hood a little more, then glanced up to the open sky. It had finally stopped raining, but the factory floor was now swimming in two inches of water. There were City Watch patrols out in the streets of the restricted zone, and he moved carefully, not making a sound. Not that it was difficult for him. Silence, stealth and secrecy had been his bread and butter once. And now, after all this time, it had been easy to fall back into the old ways.

Perhaps a little too easy.

He stopped and exhaled slowly, controlling his breathing and the growing feeling of doubt that was blossoming in his belly.

He was too late. It wasn't here. Maybe it never had been. Maybe the stories were just that.

That was when he heard it—a splash, boots slopping through water, someone clumsily entering the factory, thinking they were alone.

Daud immediately crouched into a combat stance, years of training and a lifetime of experience guiding him almost without conscious thought. Still hidden in the dark he darted away from the rubble, toward a long rectangular depression cut into the factory floor to his right—a whale oil overflow tank, choked with debris and filled with water. But there was still enough space to crouch low and observe the intruder unseen.

The light from a hooded lantern caught the wall on the other side of the factory, then swept around as the newcomer moved forward, out of the shadows near the street entrance and into a shaft of moonlight streaming in through the broken wall. The intruder wasn't a guard of the City Watch, out on his patrol. The man belonged to another kind of order altogether—an order infinitely more capable and dangerous.

The intruder wore black breeches underneath a long charcoal-gray tunic, belted at the waist and harnessed with narrower leather straps over the shoulders, the wide cuffs embellished with bold gold motifs woven into the cloth. His face was hidden behind a golden mask, the features molded into a scowling, twisted visage of anger, the forehead engraved with a symbol, a horizontal pitchfork passing through a large capital C.

An Overseer, a member of the militarized faction of the Abbey of the Everyman. Brutal zealots, deployed only for very particular reasons, situations where black magic and witchcraft—*heresies*—were suspected.

Now, that was interesting. An Overseer in the ruined factory. No wonder the authorities wanted to keep people away. Which meant…

The stories were true. It had been here. And they were still looking for it.

The Twin-bladed Knife was *real*.

And he was getting closer.

The Overseer strode across the factory floor, passing his lantern beam over the rubble, over the walls, making no attempt at stealth.

Of course, it was no wonder the City Watch patrols had been so clearly disinterested in their duties that Daud had been able to practically walk straight past them. The City Watch and the Abbey of the Everyman had an uneasy, suspicious relationship—or at least they had, when he had last been in Dunwall. If the Overseers were here, then the Abbey was in charge. The City Watch would resent their authority and would resent being assigned to simple guard duty while the Overseers gave the orders.

He hadn't seen any other Overseers on his way in, but then again, he hadn't exactly dawdled outside. With the cordon in place, his primary goal had been to get into the factory quickly. It had been sheer luck that he hadn't run into them.

And it was sheer luck that one had come in now, alone.

The Overseer turned, facing away from the debris-filled whale oil tank.

Now was his chance. Time to truly test himself, to see how much of the old ways he really did remember.

Time for the Knife of Dunwall to come out of hiding.

Daud raised himself up, fists clenched. He exhaled slowly, focusing his mind, drawing on a tether to somewhere else. A tether he'd grown increasingly reluctant to use. But Daud was nothing if not practical—if you had a tool, it was stupid not to use it. An opportunity like this wouldn't present itself again, of that he was sure.

As the Overseer moved away, Daud dashed forward, boots silent in the two inches of water on the factory floor. He reached out with his left hand, the Mark of the Outsider engraved into the back of it burning fiercely under his glove as he drew on the power that had been granted to him so many, many years ago.

The Overseer had no idea what was coming as Daud leapt through the Void, transversing the fifty yards that separated them in a blink of an eye before grabbing the Overseer around the neck with a forearm and pulling backward, dragging him off balance. The Overseer grunted and dropped his lantern, his feet kicking in the water as Daud reached out again, transversing the pair of them up onto the top of one of the makeshift props that held up the wall opposite, then again, up over the crumbling wall of the factory and onto the moonlit rooftops of Dunwall, dragging the now unconscious Overseer with him.

It was time to get some answers.

2

A (VERY) HIGH ROOFTOP, TOWER DISTRICT, DUNWALL
18th Day, Month of Earth, 1852

"The last Overseer, no doubt consumed with terror at seeing his brothers fall so easily, sank to his knees and begged for mercy. Daud spoke a single word that made my entrails squirm in my belly upon hearing it. The Overseer shrieked like a madman until his mask split in two, as though struck by some hammer and chisel, and a stream of blood gushed forth from the crack, bathing Daud's boots.

I closed my eyes at that point, too overwhelmed to witness any further atrocity. I could only hope that if that foul heretic discovered me next, my life would end swiftly. But when I opened my eyes, Daud was nowhere to be seen. That was the last I ever saw of the Knife of Dunwall."

—THE KNIFE OF DUNWALL, A SURVIVOR'S TALE
From a street pamphlet containing a sensationalized
sighting of the assassin Daud

Daud leaned back against the damp old brick of the gargantuan chimney, and watched as the sun rose over the city of Dunwall. The sky was clearing, but enough thick clouds lingered to turn the sky brilliant banded shades of yellow, orange, red, even purple, and in the growing morning heat the rain of the night was evaporating from the ocean of slate that made up the collected rooftops of the city, creating a thin mist that smelled of clean stone. From this altitude, standing on the high metal gantry that orbited the chimney at nearly its summit, the view was nothing short of spectacular. Stretched out all around, Dunwall glittered, as though the entire city had been scattered with diamonds.

It was beautiful. Daud allowed himself a small smile as he finally admitted that fact. He'd been away so long that he'd forgotten the true splendor of the Empire's capital, the largest, densest city in all the Isles. His memory, he realized, had been selective, his subconscious choosing to remind him only of the stench, of the rot and decay, of the violence and pain and death between narrow alleys of crumbling stone.

Of course, those memories, along with the feelings they elicited, were genuine. Decades ago, Daud had made Dunwall his home, and here he had done terrible things under the cover of the city's shadows. The side of the city that he knew—the side that had been his home, with all its danger and darkness—had been the underbelly.

But there was another side to the city, one that, perhaps, Daud had not seen enough of. Up here, he at least had a glimpse of that splendor.

Daud grunted a laugh, amused at the way his mind had wandered. It wasn't like him to think this way, but then he had been away a long time, and he was older than he cared to admit and had perhaps changed over the years more than he realized. The city had changed too. His time as leader of the Whalers was so long ago, the activities of his group no doubt now just an unpleasant footnote to an unpleasant period of the Empire's history. A period he had played a key role in. Not a day went by when he didn't remember, and he knew he would carry those memories—memories that grew heavier and darker with each passing year—to his grave.

He had tried to forget. Exiled from the city on pain of death at the hands of the Royal Protector, Corvo Attano, Daud had run. He'd got as far from Dunwall—from Gristol itself—as he could. He went to Morley, where he lasted a year in Caulkenny before getting tired of being around people. He went to Tyvia, settling not in Dabokva or Tamarak but heading inland, skirting the tundra and finally settling outside a village near Pradym, in the barren northern territories. There he built his own shack and spent the days harvesting lumber and the nights carving the endless cords of chopped wood into intricate animal forms: bears, wolves, owls. He was especially fond of carving owls.

His hair and beard grew long and he spent six years avoiding the curious residents of the village as much as he could, until one night he saw them gathering with torches and he slipped away before they came to burn his cabin down, the more suspicious village leaders ready to accuse the strange hermit in the woods of witchcraft.

He had walked north and had thought of nothing but Dunwall. It seemed that the farther he got from the city the more the place pulled at him, like he was tied to its very stones, in the same way that the Mark of the Outsider had tied him to the Void. Daud almost turned around, surrendering to his doom and the inevitable return to Dunwall, but once he reached Wei-Ghon, he felt a change come over him. He had never been one to give much thought to any kind of greater meaning in life, but in Wei-Ghon, at last, he began to wonder whether he could finally let go of his past—or if he could go further. Reinvent himself. Take a new name, start a new life. He even began to sleep again—properly sleep, not the semi-conscious doze his body was used to, his mind slumbering but ever alert for approaching danger.

For the first time in *years*, Daud dared to wonder if he had found a life he could actually live.

And then the dreams started.

They were all the same. He was a Whaler, holding a bloody knife as he stood over the body of Empress Jessamine Kaldwin. The city of Dunwall was crawling with an infinite swarm of rats. They raced up his legs, covering his body, crawling behind his mask, clawing at his eyes, eating his face. And through the bloody ruin of his eyes, Daud saw the Outsider standing before him, arms folded, silent, watchful, the corner of his mouth turned up in an evil, knowing smirk. And then the Outsider turned, gesturing the landscape around them, and Daud's final dying vision was not of Dunwall but of Karnaca—the city of his birth, a city he had not seen in more than twenty years—on fire. The air filled not with smoke but endless black clouds of bloodflies, the beating of their wings the sound of the end of the world.

Daud woke up screaming the first night. The screams became less frequent over the days and weeks that followed, but only because he found himself afraid to sleep. But the night terrors didn't stop when he was awake, because all he could see when he closed his eyes was the Outsider's face. His black eyes; his black smile.

Daud left Wei-Ghon and headed south to Karnaca, the capital city of Serkonos and the southernmost country of the Empire of the Isles.

His home.

The journey had been long, but Daud had used the time well. He had come up with a plan that would free him from his past, once and for all. He gave himself one last task that he hoped would atone for his lifetime of anger and hate and violence and deceit. One final mission that would release him, forever.

And not just him—if he was successful, he would free the whole world from the grip of the interfering black-eyed bastard.

Daud was going to kill the Outsider.

The only question was how? The answer eluded Daud for a long time—until he began to hear rumors of something that sounded like the solution. It started with a story whispered in a back-alley drinking hole, a story that had taken Daud six weeks just to get one complete, vaguely linear version of.

It wasn't much, but it was enough—and Daud took the fact that the rumor had reached him just as his nightmares reached their peak as a sign. From where, he didn't care to speculate—his own addled mind, probably. But now Daud knew his self-declared mission wasn't just the product of an aging and bored mind fighting against an empty and directionless life.

The mission was real. More than that, it was *possible*. The Outsider would die by his hand, and he knew exactly how to do it—and with what. Because the rumors told of an artifact, an object straight out of myth and legend. A relic of another time, another place. A weapon—a bronze knife with twinned blades.

The knife that had *created* the Outsider.

It was real, and it had reappeared in the world. Or so the rumor went, the story fueled not by some cultish interest in the heresies of the Outsider but speculation as to how much such an object would be worth on the black market.

There was a small, secretive trade in magical artifacts; Daud knew that well enough. And the Twin-bladed Knife would be the most sought-after relic of them all.

And as the Twin-bladed Knife had brought the Outsider into being, it was—so the legend went—the only weapon in existence that could end him.

That was good enough for Daud. And now his mission had a concrete objective, because to fulfill it—to kill the Outsider, to free himself and the world from that malign influence—he had to find the knife.

His search began where the rumors ended. In Dunwall, at the ruined factory.

"Urghhh…"

Daud's reverie was interrupted by the moan from the body at his feet. The Overseer lay on his back on the gantry, mask still in place and reflecting the growing dawn light. As he began to stir, Daud nudged his head with the toe of his boot. The Overseer jerked awake.

"Where am I?"

Daud swung his leg over the Overseer and stood astride him. The Overseer jerked again, sucking a lungful of air in through his mask before coughing violently. He lifted himself up onto one elbow and leaned over to spit a rope of watery mucus through the mask's grimacing mouth.

Daud lifted one boot and planted it on the Overseer's chest, shoving the man back onto the platform. The Overseer's fingers clawed at Daud's calf as the assassin pushed down, hard.

"Please! What are… you… doing…?"

Daud moved swiftly, dropping down onto one knee, the impact winding the man beneath him. Daud grabbed a handful of his coat at the collar, pulling the man up from the gantry as much as he could. Daud leaned down until the tip of his beard touched the metal chin of the

Overseer's mask. His voice was a low growl. "You'll speak only to answer my questions. If you ask any of your own, you die. If your answers are not to my satisfaction, you die. If you tell me any lies, I'll know, and you die." He tightened his grip on the tunic. "Do we have an understanding?"

The Overseer breathed hard. This close, Daud could see the man's eyes through the mask. They were very blue, very wide, and very wet.

Daud took a deep draw of the cool morning air. He could smell the sharp electric tang of the metal platform beneath him as it warmed in the sun. He could smell the earthy scent of the Wrenhaven River. But there, faint now but growing stronger, the acrid, sour stink of fear wafting from the Overseer beneath him.

Now *that* was the Dunwall he remembered.

"Nod if you understand," he said. At this the Overseer nodded quickly. A whimper sounded from behind the mask. Daud paused. Was the man... was he *crying*? Daud snarled and yanked the mask off. He frowned. Daud wasn't sure what he expected to see underneath, but part of him was surprised.

Daud was older than he cared to admit, and he had been away from Dunwall for a long time. But he honestly didn't remember Overseers being this young. His captive looked like a boy, surely not even in his eighteenth year? His clean-shaven face was round and still filled with baby fat, his skin red and flushed and wet with the tears that continued to stream from the boy's big blue eyes—eyes that stared at Daud's face in pure, wide terror.

At least Daud knew he wouldn't be recognized—his beard was long, the black whiskers streaked with white. And the Overseer was just too young to know who he was anyway. The boy—the *man*, Daud corrected himself—would have been a child during the rat plague, when the Whalers had stalked the streets of the city. Back then, Daud's face had been plastered everywhere: posters offering a reward for his kill or capture appeared in almost every tavern and every alley in every district of the city.

Daud opened his mouth to ask his first question, but it was the Overseer who spoke first, despite his captor's threats.

"You're him, aren't you?"

Daud froze. The Overseer squeezed his eyes shut tight and held his breath, his lips pressed together until they were almost white.

"You don't know me, boy," Daud said through clenched teeth. He paused, considering his options. The boy was terrified—but hopefully still able to answer Daud's questions. "What's your name?"

"Woodrow," said the Overseer. "Hayward Woodrow."

Daud snarled and slid his knee off the Overseer's chest, then leaned back, pulling the Overseer up with him by the neck. "Listen to me, Woodrow—"

"The Knife of Dunwall. You're him, aren't you?"

Somehow, after all this time, despite his own changed appearance, this Overseer—this *boy*—knew who he was. Knew—or guessed. Daud considered. Maybe it didn't matter. He was surprised, yes, but he also knew it wasn't really *him* that the boy was babbling about. It was his *legend*.

Woodrow swallowed. "It's only… I mean… I'm sorry." He stammered, looking for the words. "Only… the Knife of Dunwall, we still talk about him and what he did. Before my time, of course. I'm only a First Initiate. I mean, I never… he's just a legend. The older ones… I mean, the more senior members of the Abbey, they mention him. That's all. A story to remind us of the past and what happened to the city. Of what *could* happen. So we can make sure it doesn't happen again."

Daud tightened his grip on the Overseer's neck and pushed the young initiate back, slamming him onto the gantry. Woodrow cried out in surprise as he realized, finally, where he was.

"What... How did we get up here? How did we—"

"Listen to me, Woodrow," said Daud, his beard once more brushing his captive's face. "We are going to get along just fine. We will become great friends and we will talk and sing long into the night, and the day you met the Knife of Dunwall will be the greatest day in your entire life. Because if you answer my questions truthfully and you give me the information I require, I will let you live, and for the rest of your days you will be thankful for every breath of air you take."

The Overseer whimpered and tried to nod his head as best he could.

"And if you don't," said Daud, "I will throw you off this platform and the Abbey of the Everyman will be less one initiate."

Woodrow's eyes widened again. "Please, just... please—"

"What are the Overseers doing at the factory?"

The boy gulped in air. He had stopped struggling, but Daud kept a tight grip on his neck, although he could still breathe... just.

"Patrol," said Woodrow. "I was on patrol at the slaughterhouse. Change of shift. You must have seen the others."

"Why is the factory important?"

"I, er..."

"*Why is the factory important?*"

"Heresy!" Woodrow screwed up his face. "A black magic rite—witchcraft! Something unspeakable happened."

Daud narrowed his eyes. "Explain."

"There was a man. A stranger, from… somewhere else. Tyvia, some said. A traveler. He gathered a group of mercenaries around him and they used the factory as a base of operations."

"For what?"

"He had an object. An artifact."

There it was. "What artifact?"

"I don't know."

"You're lying."

"Nobody knows!"

"You're *lying*!" Daud lifted the Overseer by his collar and swung him over to the edge of the gantry. The Overseer cried out and twisted his neck around to look down. There was nothing between him and the roof of the mill except two hundred feet of air.

"Nobody has seen it!" Woodrow turned his head back around to stare up at Daud. "We only know what the Sisters of the Oracular Order have told us."

Daud cocked his head. "The Sisters saw it in a vision?"

"Yes. Yes!"

"What did they see? Speak!"

At first the Overseer shook his head, then he nodded, spit flying from his mouth. "Some kind of weapon. That's all I know, I swear to you. That's all any of the initiates in my chapterhouse were told."

So, the stories were true. He was following the right path after all.

Overseer Woodrow gasped, but Daud relaxed his grip on the youth's neck. Woodrow gasped again, his chest heaving.

"So that's why the Overseers are here, isn't it?" asked Daud. "This stranger brought the artifact to Dunwall. Whatever he was doing at the factory, something went wrong. He was killed and the Abbey of the Everyman think the artifact is still here. So the Overseers have spent eight months sifting through the wreckage."

"It's dangerous," said Woodrow. "Heretical artifacts cannot be allowed to exist."

"You never found it," Daud said. "You're still looking."

"Please! Don't let go! Don't let go!"

Daud leaned down over the Overseer. "Then keep talking. What else have you heard in your chapterhouse?"

"Now they're saying the artifact was taken! Someone came in, after the explosion. They found it and took it. Before the City Watch had the cordon up. Before the High Overseer called us in to search."

Daud snarled. "Who took it?"

Woodrow shook his head. "I don't know. I don't know. The senior Overseers don't believe the story. That's why they keep looking. But I'm only telling you what I heard."

Then Woodrow closed his eyes and began to speak, softly, and quickly, the words tumbling out without pause. "Restrict the Wandering Gaze that looks hither and yonder for some flashing thing that easily catches a man's fancy in one moment, but brings calamity in the next."

"Woodrow."

"Restrict the Lying Tongue that is like a spark in the heathen's mouth."

"Woodrow!"

There was a crack of gunfire, a shouted warning, once, then twice.

Daud looked up, his grip on Woodrow relaxing. The Overseer slid a few inches further toward his demise and cried out in terror before Daud caught him again. Daud frowned, peering in the direction of the sound.

The gunshot had come from the east, somewhere toward Dunwall Tower itself, the imperial palace just a few streets away. Daud's eye was caught by movement below; looking down, he watched as officers of the City Watch appeared from several different streets around the mill, grouped together like ants after their nest had been kicked, then ran toward the Tower.

Hanging from his arm, Overseer Woodrow jerked into life. "Help me! Somebody, help me! Help me—"

Daud swung Woodrow back up onto the gantry and spun him around, wrapping an arm around the man's neck. Woodrow's eyes bulged and he scrambled to get purchase, but it was no use. Five seconds and Woodrow stopped struggling. Ten and the Overseer was out cold, his body slumping against Daud's chest.

Daud let Woodrow's unconscious form slide down against the curve of the chimney.

Two more gunshots sounded and more shouting, far away.

Daud crouched on the edge of the gantry, and from inside his jerkin pulled out a small spyglass. As he focused on the commotion, he felt a rush of adrenaline, the stirring of a long-distant memory rising up from somewhere in his mind.

Daud scanned the streets close to Dunwall Tower through the eyepiece. Soon enough he found four guards running down a wide avenue. Daud tracked them until they joined a larger group in a small square. The men pointed and shouted, the morning sun reflecting off their bandolier buckles. Some of them had their swords drawn. An officer had his pistol in his hand, and he used it to point toward the Tower. Some of the guards broke off and headed in that direction. The others milled around, looking up at the buildings around them.

Daud lowered the eyepiece and shrank back a little from the edge of the gantry. He frowned. He didn't know what was going on, and he didn't care. It couldn't be him they were after—true enough, the unexplained absence of Overseer Hayward Woodrow would probably have been noted by now, but they were on the other side of the city from Slaughterhouse Row. Whatever was happening was centered on Dunwall Tower itself.

He looked through the eyepiece again. There were more guards now, the officer with the pistol apparently trying to organize a more structured search.

A search for what?

Daud twisted the eyepiece, adjusting the focus and range as he scanned the district.

And then he saw it—the unmistakable form of someone running across a sharply angled rooftop to the west of Dunwall Tower before vanishing into the shadows. The figure was three hundred yards, three-fifty maybe, from Daud's position.

Daud fixed the eyepiece on the rooftops near the Tower. The shadows were black and there was no movement at all, for nearly a minute.

And then the figure broke cover and ran.

They were good. Daud watched as they kept to the morning shadows, the busy, crowded stone architecture of the city's skyline providing plenty of hiding spots as the figure fled.

Daud turned the eyepiece back to the streets. The City Watch hadn't fired a gun in a few minutes, having clearly lost whoever it was they were trying to track. They were gathering in growing numbers, spreading out from the square, but down at street level they had no hope of finding their quarry, not when that quarry was so able, so adept.

Daud wondered just who in all the Isles it could possibly be.

From his position, Daud had a perfect view of the fugitive as they leapt from one building to the next, soaring across the narrow alleyways, flying directly over the heads of the guards looking for them.

Daud watched, fascinated. The figure was small. Lithe. A child perhaps—no, older. Teenage. A runaway? Or perhaps, given their skills, a thief or a young gang pledge on the run after encountering the City Watch, proving their worth to the underworld boss they hoped to impress. *Once,* Daud thought, *that might have been me.* But now—

Daud felt the breath leave his body. He lowered his eyepiece, as though he could see better over the distance with his naked eye, then raised it again, refocusing, twisting the barrel to zoom in and get a closer look. He struggled to follow the figure smoothly at that level of magnification.

It couldn't be, could it? Daud watched as the figure jumped and ran, then scaled a vertical wall, the difficulty of the task not slowing them by a second.

Slowing *her.* Because the escaping figure was no teenage runaway or would-be gang cutthroat. It was a young *woman*, dressed in fine clothes—a black trouser suit with a flash of white at the collar.

Daud recognized her at once. Her portrait hung in every city in the Isles, her silhouette stamped into every coin of the realm.

Emily Kaldwin: the Empress of the Isles herself.

On the run.

It had been fifteen years since he had last seen her in person. Daud began to laugh, quietly at first, but soon the low rumble in his chest grew and grew. He shook his head in disbelief and watched as the Empress vanished from sight over a rooftop.

No wonder the City Watch was a flurry of activity. The Empress had, for some mysterious reason, fled her tower, and was clearly running for... what? Her life? It certainly looked that way, if her own City Watch were after her.

But the reason for her flight would have to remain a mystery. Daud wasn't about to get involved with anything—*anything*—that wasn't connected with his mission. And besides, Emily would never accept his help, even if he was inclined to offer it.

The Empress was out of sight now, but she had moved with considerable skill and grace. It was obvious that her athleticism as she escaped across the rooftops was down to more than twice-weekly fencing lessons.

She had to have been trained.

Daud laughed again. *Of course.* Corvo Attano. Royal Protector and Emily's father. The pair *had* been busy in the last decade and a half, the Empress perhaps convincing her father to train her to defend herself if ever the Royal Protector could not. And after the murder of her mother, Empress Jessamine, and her kidnapping, Daud didn't blame her.

He blinked, his mind flashing back to that day fifteen years ago. To the assassination and the reckoning with Corvo Attano. The fight that had ended with Corvo banishing Daud from Dunwall.

Daud didn't know how Corvo had found the strength to spare him. He should be dead. And perhaps he wished that Corvo had been... what? Stronger? Weaker? Which was the better decision, the moral choice? To banish him or kill him? Daud had murdered Empress Jessamine Kaldwin—Corvo's lover—and although he had only been a hired mercenary, following the orders of Hiram Burrows, his actions had nearly brought about the end of the Empire itself.

Maybe he'd deserved death. Sometimes he'd certainly wished for it. Corvo had given him a second chance, but as Daud spent the years afterward wandering the Isles, searching for a purpose and a new life, he felt like what time he had left remaining was just wasting away.

Until he found his mission.

He glanced back to the rooftops as Emily reappeared by the small industrial dock on the riverside. She carefully stepped along a narrow outflow pipe, then at the end dived off into the water, breaking the surface a few yards later as she headed for the single ship in port, a battered steamer called the *Dreadful…* something. It was too far to read and the angle of the sun was all wrong.

Daud sighed. He told himself that whatever was going on was none of his business. The world could split in two. The Empire of the Isles could fall into the sea. None of it mattered. He could not—and would not—deviate from the mission.

Find the Outsider.

Kill the Outsider.

And to do that he needed the Twin-bladed Knife. It had been here, in Dunwall, at the factory. The Overseers were still looking for it.

Daud looked down at the body of Overseer Woodrow as he lay huddled against the chimney. The young man was gently snoring, his lips quivering, his eyes flickering behind closed lids. The Overseer would be missed, yes, but someone would find him up here, on the almost impossible to reach platform.

Eventually.

Daud cocked his head. Perhaps the story Woodrow had heard in his chapterhouse was right. Perhaps the reason why the Overseers hadn't found the knife was because someone had found it before them.

Heretical artifacts were rare, but not unknown, the black market trade in them—along with bonecharms and other more common objects touched by the black arts—could be surprisingly busy. And if the stories of the reappearance of the Twin-bladed Knife had reached Daud on the other side of the Isles, then its existence would be common knowledge here in Dunwall, if you knew whom to ask.

And as it happened, Daud did, because if you were interested in the heretical and the arcane, there was just one place to go. It was a place he hadn't visited in a *long* time—even as a Whaler, he had had no cause to enter the territory, and he knew that most of the other gangs of Dunwall felt likewise.

But it was a place to find answers and a place to pick up the trail.

Wyrmwood Way.

And once he got there, Daud knew exactly who he had to see.

3

THE STREETS OF DUNWALL
18th Day, Month of Earth, 1852

"With regard to Section 5, subsection 1, paragraph 4, clause 7B, officers of the City Watch are obliged to report to their posts upon enaction of Special (Executive) Orders, Protocol 6, thus authorizing the establishment of cordons and restricted zones of access; further, that upon enaction of Special (Executive) Orders, Protocol 7, the City Watch shall be empowered to enact and enforce a curfew, the parameters and limits of which shall be at the discretion of the commanding officers, upon the orders received through the City Watch Command, the Royal Protector, and/or the Imperial Throne of the Empire of the Isles, whomsoever has been declared to occupy such positions of state."

—ADDENDUM TO SECTION 5, NOTES ON
EXTRA-ORDINARY COMMAND AND
EMERGENCY PROCEDURES
Extract from the City Watch Operational
Manual (twenty-seventh revision)

The journey across Dunwall from the Tower District to Wyrmwood Way had been an interesting one, and had taken Daud far longer than he had intended, even though he'd traveled in the open for the most part. Daud had decided to forgo the shadows and rooftops and had stuck to the streets. It had become clear soon enough that with all the commotion, nobody was going to stop him, or even give him a second look.

Dunwall was in uproar. The initial activity of the City Watch as they tried—and failed—to pursue their own Empress had quickly spread into a city-wide mobilization, the streets filled not just with guards but Overseers too. In contrast to the slight panic of the City Watch, the Overseers moved through the streets with a sort of austere calm, their masks a menacing presence as they lurked in smaller numbers among the increasing numbers of ordinary citizens who were now taking to the streets, as word of what was happening in Dunwall Tower coursed through the city like a fire. The information was sketchy, incomplete, and in parts contradictory, as news of this kind always was this soon after the event in question had taken place.

There had been a coup. The Empress had been deposed—some said she was dead, some said she was in hiding. Daud, at least, knew the truth, although as he made his way through the crowds he kept his mouth firmly shut, listening to the gossip swirl around the crowds like gnats dancing in the summer sun, but contributing nothing himself.

This had nothing to do with him. He existed apart, an observer—no, an *outsider*, he realized, not without a small sense of irony.

Daud tried to move off the main avenue, his progress becoming slower as the crush increased, but he found most alternative routes cut off by City Watch and Overseers as they began to funnel the crowds into more easily controlled spaces. That was logical and didn't surprise him.

What *did* surprise him was the discovery of a third faction of quasi-military officials, helping—no, *commanding*—the others. They were dressed in uniforms of baggy beige pants and short-sleeved tunics that were a blueish-green for most, a darker red for a couple of others, in each case contrasting with the white leather belts and bandoliers that crossed them. They all wore tall white caps with a short brim at the front and a longer one shielding the back of the neck. On the front of the caps was a silver badge, signifying the authority for whom these strangers worked.

Daud knew the uniforms and knew the badge. He had known them his entire life. They were the Grand Serkonan Guard, a long way from home, but here in Dunwall, in the middle of a coup, and apparently in quite some numbers. And, more importantly, it was the red-coated veterans who appeared to be giving the orders—to their own men, and to the Dunwall City Watch and even the Overseers as well.

That, Daud thought, was interesting. Whatever had gone down at the palace, clearly the Duke of Serkonos himself, that pig Luca Abele, had something to do with it.

Daud watched as officers of the Grand Serkonan Guard conferred with their counterparts of the City Watch and the Overseers, as more members of each faction began assembling in the narrow street behind them. They were about to move on the crowd, with the intention of driving them back inside, and no doubt ordering a curfew. But they would need to act fast—it had taken Daud two hours to get just this far, and the crowds showed no signs of shrinking. In no time at all, things would turn ugly, the spontaneous gatherings of concerned citizens a powder keg. Daud knew what would happen next. The crowds would riot, and the authorities—whoever was in charge now, perhaps Duke Abele himself—would order a crackdown. It would be bloody and violent. Daud had to get out; this sudden instability threatened his plans. He had to get to Wyrmwood Way, get any and all information he could about the Twin-bladed Knife, perhaps even find the artifact itself, if it was still in the city after all this time. And if not, he needed to discover where it had gone, who had it now, and what he needed to do to get it for himself.

The scrum of citizens began to surge. Daud could sense the atmosphere changing as people began to notice the guards gathering. Curiosity, confusion—even a little excitement—had given way to uncertainty, to *fear*.

It was going to happen, and soon.

He slipped from the storefront, skirting the crowd, giving him a clear path down the street. Farther away, the crowd thinned, and the side streets and alleys seemed free of guards.

This is not *my problem.*

Ahead of him a group of City Watch marched forward. They seemed uncertain, jumpy. Daud didn't blame them— they probably knew as much, or even less, about what was going on than he did, and were no doubt less than happy to be under the command of the Grand Serkonan Guard. Daud didn't want to risk any confrontation; he had wasted enough time already.

One of the approaching guards pointed at him.

"You there. Where are you going? The city is now under curfew."

Daud stopped and raised a hand in what he hoped was a friendly greeting, but that only made the guard frown. He and his companions were still fifty yards away but now they began to jog toward him.

Darting forward, Daud turned sharply into a narrow alley. The buildings on either side were tall and the walls were flat but covered in a network of iron stairwells, their descending ladders locked at least ten feet from the street, safely out of reach.

The sound of the approaching City Watch grew, their boots heavy on the cobbled street.

Daud took a deep breath, then let it out slowly. He didn't want to use magic, but, once again, he found himself forced to. He needed to be fast. Time was of the essence— more now than ever, it seemed.

He looked up, judged the distance, then reached out with his left hand. The Mark of the Outsider blazed like a brand on his skin, flaring once, twice, three times as Daud traveled up the stairwells, then up onto the roof. He paused and looked down over the edge as the City Watch patrol entered the alley and looked around like lost children, then he turned and continued on his way.

4

WYRMWOOD WAY, WYRMWOOD DISTRICT, DUNWALL
18th Day, Month of Earth, 1852

"For the more intrepid traveler seeking to discover the true nature of the city, and who is perhaps willing to experience a side of Dunwall not commonly encountered, a visit to Wyrmwood Way may be considered. The so-named street is itself merely the main thoroughfare of a small, though rather densely built, district hidden in the southwest of the city. Here the traveler may browse stores unlike any found elsewhere in the city, catering to more unusual tastes. However, the traveler is advised not to stray from the cobbles of Wyrmwood Way proper; it is also recommended that a personal bodyguard be hired to curtail the risk of any unpleasantness. For while Wyrmwood Way is in truth an excellent and most fascinating area to visit, the district at large has been for many years under the watch of a variety of underworld organizations prepared to tolerate visitors only so long as they are not tempted to stray where they are not welcome. Foolish is the outsider who wanders from Wyrmwood Way, and travelers are reminded that the City Watch will not respond to calls for assistance south of Darrellson Street. Discretion is advised."

—THE SECRET SIDE OF DUNWALL:
WYRMWOOD WAY
Extract from *The Eclectic Traveler's
Guide to the Isles* (fourth edition)

Daud looked down at the street below from the safety of the sharply angled gable of a tavern on the corner of Darrellson Street. This part of the city, in contrast to the chaos farther north, was quiet, but not because of any curfew or threat from the City Watch and the other quasi-military forces now patrolling Dunwall. It was quiet because it was always quiet at this time, and today was no exception.

Wyrmwood Way itself ran parallel to Darrellson Street, which itself acted as a kind of border, effectively separating Dunwall from the Wyrmwood district itself, an area that was definitely different, distinct from the rest of the city. The architecture seemed older, the streets that spidered out from the spine of Wyrmwood Way narrow and twisted, the buildings that lined them lopsided and leaning. The area looked old and the stones were worn, as though this small wedge of Dunwall was somehow a good few hundred years older than the rest of the city. Perhaps that was true. Perhaps Wyrmwood Way was the original old town, the seed from which Dunwall grew, expanding outwards to conquer the southern banks of the Wrenhaven before spreading even farther north, becoming over time the largest city in all the Isles and the capital of the Empire.

Perhaps. Daud wasn't sure, and he wasn't interested.

Wyrmwood Way and its environs were the one area of Dunwall with which he wasn't intimately familiar. But he knew enough. Enough to know he had to be very, very careful as he went about his search. It would have been difficult enough without the frisson of fear that had gripped the city after the sudden coup at the Tower.

But he had no choice. It was now, or never.

Wyrmwood Way was different—*separate*—from the rest of Dunwall for another reason that was unrelated to its architecture or history: its gangs—or, specifically, one gang. The most dangerous, most cutthroat, most violent gang in all of Dunwall's history. They weren't generally mentioned in the same breath as the other, more well-known groups that stalked Dunwall's underbelly—the Hatters, the Dead Eels, the Bottle Street Gang, and, more recently, the Roaring Boys—because their activity was confined within the boundaries of the Wyrmwood district. Most of the citizens of Dunwall, although they would have heard of Wyrmwood Way—may even have ventured into the mouth of it, hunting for rare antiquities or unusual trinkets, blissfully unaware of the darker kinds of markets that operated in the area—had never even heard of the gang.

They called themselves the Sixways Gang. They were led by a man called Eat 'Em Up Jack. Their base of operations was a tavern called the Suicide Hall.

Daud had come to see them because there was one very particular type of business the Sixways controlled within their Wyrmwood empire: smuggling. Art treasures, stolen property, kidnapped people, heretical artifacts—or just plain old coin—if you needed to get it out of Dunwall without anyone knowing about it, you employed the services of the Sixways Gang.

If anyone knew what had happened to the Twin-bladed

Knife, it was going to be Eat 'Em Up Jack. And Daud was going to ask him in person.

He only hoped he wouldn't have to kill them all to get out alive.

Daud made it down to street level and headed directly for Wyrmwood Way. He was alone for a few dozen yards, and then he wasn't. A few more paces, and he turned and saw that he was being followed openly, by two people—a man and a woman, both wearing immaculately tailored suits of the kind favored by bankers and accountants. But these were not business people. The man's neck was thick and muscular, and he wore a heavy moustache with upturned waxed ends, while his companion's long hair was wound into a tight bun on the top of her head, and her round-collared shirt did little to hide the tattoos on her neck. Their jackets had had the lapels roughly cut away, leaving a jagged, almost torn edge with white threads trailing against the dark fabric.

It was clear these were lookouts for the Sixways, stationed at the start of Wyrmwood Way, not so much to guard the approaches but to see that whatever was going on in Dunwall did not interfere with operations here in their own territory. Word of the coup must have reached them.

Soon the two lookouts were joined by another two men, and another couple, peeling casually out of doorways to follow the stranger walking so boldly into their domain.

Daud took this as a good sign, because it meant that the Sixways were still in operation—and that there was a chance he could get the information he had come here for. *And just in time, too,* he thought, as he passed the burned-out skeleton of a building on his right. The Overseers periodically came into Wyrmwood Way and set fire to buildings in somewhat half-hearted attempts to halt the trade in heretical and arcane goods. That they never managed to do much damage was largely due to the fierce street fighting they had faced when, on one historic occasion, they had penetrated right to the heart of the Sixways territory and faced an army of gangsters who left dozens of Overseers dead and drove the rest out. Since the Battle of Mandragora Street—as the event had become known—the Overseers never had much interest in devoting the time and manpower that would be needed to truly flush the Sixways from the district.

As Daud continued his journey, followed now by six lookouts, he wondered how long that impasse would last now. If there was a regime change at the Tower—if Duke Luca Abele of Serkonos had installed himself as ruler—then he doubted Wyrmwood Way would remain untouched for much longer.

Which is why there was no time to waste. He had to get in, get the information, find out who had taken the Twin-bladed Knife and where.

He marched onward, head up and hood pulled back enough so his face wasn't hidden. Further down Wyrmwood Way, there were more lookouts of various ages and builds, a more or less even mix of men and women, all clad in their suits, jacket lapels shorn away, men with round hats and moustaches elegant and waxed, the women with their hair in topknots. They stood in doorways and against walls. They sat on steps and leaned against rails. And it wasn't just at street level. Daud glanced up and saw more leaning out of open windows or looking down from behind closed ones.

They all watched Daud as he walked down the street, his escort now twenty paces behind him. He ignored it all and kept walking in a straight line with his eyes fixed ahead, his expression firm. He hoped that his manner suggested he was here quite deliberately, not for a fight, but for business.

The road was quite long and fairly straight, the quarter mile thoroughfare terminating at a large intersection, right in the heart of the district, where five other streets converged—two major arteries, Wyrmwood Way and Mandragora Street, and three smaller roadways—the area forming a fairly large, open circular space surrounded by tall buildings. The center of the intersection was clear, but around the edges were more gangsters—perhaps fifty, all dressed in the uniform of the Sixways Gang. Daud stopped, unable to hide the hesitation in his step. The gang was on alert, no question about it. Because unlike his escort of six, and the others who had watched him, the gangsters here made no attempt to conceal their weaponry. Each had two pistols stuffed into their belts, and from each right hand dangled a leather blackjack, the way their bulbous ends swung in the air telling Daud they were filled with lead.

Nobody spoke or moved. Behind him, Daud's escort stopped, keeping their distance.

This was the Sixways itself—the heart of Wyrmwood—from which the gang that ruled the district took their name. There were two big buildings dead ahead, on the other side of the intersection. One was a blackened shell of an old building, the doors and windows gone, brick sooty and crumbling, a collapsed roof, and gaping holes for windows that were like the empty eye sockets of a dried-out skull. The structure was not unlike the ruin of the slaughterhouse that had led Daud here in the first place, the burned-out shell here left as a memorial of the Battle of Mandragora Street.

It was the ruin's intact neighbor that Daud had come to visit. The building was dark brick and five floors high, the front three windows wide but no more. The windows were closed and shuttered, save for one on the fourth floor; Daud could see two people moving behind the glass, watching the street. More Sixways lookouts.

The building was a tavern, that much was obvious from the ocean of green curved tile that formed the entire façade of the first floor. The main door was accessed by a short flight of steps set between two wide verandas, the windows of which were large and shaded by awnings striped in faded green and white. If the tavern had had a name before, Daud certainly didn't remember it—there was a sign, or what was left of one; most of it had been torn off to leave just three large gilt letters—BAR—with elaborate curlicues over the doorway.

Daud knew the building by another name, as did everyone else in Wyrmwood, along with those in Dunwall who made it their business to know, whether they were officers of the City Watch, senior members of the Abbey of the Everyman, or those who had a certain kind of business that required the services of the Sixways Gang.

This was the gang headquarters, and home of their boss, Eat 'Em Up Jack, the Suicide Hall, so called because if you went inside without an invitation or a business proposition, you wouldn't come out alive.

Daud rolled his neck and patted the right breast of his jerkin. The pouch was still there, nestled against his chest. He didn't want to use what was inside, but it was just for something like this that he had brought it along.

Armed with his contingency, Daud gritted his teeth and walked into the bar.

5

THE SUICIDE HALL,
WYRMWOOD DISTRICT, DUNWALL
18th Day, Month of Earth, 1852

"You know how the Sixways Gang has operated all this time, for all these years? Well, I'll tell you. Fear. It's as simple as that. And their leader, Eat 'Em Up Jack, is the master of fear—he is the ringmaster of terror, and all of Wyrmwood Way is his circus. He understands that to instill fear—to truly make people believe it—requires more than just talk.

Fear needs spectacle.

Someone steals from him: he cuts off their hands. Someone speaks against him: he cuts out their tongue. Someone challenges his authority: he cuts off their head, sticks it on a pole, and dangles it out of the top window of the Suicide Hall for all to see.

And that's just within his own family.

Fear is a powerful tool indeed."

—WYRMWOOD WAY AND THE SIXWAYS GANG
Excerpt from a journalist's report
on organized criminal activity

The inside of the Suicide Hall was clean and tidy, the very picture of a respectable hostelry and no different to any of the upmarket inns that dotted the more inviting districts of the city. The public room was large, full of low beams and dark wood that were complemented by the green-and-white-striped upholstery of the booths that lined the walls. Despite the daylight outside, it was dark and cozy inside, the lighting turned low and the big windows looking out onto the veranda were frosted for privacy. Directly ahead of Daud, on the other side of the room, was the bar itself, the well-stocked shelves surrounding a large mirror. Daud looked at his own reflection, and the reflections of the twenty heads of the gangsters who were sitting around the room, all eyes on him.

His view was blotted out as one of the Sixways strolled over and stepped directly in front of him. The woman lifted her pistol, placing the barrel directly against Daud's forehead and pushed, hard.

"That's far enough."

Welcome to the Suicide Hall, thought Daud. He glanced over the woman's shoulder, scanning the words carved into the brown wood panel over the bar, the jagged white scar of the letters the only thing—gangsters aside—that seemed out of place.

BETTER OFF DEAD

Daud smiled, and lifted his empty hands. "I'm just here for a drink."

The gangster didn't move a muscle. Daud felt the gun barrel drilling a circle into the flesh of his forehead.

"That so?" asked the woman.

Daud's eyes darted around the room, meeting the gaze

of the watching gangsters, some sitting in the booths, some leaning against the dark-wood pillars, all armed with pistol and blackjack. There were no tables or chairs or stools at the bar—less makeshift ammunition in case of a fight, perhaps—and despite the myriad liquors on display behind the bar, nobody was drinking.

Daud's focus returned to the mirror, his view obscured by the woman holding the gun to his head. He very carefully leaned to his right.

"And a talk," he said, to the mirror. It was a two-way, of course. Facing the door, the perfect way to see who was coming and going. Someone was watching the scene now, he knew. Maybe even Eat 'Em Up Jack himself.

Nobody spoke. That was fine. Daud could wait.

He had no choice, anyway.

After a few moments there was a creak, then a heavy door slammed shut, and a man appeared from around the curve of the bar. He had a moustache like the rest of the men, but he was a good deal older and he wore no hat, his thinning gray hair immaculately combed and glistening with tonic. He wore no jacket either, and the sleeves of his collarless shirt were held halfway up his forearms by silver armbands that sat above his elbows. Around his waist was a green-and-white-striped apron, and over one shoulder was a towel in the same pattern.

The man may have been older than the rest of the gangsters assembled in the Suicide Hall, but he was completely in his element. His neck was thick, his broad shoulders stretching the fabric of his shirt. When he planted his arms on the bar, locking his elbows, Daud could see his muscles flexing.

"Well?"

Daud paused. Was this Eat 'Em Up Jack himself? Was this how he played it, pretending to be the barman in order to scope out potential clients, or victims?

Daud didn't speak, but he did raise an eyebrow.

The barman stared at him. "You said you wanted a drink."

Daud glanced at the woman with the gun, then he took a half-step back and casually brushed the barrel aside with one hand. The gangster let the weapon fall and looked over her shoulder at the barman. The barman nodded and the gangster stepped back.

Daud ran a hand over his beard and moved toward the bar, aware of his every move, aware of all the eyes watching him. When he reached the bar he was careful to place both hands on top of it, in plain view.

"Well, you know what they say in Morley," said Daud.

The barman said nothing. He fixed Daud with a steely look. Daud could see the green edge of a tattoo just at the edge of the man's collar.

"No," said the barman. "What do they say in Morley?"

"That the sun is always high enough somewhere in the Isles for a drink."

Daud held the barman's stare for five long seconds that felt like an eon in the dim stillness of the Suicide Hall. Then the barman turned to the shelves behind him. With his gaze firmly on Daud's reflection in the mirror, he pulled a thin, dark bottle from the back of the second shelf—Serkonan spiced rum—then he turned and produced a square cut-glass tumbler from under the bar. He placed both in front of Daud, then he returned to his previous pose.

Daud glanced at the bottle. The label was faded and old, but the liquor was good. He glanced at the glass, then back up at the barman's impassive face.

"Wrong glass," said Daud.

The barman said nothing.

"Serkonan rum is traditionally served in a tall glass with a wide bowl," said Daud, "to let the aroma develop."

The barman remained silent. Daud dropped his hands.

"Of course, you'd know all about that, southerner."

Daud turned at the voice. It was female and came from one of the booths by the window, where two men were sitting, built out of the same slabs of solid muscle as the rest of their Sixways brethren.

Dwarfed behind them, tucked into the corner of the booth, was a woman. She was dressed the same as the others —tailored jacket with the lapels shorn off, white shirt with high, round collar—but unlike the other women, her red hair was not in a topknot, but was cut short and slicked back with tonic, like the barman's. Daud placed her at perhaps twenty, twenty-five years old.

The same age as the Empress, he thought, remembering Emily's flight across the rooftops. That felt like *days* ago, even though it had only been a few hours.

Behind him, Daud heard a gentle *thunk* on the bar top. He turned, and found another square tumbler had joined the first. He and the barman looked at each other before the barman turned and, yanking the towel from his shoulder, began cleaning the bar under the mirror.

The woman laughed. "Are you going to stand there looking like you're ready to pull the City Watch apart with your bare hands, or are you going to join me for a drink?"

Daud licked his lips, his gaze darting around the room once more. Everyone—except the barman—was still watching him. He grabbed the bottle and the two glasses and walked over to the booth. He stood by the table, his eyes on hers, ignoring the two thugs with her.

The woman nodded, and the men stood and walked away, leaving the leather booth seats hissing in their wake. Daud put the bottle and glasses down and slid into the booth across from the woman. They looked at each other for a moment, a faint smile playing over the woman's lips. Daud reached for the bottle, removed the stopper, and poured two glasses of Karnaca's finest. He pushed one toward the woman before raising his own and draining it in a single gulp. He felt the liquid coat his mouth and throat, filling his senses with fire and notes of coffee and vanilla. When he filled his glass for the second time he did not drink. Instead, he nodded at his companion.

"Eat 'Em Up Jack, I presume?"

Ignoring the glass in front of her, the young woman lifted the liquor bottle and took a long swig, her eyes on Daud's. She put the bottle down, but left her hand on it.

"You presume correctly."

Daud lifted his refilled glass and raised it to her, then drained it again in one.

"Enjoy your drink," said Jack. "It's on the house."

Daud nodded his thanks.

"Because when you're finished," Jack continued, "you're going to have to come up with a very good reason why I should let you walk out of here alive."

6

"What will we do with the drunken whaler?
What will we do with the drunken whaler?
What will we do with the drunken whaler?
Early in the morning?

Feed him to the hungry rats for dinner?
Slice his throat with a rusty cleaver?
Shoot him through the heart with a loaded pistol?
Early in the morning."

—HARPOONER SONGS
Excerpt from a book of sea shantys sung by sailors

"I'm not here for a fight, Jack," said Daud.

Jack lifted the bottle again. Daud watched her drink, this tiny, pale, red-headed woman. Was she really Eat 'Em Up Jack? Daud thought back, dredging up old memories of his time in Dunwall. As far as he could remember, the leader of the Sixways Gang had *always* been Eat 'Em Up Jack—stretching back to before this young woman was born. The name, then, must be a title, one handed down across the years from leader to leader.

If there was one thing that was good for business, it was continuity. And for Wyrmwood Way and the Sixways Gang, *everything* was about business.

The young gang leader and the exiled assassin regarded each other across the booth table for a while, the bottle of Serkonan rum half gone. Daud kept his expression set as Jack regarded him with a tilted head.

Daud ran a gloved hand over his beard. He liked the sensation. It helped him think.

Finally she spoke. "I've changed my mind."

Daud pursed his lips. "About what?"

"I don't want just one good reason why I shouldn't exsanguinate you on the doorstep."

"Oh?"

Daud's gloved hand found the bottle. Jack leaned forward across the table and draped her own hand over Daud's. She had long, delicate fingers, the nails trimmed short. *For fighting,* Daud thought. He looked into her eyes, and she gently pulled the bottle away from him.

"No," said Jack. "I think I'm going to need at least four good reasons."

Daud chuckled, the low, gravelly sound rising from somewhere deep in his chest. *Oh, why does this have to get complicated?*

"Is that so?"

"Make it five," she said.

Daud sat back and sighed. "I said I wasn't here for a fight. And I can only give you one reason not to kill me, but you'll like it."

At that, he reached inside his jerkin and pulled out a small leather pouch, then tipped out a single circular ingot of pinkish-white metal onto the table. It was about the same size as a coin of ten, but twice as thick—it was ninety-eight percent pure platinum, and a small part of the cache he had taken years to accumulate, the money hidden in safe houses scattered across the Empire. In terms of theoretical value, it made Daud a rich man. Practically speaking, it was a difficult form of currency to cash—but useful in situations like this.

Jack's eyes flicked to the ingot, then back to Daud. She picked it up, weighed it in her hand, then turned it over. A semicircle and a pitchfork were stamped on the back.

Jack let the ingot drop back onto the table. "Stealing from the Overseers?"

Daud shrugged. "Does it matter?"

"It does if they want it back."

"Then melt it. I don't care. I'm here for business." Leaving the ingot where it was, he pulled the drawstring of the pouch tight, then pushed it across the table toward Jack. "That's more than enough payment for your services."

Jack cocked her head again. "You want something moved?"

"Actually, no. I'm looking for something. An artifact." Daud glanced at Jack and saw her forehead crease in confusion.

"That's not how we work," she said. "You want to spend your stolen money on bonecharms, go right ahead. The storekeepers of Wyrmwood Way will be more than happy to assist."

"All I want," said Daud, "is information. There was an artifact in Dunwall recently. It was brought in to the city, but then taken out again. I need to know where it went."

Jack didn't speak.

"It's a knife. Bronze, twin blades. Could be big or small, I don't know. Might look ordinary. Might look like nothing you've seen before. It was brought to the city maybe eight—"

That was when Jack laughed, and the laughter spread across the room. Daud turned in his seat, and saw the members of her gang joining in with their leader.

Daud turned back around and nudged the ingot and the pouch toward Jack. "Nine ingots. Consider this a down payment. Name your price."

Jack's eyes narrowed. "Listen, my friend from the south. The Sixways operates a very particular kind of business. Our services have been employed by the good people of Dunwall for a long, long time—services that are not discussed outside of this room." She sat back against the booth, the leather creaking under her. "Now, a stranger comes in, with Overseer money, and says he's looking for something he thinks we moved for someone else? I'm sure there is a quicker way to die, but I haven't heard of it myself."

Daud turned to the window. "Do you know what's going on out there, beyond the walls of your little empire?"

Jack shrugged. "Word is there was a coup at the Tower. The Duke of Serkonos has dug up a skeleton from the Kaldwin family closet, apparently. Good for him."

Daud looked at her. "You really think you're that untouchable?"

"They won't come here."

He curled his hand into a fist and resisted the urge to slam it down on the table between them. "Listen to me, *Jack*. You may think you're safe in here with your own private army, but they *will* come for you. Believe me, they will come." He jerked a thumb at the window. "You think the Duke of Serkonos doesn't know about Wyrmwood Way and the Sixways Gang? Maybe you're too young to realize, but a coup like this takes planning. Months of it. He's got it all laid out. Marching his men into Dunwall Tower is just the start. And it wouldn't have been possible in the first place without collaborators working on the inside." Daud leaned forward across the table. "They will be here by nightfall. On that you have my word. And they won't be scared by the Sixways Gang." Daud leaned back. "It's happened before. The Overseers have come in, time and time again, to burn the place out, to clear it of vermin—and that includes the Sixways. You may think that the Wyrmwood is special, and it is, but it's also a part of Dunwall. And whoever sits on the throne in the Tower owns this city—and they own you."

Jack frowned. She slowly reached for the bottle, took a swig, and put it back down. "Is that some kind of a threat?" she asked finally.

Daud spread his hands. "I'm not threatening you. I'm *warning* you. I'm not the only one running out of time here. I came for information. Information I *need*. Once I have it, I'll be gone. And I suggest you go too. At least for a time, until things settle. I'm just trying to help you, so maybe you'll consider helping me."

Jack's eyes flicked over Daud's shoulder, and from behind him came the unmistakable sound of roughly two dozen gangsters with short tempers and a desire for violence standing quickly, followed almost as fast by a sequence of clicks that was almost musical.

Daud glanced over his shoulder. Everyone in the Suicide Hall was now standing and each had a pistol cocked and aimed right at him. The barman watched from the back, the only person in the place other than Daud and Jack not holding a weapon.

"You, my southern friend, are better off dead," said Jack.

Daud turned back around. "If you don't listen to me, you're all dead. Trust me."

Jack shook her head, picked up the bottle and settled back into the corner of the booth, cradling the rum against her chest. The glass clinked against whatever she had in her top pocket.

Daud had expected—or perhaps hoped—that his conversation with the notorious leader of the Sixways Gang would go better than this. The platinum ingots were a portable fortune, more than enough to pay for information. But of course, they could just kill him and take the money anyway. He had hoped his warning about their approaching trouble with the Duke would motivate Jack to be a little more cooperative, but she clearly thought the Sixways were untouchable.

She was too young. She wouldn't remember the days of the Rat Plague, the Regency, the terror the gangs of Dunwall—the Whalers included—brought to the streets. The Battle of Mandragora Street was probably just a bedtime story for her, told by whoever held the title of Eat 'Em Up Jack before her.

He looked at Jack. "I need to find the artifact—the Twin-bladed Knife. The Sixways Gang run the biggest smuggling operation in the Empire, and I know for a fact that there is nothing heretical or arcane that moves into or out of the city that Eat 'Em Up Jack doesn't personally know about. I've given you money. I've given you advice. That's payment enough. I'm not asking for details, I just need a name or a place, and then I'll leave you in peace. I don't work for the Overseers. I have nothing to do with the coup. Whether you take my advice and get out, or whether you begin preparations for war, that's not my concern, but I hope my warning to you has some value— value enough to strike a deal."

Jack's tongue ran circles around the inside of her cheek. Then she nodded to one of her lieutenants.

"Take him outside." She looked at Daud. "Time to have some sport."

7

"A mystical woman, Delilah she's called,
Claimed rights to the throne, and the Duke she
   enthralled,
Some called it magic and some called it fate,
Did she do it for love, did she do it for hate?

Now I'm just a poor singer, recounting this tale,
If I sing it wrongly I'm dead as a whale,
The Duke rules us now, and we know him, we do,
So let's raise a glass to our Duke and the coup!

A coup, a coup! What is it to you?
A feast or a famine, a nail or a screw?
A Duke from the south, a vile witches brew
A coup, a coup! What is it to you?"

—THE COUP
Fragment of a popular song, composer unknown

Daud was led out through the main doors of the Suicide
Hall and down the steps. Out on the intersection, the

members of the Sixways Gang who had been stationed around the surrounding buildings had moved out into the road, assembling into one large mob. Daud saw pistols, knives, and blackjacks.

They were ready.

Daud rolled his neck. This wasn't how he wanted it to go, but maybe he could survive this. It would be difficult. But not impossible.

At least that's what he told himself. Once again, he found himself in a figurative corner, where the only escape route possible was the one granted to him by a supernatural being he wanted to kill.

The Outsider.

Daud closed his eyes, drawing on decades of experience to focus himself.

Behind him, the door of the Suicide Hall swung on its hinges and he heard the bar empty, the heavy footsteps of Jack's personal bodyguard thumping down the stairs. Jack stood at the top of the stairs, hands on her hips as she surveyed her territory, stepping aside only briefly to let the barman past as he came out and thudded down the steps. He may have been older than Daud, but he was built like an ox.

No match for Daud, of course, not with the Mark of the Outsider at his beck and call. He was just grateful that nobody seemed to know who he was, otherwise Jack—if she had any sense—would have had him shot through the back of the head inside the bar.

Daud spread his hands as he addressed the gang's leader. "I came for information. Tried to pay you, and even gave you my advice. Now I'm going to slaughter most of you and take what I want from whoever's still breathing."

Jack ignored him while the barman smiled. In the daylight, Daud saw that nearly half of his teeth were gold.

"Perhaps Jack gave you the wrong impression," said the barman, his booming baritone echoing loudly around the buildings that crowded the Sixways. "And perhaps that impression was that your head was going to remain attached to your body."

Behind him, at the top of the stairs, Jack laughed.

The barman took a step forward. He shook his hands out from his sides, flexing his fingers, the hard muscles rippling underneath his tight shirt. He pointed at Daud.

"You are better off dead." He lifted both arms and began to walk in a circle, encouraging the others to join in. Soon enough, everyone had picked up the chant.

"*Better off dead! Better off dead!*"

Daud waited until the barman had his back to him. Then he concentrated, the Mark of the Outsider burning on the back of his hand, the pain hot and sharp and clean.

And then he *moved*.

Jack called out as Daud materialized behind the barman. Before the big man could turn in surprise, he'd planted his boot in the small of the barman's back. His body was as thick as an oak tree and felt just as immobile, but the Mark of the Outsider gave Daud more than just stealth and subterfuge.

It also gave him strength.

The barman toppled forward, tried to regain his footing, but was unable to balance himself. He crashed to the cobbles, chest-first, but reacted quickly, pushing himself back up and swinging his arm out. Daud ducked and kicked again, this time connecting with the man's knee. There was a crunch. The barman fell down onto his backside and tried to get up, but his leg was bending in the wrong direction. Crying out in pain, he shuffled backward along the cobbles, clearing room for his companions to get to work.

Daud sensed, rather than heard, the movement behind him. He spun around to see that the Sixways Gang had now formed a semicircle around him. Some of them were grinning; they were enjoying this. Those at the front had put their pistols away, and were now swinging blackjacks and blades. Guns were too easy. They wanted this fight to last as long as possible.

Daud inhaled through his nostrils, the air suddenly cool and electric. The back of his throat tingled and the back of his hand burned and he could feel his heart pump in his chest as the first flush of adrenaline faded.

He had to admit: it felt good. Maybe this was what he had missed. Maybe it had been wrong to steer away from violence for so many years after his exile. Who was he trying to fool? He was Daud, the Knife of Dunwall. He was a killer, an assassin. Even without the Mark, he was a sublime fighter, his skills unparalleled in all the Isles. Age had done nothing to weaken him. And with the gift the Outsider had bestowed upon him, the power he was able to draw from the Void, he was invincible.

Perhaps in reaction to his thoughts, Daud's left hand lit in exquisite pain, the Mark of the Outsider burning white hot. The agony was so excruciating he wanted nothing more than to tear his hand off with his teeth if he had to.

And then, no sooner had the pain flared into terrible being, it faded, leaving nothing but a dull ache. His entire left arm suddenly felt like a lead weight.

Daud wondered if the Outsider was watching him. Wondered if the Outsider knew what he was thinking, if the Outsider was *playing* with him.

He wondered if he would ever be free of that parasite.

In front of him, some of the Sixways Gang danced on the balls of their feet, others rolled their necks, flexed their shoulders.

Then three men lunged forward. Daud waited until they were in striking distance, then feinted for the one on his left, the man ducking back in reflex then swinging his blackjack, before realizing Daud was out of range, having pushed off with his left leg, darting instead to target the thug in the middle. Forearm horizontal, elbow braced, Daud's arm collided with the man's throat, crushing his larynx. The gangster staggered and swung, but the attack was weak; Daud parried the soft blow easily with his still-raised forearm, then slammed his boot into the man's thigh. There was a crack and the thug sagged forward, head down, presenting the back of his neck to Daud. Daud didn't waste the opportunity and slammed down on the back of the man's skull with both hands. Vertebrae crunched and the thug dropped, his chin met by Daud's swiftly rising knee. Teeth went flying as Daud sidestepped, letting the gangster's body drop to the road.

Two tree-trunk arms wrapped around his torso, pinning his arms to his sides. The man hissed in Daud's ear, his breath hot and smelling of sour onions.

He couldn't see his attacker, but the man was big. The gangster reared up, lifting Daud clean off his feet, as two more men lunged in to join the fray. Daud lifted his legs and kicked out, his boots connecting with their faces, sending them staggering backward. The gangster holding him roared in his ear and squeezed as he adjusted his footing for better balance.

Daud used this to his advantage, rocking his upper body forward just as the gangster thought he was stable. The sudden shift in Daud's center of gravity caused the man to tilt forward, his grip loosening. As Daud's feet touched the ground, he winged his arms out, breaking the gangster's grip. He ducked left and then right as he dodged two swinging blackjacks, before weaving in the opposite direction to deliver nose-breaking punches with the heels of his hands, left then right.

There was a bang, and Daud felt the trailing hood of his jerkin puff out, pulling sharply on his neck. Daud glanced to his right and saw smoke rising from a pistol. Someone was obviously keen to bring the fight to a conclusion before more of the gang were taken out. The shooter paused to check her aim, sighting down the barrel with one eye closed.

Daud dropped as the pistol fired again, the shot safely wide. Daud ducked down and darted forward before pushing himself up and throwing himself at the shooter. He caught the woman's wrists, flinging her arms high and sending the gun spinning into the air. The woman fell and hit the cobbles on her back, while Daud directed all the force of his own landing into the woman's chest, slamming his knees into her body with a satisfying crunch. The gangster's mouth flew open and her eyes bulged as something broke inside her. Daud quickly rolled off, easily escaping the woman's flailing hands.

On his feet, Daud spun around ready for the next attacker. There were bodies on the ground, but there were a great deal more still standing—and now they were angry. Back over at the Suicide Hall, Jack was shouting orders Daud couldn't quite make out.

The Sixways Gang surged forward as one, their sport forgotten. They were now operating as a pack, and were going to take him down by sheer brute force and overwhelming numbers.

Daud felt the Mark of the Outsider flare on his hand. After so many years of refusing to call on the power, the rush he now got from it almost overwhelmed his thoughts. He shook his head, trying to clear it. The Mark gave him power, but if he couldn't focus it, that power would become a liability.

The Sixways Gang charged, blackjacks and knives held high, roaring a battle cry. Daud braced himself, ready to absorb what hits he could, ready to use the strength of the gang against them. And he succeeded, ducking and weaving and diving, following through with his own punches and kicks, each carefully aimed, despite the chaos, to cause maximum damage.

At first, anyway.

There were too many of them, coming too quickly. He mistimed a punch, threw his body off balance, and a blackjack connected with his shoulder, sending him tumbling. He went with the movement, ignoring the pain, ready to spin back around and catch the attacker unaware from his opposite side, but suddenly there was no room. The gang crowded close, forming a scrum that surrounded Daud, forcing him to curl into himself, even the light of the day dimming as the gangsters yelled and screamed and, too close to use their weapons, began to tear him apart with their bare hands.

Daud held his breath and clenched his fists.

Enough. *Enough*.

The Mark of the Outsider flared into life on the back of his left hand and he was ready to unleash the full power at his disposal, when a sudden hush descended on the group. The crush eased as the gangsters backed off.

Daud looked around, getting his bearings. He was in the middle of the Sixways itself. The Suicide Hall was behind him. Dead ahead was the end of Wyrmwood Way, the street that led back into Dunwall proper. Between him and escape stood the barman. The giant of a man moved forward, limping on his injured leg, his lip curled, gold teeth shining. The rest of the gang moved to give him some room.

The power of the Void flooded through Daud, making him feel light, alive, *dangerous*.

That was when he heard it.

Metal on stone, rhythmic, heavy.

Getting louder. Getting *closer*.

The others heard it now. Feet shuffled as the gang turned toward Wyrmwood Way.

The barman stayed just where he was, staring at Daud.

A gasp went around, and everyone moved back toward the Suicide Hall.

The machine was bipedal, a skeletal structure of metal and wood that towered over the heads of even the tallest members of the Sixways Gang. The thing's head was a carved wooden beak, long and pointed like the skull of a mythical giant bird. The chest was boxy and compact, comprised mostly of a large geared wheel on the left, and three glass cylinders on the right, rising in an arc out of a machined metal cover. There were four arms, long and hinged, angled up and out like the legs of a spider sitting at the center of its web. The upper portions of each were short, encased in amber-colored wood, but from the elbow down they were nothing but steel blades, so long their wickedly sharp tips could easily skim the cobbles some six or more feet from the articulated shoulder joints.

Daud had never seen anything like it, and gauging by the reaction of the Sixways, neither had they. The technology was amazing, breathtaking.

Deadly.

It walked into the Sixways and stopped, its whole structure vibrating as it lifted its great arms high over its beak-like head. Over the scuffing of the gang's boots on the cobbles, Daud could hear a faint ticking sound. The gear wheel in the machine's chest spun and the glass bulbs glowed. Daud saw the air shimmer over the joints at the shoulders and the waist as though there was another force at work, in addition to the clockwork, holding the whole construction together.

Daud looked at the barman, who finally turned around to see what had arrived in the Sixways.

"What in the name of the—"

He never finished his question. Almost as soon as he had opened his mouth, the clockwork soldier sprang into life, moving forward and rubbing its blade-arms together like a chef sharpening his knives.

"*Combat protocol four. Combat protocol four,*" came the tinny voice from somewhere inside the machine's boxy torso. "*Civilian profile but hostile. Entering combat state.*"

The barman drew breath to speak again—and then it was over, his head severed from his body by the scissor-like action of two of the clockwork soldier's blades, snapping together with perfect precision, shearing through flesh and bone in an instant.

Arterial blood, scarlet and hot, was pumped high into the air. The barman's body dropped to its knees, then forward onto its chest. His head bounced on the cobbles and came to rest by Daud's boot. He looked down at the grimacing dead face of the gangster.

The games were over. Daud was no longer the concern. As one, the gang turned and watched, stunned into a terrified silence, as the machine creature stood, blade-arms twitching, gear wheel spinning.

The machine raised its arms into the air once more, the sun reflecting off the four polished blades.

Whatever it was, whoever had built it, its function was clear.

It was a killing machine, pure and simple. And it was here to make sure nobody got out of Wyrmwood Way alive.

8

THE SIXWAYS,
WYRMWOOD DISTRICT, DUNWALL
18th Day, Month of Earth, 1852

"Dear readers, you will be fascinated to know that earlier models of the Clockwork Soldier had human-like faces! Allow me to explain. As you know from Chapters 18 through 22, I had been testing the Clockwork Soldiers against a wide range of enemies. Early in this process a problem emerged. The would-be thieves and assailants were not intimidated by the delicate ceramic faces of the earlier prototypes. One criminal even believed he recognized an uncle and attempted conversation!

Undeterred, I set about redesigning the head mechanism, encasing it with a terrifying visage! I knew I had found the right design when my first test subject fell to their knees in fear."

—THE ASTOUNDING CLOCKWORK SOLDIERS
A Precise History by the Creator Himself, Kirin Jindosh,
Grand Serkonan Inventor (Chapter 23)

In almost perfect unison, the Sixways Gang pulled their guns out and opened fire at the clockwork soldier. Daud ducked down and dived sideways, just in time, as the fusillade sparked against the chassis of the machine creature, sending bullets and shrapnel everywhere. The clockwork soldier shook under the attack, its casing remarkably resilient, but not indestructible. The amber-wood panels began to chip and there were blackened marks on the metal parts of the machine as bullet after bullet found its mark.

But the machine was too strong and the gang's ammunition was limited. In just a few moments the gunfire began to quieten, then stopped entirely.

The machine shuddered but did not move. The big gear wheel continued to turn, and the bulbs on the chest flickered in sequence, like the machine was plotting a response to the attack.

Whatever it was, Daud knew the gangsters didn't stand a chance. Ducking under the low-hanging eaves of a building, he looked over his shoulder, searching for Eat 'Em Up Jack. She had retreated back toward the Suicide Hall's doors, and was staring at the monstrous machine.

The gang began to reorganize, casting aside their empty guns and switching to the blackjacks, perhaps hopeful the partially exposed, seemingly delicate mechanisms of the machine creature would succumb to a brute force attack.

The clockwork solider jerked into life, stepping toward the gang. Daud could only watch as the horror unfolded before him.

The first two died quickly, impaled through the stomach on a blade-arm each, their bodies then lifted clear of the cobbled street and tossed to one side without any apparent effort. With the machine's beak-head turned away, two others moved in to attack what appeared to be an opening on the other side, but the first lost his arm nearly at the shoulder and the second had her forehead cleaved as the machine, clearly able to see directly behind it, swept its other arms around to defend its flank.

The rest of the gang hesitated—Daud gave them that much credit, at least—as the machine pivoted at a perfect ninety degrees and walked toward them at a measured pace. Its thin, articulated legs neatly stepped over the blood-soaked bodies on the street.

Daud ran through his options. That the Sixways were dead was a given—the machine must have been brought by the Duke of Serkonos to help with the coup, an unstoppable force to wipe out any and all opposition. There would be more of the things, too—this one had just been sent in to deal with Wyrmwood Way.

None of it mattered. He needed to complete his mission.

To do that, he needed to live—he needed to get *out*, now.

But he also still needed to know where the Twin-bladed Knife was. And there was still someone here who might have the information he needed.

He looked up at Eat 'Em Up Jack. The young woman was back at the top of the stairs, calling to her gang, but Daud could see the fear and uncertainty that was now clouding her expression.

Daud gritted his teeth as he felt the power flow through him. He reached forward and pulled himself across the Void, reappearing at the top of the stairs beside her. Jack took a single step back in surprise, then growled and reached into the top pocket of her tunic. From the concealed sheath, she drew a knife with a blade that was long and square, more like a spike. She flipped the stiletto around in her grip, placing her thumb on the pommel, ready to fight.

Daud held out his hand. "I can get us out of here."

She just stared at his hand and frowned, her brow slick with a cold sweat.

Out in the Sixways, just twenty yards away, the clockwork soldier continued its rampage, dismembering anyone within range of its killing arms. The heavy cobblestones of the intersection were running thick with blood, but the gang was clearly not about to give up. Even from this distance, Daud could see the fire in their eyes. It was the same kind of intensity, the same kind of focus he'd seen in the Whalers, back in the day. The Sixways were strong, skilled fighters, a *family* who had each other's backs—loyal to the very last.

Loyal to their leader, Eat 'Em Up Jack, they were protecting her. But it wasn't enough. The machine was making quick work of the gang, and it was getting steadily closer.

Daud turned to Jack. He reached out for her, but she pulled away.

"We're getting out of here, *now*!"

She looked at him and snarled. "No! I'm Eat 'Em Up Jack. I'm the leader of the Sixways Gang. I stay with them and I *die* with them."

Daud turned back to the fight. It was getting closer—and it was weakening, but not enough.

Could he finish the job? Save the gang—save Jack—and still get the information he needed? It was a mercenary thought, but Daud had no time for anything else.

It was do, or die.

He just needed a weapon.

Daud turned, his gloved hand snatching at Jack's. She swore and swung with the stiletto, but Daud was faster. He grabbed her wrist and twisted, forcing her to loosen her grip. Then he slid his hand up and tore the knife away from her.

A stiletto was not Daud's favorite choice of blade, but it was better than nothing. He moved to the top of the steps and reached forward.

In the blink of an eye he had crossed the Sixways, appearing *behind* the clockwork soldier. Before the machine could react, he stepped up onto the crook of the thing's knee and lifted himself onto its back. The torso was covered with amber-wood plates, but the complex mechanisms underneath were within range of his blade.

The mechanical creature spun around, momentarily unable to determine where this new attacker was. The blade-arms flailed, snapping back and forth, but Daud, his head ducked down, remained out of reach. He clung on, ignoring the machine as it announced a new string of protocols, and peered between the plates on the thing's back.

This close, the machine's heart looked so delicate and fragile—the narrow stiletto was the ideal weapon. Ignoring the large spinning gear wheel that was sure to snap the small blade in an instant, Daud slid the knife under the lip of an amber-wood plate and used it as a lever. He pushed the stiletto up to get a better angle, then plunged it downwards.

There was a spark, and the hot smell of oil, but if he had managed to inflict any damage, the clockwork soldier didn't show any ill effects. It whirled again, having now realized its attacker was clinging to its back. Servos whirred as the machine pivoted violently at the waist, trying to dislodge him. The surviving members of the Sixways Gang dodged out of range of the long bladed arms as the clockwork soldier jerked and staggered around in a small circle, fighting to get Daud off.

Daud's grip slipped, momentarily. He needed a new plan—the internal mechanisms of the creature seemed to be just as tough as its exterior framework, and with the machine determined to get rid of him, he knew he would be thrown off any moment.

Then the machine pushed its torso forward, bending sharply at the waist. Surprised, Daud slid up its back, until he was forced to loop an arm around the clockwork soldier's neck just to stay on. Then the machine straightened, Daud's legs flying out behind as he struggled for purchase.

He felt the sharp sting as his leg was glanced by an oblique sweep of one of the blade-arms. Daud hauled himself up the machine's back, straddling the shoulders, the back of the carved wooden head pressed against his chest.

He was in a vulnerable position. There was little to hold onto, and he was exposed to the four swirling blades.

The head was large, from the tip of the beak to the base of the skull-like shell almost as long as Daud's arm—but the neck mechanism on which it sat seemed ridiculously slender, no more than a spinal rod and three piston-like struts with universal joints, allowing full freedom of movement. Daud rammed the stiletto into the machine's neck, sliding the blade between one of the struts and the central column rod until the hilt stopped any further progress. Then, grabbing the small handle with both hands, he pushed the weapon sideways. Something was going to give—either the machine's neck, or the knife.

He needn't have worried. The stiletto was a fine piece of metalwork, and one of the clockwork soldier's neck supports snapped cleanly, breaking like a twig. The thing's head lolled and the machine's blade-arms fell as its whole body listed to one side for a moment. With the struts on the other side of the neck now presented to him, Daud jammed the knife home again, shoving it with the heel of both hands, and broke both universal joints on the support rod. The rod came out entirely and dropped to the cobbles with a clatter.

The machine made a sound like the brakes failing on a rail carriage and it reared up again, another attempt to rid itself of its attacker. Daud shifted up so his knees were on the machine's shoulders, locked his fingers underneath the thing's beak and yanked upwards.

With a spray of sparks, the creature's head came off in his hands and Daud fell backward, bracing himself as he hit the cobbles.

Neck sparking, the machine tottered on its thin legs, its arms swinging, the sharp tips of its blades gouging the cobbles, throwing up hot orange sparks.

"*Catastrophic damage to head. Increasing power to audio detection.*"

Now the Sixways Gang saw their chance. Daud counted only two men and one woman left standing, but they charged in, blackjacks swinging, easily dodging the now slow, uncoordinated movements of the blade-arms. With several well-placed blows, the machine buckled and the gangsters jumped back as the twitching creature finally folded onto the road with a crash. One of the bulbs on the front of the torso caught a cobble on the edge and shattered, and a moment later the other bulbs dimmed. The clockwork soldier twitched for a few seconds before the machine stopped moving altogether. Thick, bluish fluid—processed whale oil—began to pool out from underneath the machine, mixing with the blood of the fallen gangsters.

The three survivors stood panting and wiped the sweat and blood from their faces. The silence on the Sixways intersection was almost palpable.

Then came the sound once more.

Metal on stone, rhythmic, heavy.

Getting louder. Getting *closer.*

Jack ran down the steps of the Suicide Hall and pointed. "Look!"

Two more mechanical nightmares clattered into view, striding out of Wyrmwood Way, marching toward them with disconcerting slowness, their legs rising and falling in stiff unison, each machine lifting and re-folding their four arms in sequence, the blades snapping together, like they were marking time and drumming out a beat of death and slaughter.

And behind the machines, Daud could see the Grand Serkonan Guard, their white helmets pulled low, each armed with a heavy pistol. It was only a small squad, eight advancing at a crouch, using the pair of clockwork soldiers in front of them as the perfect cover.

Daud grabbed the shoulder of the nearest gangster.

"Get out of here! Run! *Now*, while you can. What are you waiting for?" He turned to Jack. "Tell your men to leave. The Sixways are finished. In a few hours, the whole of the Wyrmwood district will be in flames. You can't fight this. Look at them!"

He gestured to the oncoming enemy. One hundred yards and closing.

Then the gangster Daud had spoken to turned around. She jerked her head to one side.

"Get her away from here."

Jack shook her head. "I stay with my family. They die, I die."

"I'm sorry," said Daud, "but I can't let that happen. You have information I need. And I'm not going to let you die before I get it."

The gangster waved at them. "Go! We'll buy you time."

Then she made a fist and raised it. Her companions

joined him, the three beginning their chant as they walked toward the approaching machines.

"Better off dead! Better off dead!"

Daud reached for Jack. She jerked away. "Don't touch me."

"We can debate this later," he said. He grabbed her arm and yanked her toward him. Then he reached up and pulled at the world, the Mark of the Outsider alive and electric on his hand.

The pair rematerialized in one of the gaping empty windows of the burned-out building next to the Suicide Hall. Behind, Daud heard the last survivors of the Sixways Gang shout their chant and heard the nightmare machines chatter their emotionless assessment of the threat.

Then Daud shifted higher, taking Jack with him, from window to window, then to the edge of the roof. The weak structure began to crumble under their combined weight. Daud felt the tiredness, his mind beginning to blur after all the exertion, but he kept going, transversing them across the street to another roof, then farther out, across the buildings, away from the Sixways and the horror of the clockwork soldiers. He didn't know where he was going, he only knew he had to get away, somewhere safe, where he could question Eat 'Em Up Jack, perhaps finally convincing her to give up her secret. To tell him where the Twin-bladed Knife had gone.

And as they traveled, the Mark of the Outsider glowed under his glove, the pain white hot, sapping his concentration and willpower the more he used it.

Instead, Daud focused on the pain. He wanted to remember it like a song—every note, every nuance, so he could return it in full to the one who deserved it the most.

The black-eyed bastard who had given him the Mark in the first place.

9

THE SUICIDE HALL,
WYRMWOOD DISTRICT, DUNWALL
18th Day, Month of Earth, 1852

"Our investigations have proved conclusively that there is indeed operating within the boundaries of Gristol, a covert organization, apparently independent of any foreign political control, but possibly funded by a rogue branch of one of the governments of the Isles. The makeup of this organization is as yet unclear, although we know its agents are numerous and widespread; in Dunwall, we believe they have infiltrated all levels of society, from the aristocratic classes of the Estate District down to the street gangs which still plague certain quarters of the city.

As to this organization's purpose, we have yet to fully understand. But that their prime focus of attention is on the Imperial throne is a certainty, although for what purpose, we do not know.

Investigations continue; full report to follow."

—ANALYSIS OF REPORTS OF COVERT
FOREIGN ACTIVITIES
Excerpt from a report commissioned
by the Royal Spymaster

"Exquisite."

"*Absolutely* exquisite."

A curl of blue smoke headed toward the nicotine-stained ceiling, adding to the thick fog that already filled the room.

"Such lines, such movement."

"Such movement. Such exquisite movement."

The woman took another draw on her long, black cigarillo and held the smoke in her lungs. She savored the rich aniseed flavor, the tight buzz in her head. She kept her elbow crooked and the cigarette well away from her scarlet velvet trouser suit, and as she enjoyed the rush from the medicinal herbs wrapped in with the tobacco, she absently ran a hand over her coiffured blonde hair, held high in place by a long gold hairpin.

And then she exhaled, long and slow. She unbuttoned the top of her black shirt. They'd been in the room for an eternity, and with the windows closed and the door shut it was getting hot, and perspiration was most certainly not good for one's complexion.

The man next to her was clad in opposite colors: a jet-black velvet suit, the jacket double-breasted and cinched tight, his shirt scarlet and high-collared, a black silk cravat tied in a knot so elaborate it had taken him a good half hour to get just *so*, as had his slicked black hair and neatly waxed moustache. He didn't move from his position, half-sitting, half-leaning on the windowsill, arms folded tightly, his neck craned awkwardly to look down into the street below. He didn't look comfortable, but comfort, the woman knew, was far from the point. The man was posing, for her, for the invisible audience he liked to imagine was watching their every move. Nothing he did was by chance, and his position by the window was carefully arranged to be a work of art in itself, a worthy subject for a portrait.

The woman lifted her chin. Ah, if only there *were* someone here to capture this moment in oils. What would the painting be called? *The Masters at Work*, perhaps? She liked the simplicity of it. Of course, he would think differently. He liked the elaborate, and the ostentatious. He would suggest something like *The Mistress, Her Lover, and the Blood of the Others*. Garish and a little awkward, but certainly memorable.

The woman frowned and took another long suck on her cigarillo. *The Blood of Others* was good. It seemed to sum up their job rather well. And it was certainly apt today, because there was a very great deal of the blood of others being spilled as the two clockwork soldiers dismantled the bodies of the last members of the Sixways Gang in the middle of the intersection far below the window.

"Did you see the light, Mrs. Devlin?" asked the man. He ran a finger down the bridge of his nose, but didn't turn away from the window. When he refolded his arms he pulled them even tighter than before, if that were possible.

Mrs. Devlin wrinkled her own nose. "The light, Mr. Devlin?" Of course she hadn't seen any light. Her husband was making things up, as usual. Transforming the ordinary into the extraordinary.

Although there was no need for such exaggeration today. Because she'd seen it. They both had. Not *light*, as Mr. Devlin said, but something else.

A glimpse of the numinous.

"Such lines," said Mr. Devlin. "He didn't just move, he *danced*. Danced in the blue light, every muscle in perfect harmony, every element a beat in the music of the Void."

Mrs. Devlin lifted an eyebrow. "A sonnet, written in fracturing bone, my dear," she said, but she said it cautiously. She thought back to the scene they had just witnessed. The clockwork soldiers and the demise of the Sixways Gang, although somewhat spectacular in its visceral nature, was not of the least interest to her.

No, it was the bearded man with the hooded green jerkin that had had their attention. They had listened to the conversation between him and Jack down in the bar via the speaking tubes that were secreted throughout the Suicide Hall, but while they had gained little intelligence they didn't already possess, the overheard discussion had at least confirmed their own suppositions.

The bearded man—their quarry—was indeed looking for the artifact, following the rumors across the Isles, the stories that had led him to Dunwall. Stories that the Devlins had themselves heard as they had tracked their prey, keeping their distance, patiently gathering intelligence, trying not just to discover what he was doing, but to predict his next moves. That, perhaps, was the secret to their success as the greatest manhunters the Empire had ever known—their ability not just to track their quarry, but to analyze them, *understand* them, and to use their observations and data to make calculated predictions on decisions that had yet to be made, paths that had yet to be taken.

Because if you got there first, the quarry would come to *you*.

They had lost him after the factory, but that was but a minor inconvenience. They knew he was looking for the artifact, and they knew he knew Dunwall. Which meant his next port of call was always going to be Wyrmwood Way—the Sixways Gang. So they got here first and installed themselves in the Suicide Hall, Eat 'Em Up Jack's cooperation ensured by some long-held but very convenient debt to their leader back in Morley.

"Interesting, wasn't it?" asked Mr. Devlin. He glanced at his wife, the back of one finger tapping the end of his nose. "Those abilities he possessed. The way he could disappear and reappear like that. A fascinating power."

Mrs. Devlin nodded. "Quite fascinating, my dear Mr. Devlin. It seems the legends were rather more factual than I supposed."

Mr. Devlin frowned in quiet appreciation. "Indeed, my dear Mrs. Devlin. There is nobody in all the fair Empire of the Isles that has powers like that. No bonecharm, no artifact could confer such power."

Mrs. Devlin smiled and drew in a mouthful of smoke. "He *was* remarkable, wasn't he?"

"Remarkable. Exquisite."

"*Absolutely* exquisite."

"Such skill. Such *talent*."

"Never a truer word has passed your lips, my dear Mrs. Devlin," said Mr. Devlin as he unfolded himself from the window and brushed down his thick velvet jacket and straightened his cravat in what little reflection there was in the glass in front of him. Apparently satisfied, he turned and gave a short bow to his wife, his heels clicking together, the sound echoing off the wood-paneled walls.

Mrs. Devlin lifted an arm, checking the red velvet of her trouser suit for ash and brushing the sleeve even though it was entirely spotless. Then she moved to her husband and laid her hand on his shoulder. Mr. Devlin sighed.

"I do wish you wouldn't smoke that stuff, my dearest. The smoke is *so* difficult to get out of one's clothes."

Mrs. Devlin laughed and replaced her hand on his shoulder with her chin. "You know Wyrmwood Way is quite simply the best place to obtain this particular herb, my dearest."

Mr. Devlin frowned. "The delights of Dunwall know no bounds," he said. Then he moved over to his wife, and grinning, gripped her by the waist. Mrs. Devlin rested both hands on her husband's shoulders and hummed as they swayed their hips and danced in a slow, gentle circle in the center of the room.

"This coup, though," said Mrs. Devlin, stopping her humming only for her husband to take up the tune himself without missing a beat. "Dreadfully inconvenient, it must be said."

Mr. Devlin pursed his lips. "Perhaps, but an inconvenience that is none of our concern and most certainly not part of our assignment."

"Don't you find it odd that the League had no forewarning of such an event? The organization exists to protect the imperial throne, and yet the very thing it was created to prevent manages to occur without any apparent hindrance."

"As I said, my dear, this is not our concern. Our services are offered to the highest bidder. Whether the League is capable or not—or whether they decide to share any intelligence they may have that lies outside the purview of our assignment—is not our problem. All that matters is that they pay us for a very particular job and that we fulfill the terms of that contract."

"You are, as always," Mrs. Devlin said, "a font of wisdom and insight, my dear Mr. Devlin."

"Think nothing of it, my dear Mrs. Devlin." Mr. Devlin led the dance back to the window. Down in the Sixways intersection, the clockwork soldiers now stood as still as they were able, their frames vibrating slightly, their bladed arms twitching in unison as the squad of Grand Serkonan Guards searched through the piles of dead bodies scattered across the street, overseen by a red-jacketed officer at the rear.

Mrs. Devlin broke away from her husband and studied the scene.

"Whether the coup is our problem or not," she said, "I

suggest, Mr. Devlin, that we return to the League at our earliest convenience and make our report." She leaned on the windowsill and cocked her head. Down below, one of the guards was talking to the officer, and both men were now looking up at the Suicide Hall. Mrs. Devlin shrank back from the glass, in case she had been spotted. "And I suggest that moment is now," she continued. "The soldiers appear ready to search this building."

Mr. Devlin joined her. "Then I do believe I agree with you, my dear."

"How confident are we in our projection?"

"He will extract the information he wants. Daud is both ruthless and efficient. Jack is tough, but young. She will yield eventually, and he will be on the trail of the artifact once more."

"Which means he'll go after the Collector."

"He most certainly will."

"Which means he will have to head north," Mrs. Devlin said. "How very thoughtful of him."

"How convenient."

"*Delightfully* convenient."

Mr. Devlin clicked his heels again and held out his arm. "Shall we?"

Mrs. Devlin took her husband's arm and gave him a little bow. "We can go out through the cellar. Use the sewer tunnel. If we assume Dunwall is now blockaded, we should be able to get to Ranfurly before they close that dockyard."

Her husband crinkled his nose. "The sewer, my dear?"

Mrs. Devlin shrugged. "Needs must, my darling heart. Needs must."

"In which case," said Mr. Devlin, reaching for the cigarillo still burning in his wife's hand, "I'm going to need all the help I can get."

She let him take it, and he inhaled deeply, holding the

smoke in his lungs for as long as possible before exhaling. He shrugged. "I suspect we are going to smell much worse in the very near future."

Mrs. Devlin laughed. "Come now. We have our report to make to the League." She turned and headed for the door.

"They will be pleased, won't they, Mrs. Devlin?"

His wife looked over her shoulder. "The League?"

"No, Wyman."

Mrs. Devlin smiled again. "Oh yes. Wyman will be very pleased indeed. And even more so once we present them with Daud's head on a pike."

10

YOUNG LUCY'S GRAVE, GRISTOL
18th to 20th Day, Month of Earth, 1852

"Spirit of the Deep, Siren of the Dreams.

I walked for hours along the coast, leaving Dunwall behind me until the lament of the waves drowned all other feeling. I wept, knowing you would not come to me, my love.

You rule my dreams, where I behold with senses I do not possess in waking life the dark splendor of your home in the deep. There the ocean rests on your back like a sleeping child on his father's shoulders.

In these sleepless nights of despair, you appear to me not as the mighty leviathan, but as a young man, with eyes as black as the Void."

—SPIRIT OF THE DEEP
Excerpt from a longer work of fiction

Eat 'Em Up Jack led Daud silently through the night, slipping out of the barricades around Dunwall and heading into the dark countryside. They traveled swiftly and in silence, Jack not speaking until they reached the first of what Daud deduced was the Sixways' series of safe houses and waypoints, part of their infamous smuggling route that allowed illicit treasures to vanish. Daud let Jack work as she spoke to the landlord of a forlorn, empty inn balanced on a hillside in the middle of nowhere miles to the southwest of Dunwall, keeping to the shadows while Jack and the bewhiskered landlord spoke in low voices, the landlord sometimes glancing in his direction, sometimes nodding at Jack, all the while with a stern expression on his face.

They rested at the inn for several hours. Jack retired for some much-needed sleep just as dawn began to break. Daud stayed awake, as did the landlord, who sat in front of the door of the backroom, guarding his boss and watching Daud in silence.

At dusk, Jack emerged. The landlord gave her provisions—enough for two, although he never spoke a word to Daud—and they left as soon as it was dark enough. The country was rough, and the sky was heavy with clouds, obscuring the moon. But it was safer than traveling during the day.

Jack led and Daud followed. They walked through woods, across fields, through villages shut up for the night. Eventually, Jack stopped at a house and vanished inside, leaving Daud out in the deserted street. She came out a short while later and they moved on, coming to another small farming town—Fallibroome, perhaps?— where Jack spoke to a militiaman on the gates, who led the pair up onto the wall, skirting the market square before dropping down onto rocky hillside on the other side of the settlement.

Daud understood Jack was now on a mission of her own. She had had the heart cut out of her criminal empire, and as they moved from waypoint to waypoint, Daud knew she was spreading the word, telling her agents not just of the massacre in Wyrmwood Way, but of her plans to rebuild. She was telling everyone to be ready.

They spent the next day in the deep green gloom of an ancient wood. They ate together in silence. Jack slept and Daud kept watch. Their conversation may have been non-existent, but they had at least come to some kind of unspoken agreement.

At twilight, they resumed their journey, and after a few more hours of walking they emerged from the woodland and found themselves on a high bluff overlooking the sea. There, below them, was the coastal village of Young Lucy's Grave. It was cradled by steep cliffs on three sides, the fourth open to a narrow harbor, home to a tiny fishing fleet that faced the crashing waves, the vicious tide funneled between two sheer faces of black rock.

"We're here," said Jack. Daud looked down at the village and nodded. Jack watched him a moment, her eyes catching the flash of lightning in the sky. Then the thunder rolled, and as Jack headed off, leading Daud to the narrow, precarious cliff path, the heavy Gristol sky opened, and the rain began.

Young Lucy's Grave was so named for the ancient shipwreck that still remained visible out in the harbor. Beyond the cliffs, the rising skeleton of the huge whaling ship conveniently marked the location of dangerous rocks lurking just beneath the water. As they walked the cliff path, the rain pelting down, Daud found his eyes drawn to the wreck. He hadn't been here before, but, like most people who had spent any time in southern Gristol, the story of *Young Lucy* was known to him, while the village was largely overlooked—a tiny fishing community, living in happy isolation, difficult to access and protected by the cliffs, sustained by the bounty of the ocean.

And, Daud realized, the perfect cover for the Sixways smuggling route. Because from Young Lucy's Grave you could get a small fishing vessel out into open water, and— out of sight of the major shipping lanes around Dunwall— that vessel could be met by a larger boat. From there, the secret cargo could be transferred.

This was the route the Twin-bladed Knife had taken. Eat 'Em Up Jack was leading him to it.

It was another hour before they reached the village. The settlement was densely packed, consisting of perhaps a hundred buildings that followed the cliff face, with steep, narrow streets leading down to the fishing harbor, streets that were treacherous in the downpour. The village was quiet and dark, the inhabitants asleep, and the sea beyond the cliffs rolled and roared. The waters of the harbor were somewhat calmer but not by much, the black silhouettes of the fishing fleet dancing with the currents in what little moonlight penetrated the breaks in the rainclouds.

On the edge of the harbor stood a two-story building, the upper level a good deal larger than the ground floor, with large, shuttered windows looking out to sea. Jack headed straight for the structure, knocking once on the main door. A second later it opened and Jack stepped into the darkness beyond. Daud followed, water streaming off the point of his hood.

He closed the door behind him and followed Jack's shape—and the sound of another pair of feet ahead of her—up the stairs to the upper level. There was another door here; once through and closed, light flared, white and bright, dazzling after so many hours traveling in darkness. Daud squinted, and pushed his hood back.

They were standing in what was clearly the harbormaster's office. On the back wall was a large nautical chart of the harbor, extending out well beyond the wreck of *Young Lucy*. Underneath the chart was a desk that dominated the room, its surface covered with more charts and other papers, which faced the large picture window that overlooked the harbor itself. The other two walls were lined with shelves, onto which were crammed shipping ledgers and logbooks and other documentation. A large brass telescope on a tripod stood in the far corner, the harbormaster himself standing beside it, Jack to his left. The harbormaster was a large man dressed in a heavy blue coat, the buttons straining against his impressive girth. He wore a blue knitted hat on his head, and a scowl on his face. In his hand he held a pistol, which he aimed directly at Daud.

"Do I kill him?"

Jack shook her head. "No, he needs a route out."

The harbormaster frowned. The gun didn't move. "Destination?"

"Porterfell."

"Just him?"

"Just him. I'm staying here. I've got a lot to do."

Daud lifted an eyebrow. Jack met his gaze. "I'll tell you what you need to know. And Malcolm here will make your travel arrangements."

Malcolm narrowed his eyes, then he made his pistol safe and lowered it. He moved back around to his desk, all the while looking at Daud.

Then Malcolm turned to Jack. "Strange things happening in the city, so I've heard."

Daud and Jack exchanged a look, then Jack nodded. "I need to tell you what happened," she said. "I've got a lot of work to do to get the Sixways up and running again."

As Jack and her agent talked, Daud moved to the window. He looked out into the early dawn, the rain lashing the window, the sea crashing against the cliffs around the village.

Porterfell. Daud knew the name—another fishing settlement, west along the coast from Dunwall, about halfway between the capital and Potterstead.

So, the Twin-bladed Knife was still in Gristol? *Good*.

It seemed the next phase of his mission was about to begin.

11

THE CLIFFTOP OVERLOOKING YOUNG LUCY'S GRAVE, GRISTOL
20th Day, Month of Earth, 1852

"It is nothing more than a story, but then, so much of what we know of the powers of those who proclaim knowledge of witchcraft comes from such stories, sometimes no more than whispers or rumors. That we must rely on such unreliable sources of information is unfortunate, but learn what we can, when we can.

It is claimed that those touched by the Void employ servants, under some form of mesmeric influence, living for the singular purpose of serving their terrible mistress or master.

Further, it is said by those who have borne witness that the connection between sorcerer and servant is comparable to familial love, although to say this is to pervert the very concepts of family or community."

—ON THE WITCH'S MOST DEVOTED SERVANT
Excerpt from a secret report to High Overseer Yul Khulan, by Overseer Harrison

The wind battered the hilltop, the raining coming down in sheets, soaking the hunched figure that knelt by a black boulder. Out at sea, huge waves crashed around the wrecked shell of the *Young Lucy*, while closer to the village, the waters of the harbor rose and fell in dangerous swells.

The man ignored the rain. He ignored the cold. He ignored it all. He knelt on the ground, sinking into the mud, and watched the village through his spyglass, focusing on the upper level of the harbormaster's tower. The village was dark; the harbormaster's abode was not, yellow light pouring out from the window facing the harbor—facing *away* from the cliff.

The man couldn't see what was going on inside, but no matter. He had seen enough. The journey from Dunwall to here had been nothing—he had been following Daud for months, tracking him ever since word had reached his mistress that the former assassin was hiding in Wei-Ghon.

But now time was pressing—and preparations were almost complete. After so long planning, the day was fast approaching.

The spy couldn't lose Daud now, not when the culmination of his mistress's plan was so near at hand.

It was time to make his report—perhaps his final one.

Collapsing the spyglass, the man turned and hobbled away from the edge of the cliff, out of sight of any potential onlookers. It would be dark for hours yet and if anything the storm was getting worse, but there was no need to take any risks. The village—save for the harbormaster's tower—appeared to be shuttered up for the night, but there was always a chance someone was watching. His mistress called him paranoid, but the man preferred to think of himself as *prepared*. But, more importantly, he could not risk being seen now. Although he didn't place any particular value on his own life, he knew that if he *was* seen, and perhaps chased, there was no way he would be able to escape a village warden, not in these less than ideal conditions.

So no, he couldn't risk it. Sliding in the mud, soaked to the skin, his long black hair a heavy, matted weight against his back, he skidded back toward the woods. He felt no discomfort at the weather. All he could feel was the *pain*, the constant, unending agony that only one person in all the Isles could alleviate.

His mistress—his love. And she was waiting, hundreds of miles away, patiently waiting for his report.

At the edge of the woods, the ground was cratered and scattered with large boulders. The man nearly fell behind one, then pulled himself up and sat with his back against it. Wiping the sodden hair from his face, he reached inside his cloak and pulled out a brass framework, a cat's cradle of struts and panels and hinges, the basket-like object unfolding in his hands. The main part of the device consisted of four triangular brass panels, each finely pierced with geometric shapes and symbols that had their own particular meaning. Once hinged into place, the panels formed a tetrahedron, with a gap at the apex, underneath which was a three-fingered claw formed by folded-out silver prongs.

From another pocket the man pulled a dark gemstone about the size of a plum, the surface cut into a perfect polyhedron. Buffeted by the wind and rain, the man shuffled into a cross-legged position and balanced the assembled device across his knees. He took the gemstone in both hands, and carefully slotted it into the gap at the top of the device, the crystal locking in place between the claw and the three points of the brass panels.

The man exhaled.

Assembling the thing was the easy part. *Using* it was another task altogether, because communicating with his mistress over such a distance required power, and lots of it. And the only place it drew from was his own mind.

One day, his service to his mistress would kill him—he knew that, and accepted the fact. But he didn't care. If it was this last report that did it, then so be it. If he died then it would be in glorious service to his mistress, the mistress who loved him and whom he loved, the mistress who understood his pain, and who promised to alleviate it.

Even if she was the cause of it in the first place.

He stared into the depths of the dark gemstone. He gritted his teeth and began hyperventilating, in anticipation of the agony to come.

"My lady," he said, raising his voice against the storm thrashing around him. "My lady, he is here. He is come. It is as you said. He follows the path. He follows your will."

The man paused and took a deep breath. He could feel it begin, at first a soft sensation across his eyes, then slowly encircling his whole head. After a few seconds, the pressure was vise-like, his skull feeling as if it would be crushed as his life force was drained to power the communicator.

"My lady! Can you hear me, my lady? Can you *see* me? Please, speak to me, speak to me."

The wind picked up and lightning flashed, and when the thunder rolled the man couldn't hear it. He was lost in the crystal, his eyes wide and fixed on its myriad depths.

He felt the chill first, the deep ache like his bones were made of ice carved from a Tyvian glacier. From within the crystal, a blue light sparked into being, then brightened, growing and bouncing against the inside planes of the gem, until the crystal was nothing but a glowing ball of cold, blue fire.

And then he felt the pain as the pressure around his head suddenly transformed into a searing, jagged agony, bisecting his skull and then traveling down his entire body. He was rooted to the spot, every muscle in his body rigid, caught in a terrible, bone-crushing spasm. Foam flecked his lips as his frozen chest heaved for breath. Lightning flashed again, and a small part of the man's mind that remained free and his own wished the lightning would strike and put an end to his misery.

Seconds. Minutes. Maybe hours passed. All he could do was stare at the gemstone, watch with unmoving, unblinking eyes as his calloused hands gripped the edges of the communicator, the sharp edges of the frame cutting into his flesh, his blood running freely down his wrists, mixing with the rain.

Just before his eyes rolled up into his head and he passed out, he heard her voice. Her glorious, beautiful voice, carried impossibly from Karnaca, where she waited. Her words were a song, her tone a melody. At once he could feel her love and warmth, filling his mind.

She was his mistress, his everything.

She was the witch, and he the familiar.

"I can see you," she said. "You have done well. All will be prepared. He will be led home. As it has been foreseen, so it shall be."

The man felt warm and peaceful. He felt like he was floating, as though he were not in his body but rising above it, and looking down on his huddled, ruined form. He was waterlogged and blood-soaked, the communicator cradled in his arms, his cloak billowing in the wind.

"Now sleep," she said. "You have served me well and your work will not be forgotten. Sleep, then return to me, to Karnaca, to the Royal Conservatory, where the final preparations shall be made."

Lightning flashed. The gemstone flared with a deep blue light.

"Sleep, sleep."

He did.

The gemstone faded.

INTERLUDE

THE ROYAL CONSERVATORY, KARNACA
2nd Day, Month of Timber, 1841,
Eleven Years before the Dunwall Coup

"I had no doubt that Pandyssia was rich in resources. But a place must be understood if we ever hope to exploit its myriad treasures. These were my thoughts as I agreed to join the ill-fated expedition. And so it was, on the third day of the Month of Earth, under calm gray skies, the great sea vessel *Antonia Aquillo* set sail with captain, crew, researchers, and myself, (thirty-eight of us in total) for what would be the most terrifying and spiritually draining experience of my life."

—A REFLECTION ON MY JOURNEY TO THE
PANDYSSIAN CONTINENT
Anton Sokolov, excerpt from the Introduction to the
second edition, 1822

"Your Grace, my lords and ladies, fellow philosophers, gentlemen—I bid you welcome! You are gathered here tonight at the very nexus of history, the point on which the fulcrum of progress will pivot, as the Empire of the Isles searches that far-distant horizon we call the future! For tonight, we lucky few are privileged to see a glimpse of the new and wonderful age that stretches out before us!"

There was a ripple of laughter from the audience, and only the smallest smattering of applause. Standing center stage in the makeshift auditorium that, for one night only, occupied most of the entrance hall of Karnaca's Royal Conservatory, Aramis Stilton kept the smile plastered to his face, but he took a breath and held it for a moment.

Idiots. What's so bloody funny? You're not supposed to laugh. Honestly, this entire evening is wasted on you.

Then he clapped his hands and joined the audience with a chuckle of his own, but as he stepped closer to the edge of the stage he pursed his lips and gave a slight nod to his stage assistant, Toberman, who was standing in the wings, awaiting his instructions.

Good lad. Young, but keen. Works hard. Mines were no place for him. Shows initiative. Glad to have him on board.

At Stilton's signal, Toberman touched the brim of his

flat cap and ducked away. A moment later, as Stilton cast his gaze across the audience, the temporary stage lights dimmed suddenly, leaving him illuminated only by the bright white glare of the footlight directly in front of him. For better, eerie effect, Stilton leaned forward over the light—he knew just what it would look like, as he'd had young Toberman stand in the exact same spot earlier that afternoon while he moved around the hall, checking the view from every conceivable angle.

Someone in the audience gasped. Stilton's smile returned.

Now, that's more like it.

"My lords and ladies," he said, rubbing his hands together. "What you are about to see demonstrated before your very eyes this evening pushes at the boundaries of our knowledge. The topic upon which our distinguished guest is about to lecture has until now only been whispered within the hallowed confines of the Academy of Natural Philosophy in the fair Imperial capital of Dunwall."

Stilton peered out at the crowd, moving his hands to cast a shade—just for a moment—over his face so he could see through the glare of the footlights. It was another hot night in Karnaca, and the audience, squeezed into their finery, were sweating in the close and humid air of the Royal Conservatory, the fans most of the ladies were fluttering sounding like the gentle hum of bees at work.

Ticket sales had been good—*very* good—and the place was packed. More importantly, the invitations to the very highest levels of Serkonan society had been accepted with pleasure; Stilton allowed his gaze to linger over the silhouette of the Duke, Theodanis Abele, seated in a raised, walled-off area at stage left, next to his son, Luca. The pair were flanked by four officers of the Grand Serkonan Guard.

Stilton felt a swelling of pride within him. Securing

this evening's star attraction was something of a coup, certainly dispelling the whispers around Karnaca that Stilton, the wealthy businessman known mostly for his mining fortune, was indulging in childish fantasies as only the absurdly wealthy could. Some believed he was investing in the Royal Conservatory not out of any love for art or culture, but merely to have his name engraved at the top of the list of institute benefactors.

I'll show them. I'll show them all.

Stilton gave a bow toward the shadow of Theodanis.

At least Theo believes in me.

He held the moment a fraction longer, one beat, two beats, allowing the silence to grow. Then he clapped his hands.

"I have great pleasure in presenting to you, for one night only, the renowned philosopher of all things natural. A giant among men, an intellect the rest of us can only regard with an awe that is well deserved." He bowed and sidestepped, gesturing back toward the center of the stage. "Please welcome our illustrious speaker, former Head of the Academy of Natural Philosophy, now Professor Emeritus: Anton Sokolov."

The crowd erupted into applause as the curtain— another temporary fixture, but one which Stilton had insisted was somehow installed and made operational, cost be blowed—rose. He beamed, savoring the moment. The audience reaction was uproarious and, it seemed, genuine.

Of course it was. He'd been right. So, they'd scoffed at him, like they scoffed at everything he did. A lecture? An evening of soporific discussion of Natural Philosophy? Pah. They'd thought it was nonsense about newfangled mining equipment and that nobody would come. That he would be a laughing stock. Aramis Stilton and his high ideas would be even further alienated from Karnacan society.

He rubbed his hands and retreated to the wings. *Oh, how wrong they are. All of them.*

He was sure of it.

The curtain rose to reveal two reclining chairs. The chairs stood on chrome pedestals, and were spaced to the left and right of the stage, angled at around forty-five degrees so the headrests were pointing to the stage center and the tall device that stood between them.

It was a machine of some kind. A construction of brass and copper and wood, set into an octagonal base in which, facing the audience, a glowing whale oil tank buzzed. Seated above the base was a series of angled panels, covered in switches and levers and dials, and rising from the controls were three metal columns—one brass, one copper, one silver—which rose nearly two yards into the air before disappearing into the base of a large silver sphere. Halfway up the columns, attached by sliding clamps, one to the brass rod and one to the copper rod, were two articulated metal arms, joined in three places and ending in a three-fingered clamp.

As the machine was revealed, the crowd gasped in appreciation, and there was another smattering of applause. Coiffured heads turned to each other, the audience murmuring quietly. Stilton glanced over to the royal box and saw Theodanis leaning toward his son.

Then, from stage left, strode Anton Sokolov himself, resplendent in a long velvet coat, unbuttoned to show an exquisitely embroidered waistcoat. His thick mane of gray hair was slicked back and glowed in the blue light cast by the whale oil tank. As he walked to the front of the stage, he nodded in recognition of the applause, stroking his long beard and regarding the crowd from under craggy brows.

"Thank you, Aramis Stilton," he said over the noise.

Then Sokolov narrowed his eyes and regarded the audience with a cold glare. The applause quickly stopped.

"In the year eighteen hundred and eight, I set out on the *Antonia Aquillo* for the Pandyssian Continent, leader of an expedition of thirty-eight men, the purpose of which was to navigate to that great land and to catalogue its multitude of flora and fauna.

"As many of you will know, the expedition was not without danger, but despite losses suffered from the very first day of our landing, the knowledge we gained from our time on the continent was invaluable.

"But, when we returned to Dunwall—those of us who still remained, that is— many long months later, we brought back with us much more than just knowledge— we brought specimens. And not just of the plant and animal life we found in Pandyssia. Our expedition was also of a geographic and geo*logic* nature."

Sokolov turned to the couches and the machine in the center of the stage. He walked toward it, gesturing with one arm, the other tucked into the small of his back.

"Until now, certain aspects of my analysis of the particular geology of the Pandyssian Continent has not been published, nor even discussed outside the walls of the Academy of Natural Philosophy itself. What I am about to demonstrate to you this evening is the culmination of many years of research, but only represents a fraction of the knowledge and potential of what I have thus far discovered."

Sokolov clicked his fingers, and two stage hands appeared from the wings, carrying between them a rectangular wooden packing crate. They placed it beside the machine, handed Sokolov a small crowbar, then retreated silently.

Sokolov hefted the crowbar, then used it to point at the audience.

"Ladies and gentlemen," he said. "You are among a privileged few to bear witness to my research first hand. And I must admit, I had to consider the invitation to come here quite carefully for *many* weeks before I finally agreed that the time was right for a demonstration. The public have a right to know what kind of work goes on in the Academy, and while the work is incomplete, I must admit a certain eagerness to show the world the potential of my discoveries."

With that he knelt by the box and levered the lid off, then placed the crowbar carefully on the stage and reached inside. He stood, then turned and held up his hands. In each he clutched a roughly spherical object, about the size of a large apple. Sokolov paced the front of stage as he spoke, holding the objects out so the audience could get a clear look at them shining in the footlights.

They were crystals, cut with mathematical precision into multifaceted polyhedra and polished until they glowed. From the wings, Aramis Stilton squinted, peering as he tried to get a better look—Sokolov had refused to show him the stones when he had asked that afternoon. Stilton frowned. They looked interesting, and now that everyone had seen the things, surely he could persuade the natural philosopher to give him a private showing.

He wondered how much the stones might be worth. You could cut a great many individual gems from them.

As Stilton watched on, Sokolov stopped in the center of the stage.

"These are two of the largest, finest mineral samples collected during our expedition. I will not bore you with their chemical composition, but it is safe to say that their analysis took many of my finest academicians many months, and their results were still inconclusive. We spent five entire years just *planning* the very first cut and polish—

the slightest mistake, and they would be ruined, and our chance to investigate their amazing properties would be gone, if not forever, then certainly for my own lifetime."

Sokolov walked back to the packing crate and gently laid the stones back inside. He then returned to the front of the stage, clasped his hand behind his back, and lifted his chin.

"For the next two hours, I will discuss my work regarding the electrostatic potentials of these crystals and alignment of their potential with the magnetic fields of certain alloys, which when brought together allow not just the carriage of power but its *transformation* from one state to another..."

Stilton blinked. He felt his own jaw drop.

Two hours? Did Sokolov just say... two *hours*?

Sokolov paced the stage, and talked, and talked, and talked.

Two bloody hours?

Stilton felt a sinking feeling somewhere in his stomach. Of course. He should have known. Sokolov had insisted on presenting a lecture before carrying out his practical demonstration, and Stilton had been forced to agree to it just to get the natural philosopher to come.

But this?

The sinking feeling turned to nausea. Stilton reached for his inside pocket and pulled out a silver hip flask. He unscrewed the top and took a long swig. Behind him, against the wall, was a tall stool, onto which he negotiated his not insubstantial frame. He sighed, his eyes fixed on the glittering gemstones onstage.

Tuning out Sokolov's monotonous voice, Stilton tried to get comfortable and took another drink.

PART TWO
THE COLLECTOR

12

"For an empire straddling several large land masses and surrounded by a boundless ocean, the most optimal sailing routes around the Isles have, quite understandably, been navigated for centuries. The southern and western coasts of Gristol offer placid, flat seas, ideal for close coastal travel, even in conditions that would be considered somewhat unsavory in other geographies. Further to the west, a strong ocean current traveling southward enables even larger vessels to make impressive progress; however, despite this advantage, traffic along these routes is lighter than on the eastern channels, given the heavier distribution of shipping industries along south-eastern Gristol, from the capital city of Dunwall up to the western settlements of Morley to the north, most notably the major ports of Alba and Caulkenny."

—TRADE ROUTES AND THEIR NAVIGATION
Excerpt from *A Discourse on Maritime Industries*

Maximilian Norcross.
Daud had been given the name by Eat 'Em Up Jack. He

had been given the place, too—Porterfell, a fishing town on the southern coast of Gristol—and he had been given transport. A steam-and-sail clipper used by the Sixways Gang to transport goods, piloted by a captain who wouldn't speak and a first mate who couldn't, on account of his tongue having been cut out.

The harbormaster at Young Lucy's Grave, Malcolm, had personally rowed Daud out to the clipper, which was anchored in the open sea beyond the harbor. In the driving rain and howling winds, the sea seemed impossible—to Daud, anyway—to navigate in so insubstantial a craft, but Malcolm proved to be an able seaman indeed, and the journey had only taken an hour.

The next phase began immediately. With their passenger aboard, the captain ordered his mute first mate to set course, and they ploughed through the somewhat less violent seas, heading first south, and then west.

The journey was uneventful, and for that, Daud was grateful. The smuggling route the Sixways ran between Dunwall and the western settlements of Gristol was totally unmolested by any official patrols, although whether that was because of the situation in Dunwall or not, Daud wasn't sure. His two companions for the six-day expedition gave no indication that anything was particularly unusual about the trip.

But after getting caught in the aftermath of the coup, and after the narrow escape from Wyrmwood Way, Daud had no problem with a few days of relative solitude. It gave him time to think and plan.

Maximilian Norcross.

Norcross was a collector, not exactly famous, but well known in certain quarters for not only owning one of the largest private museums in all the Isles, but for being an astute, practical businessman. He acquired art and treasure for personal enjoyment, but buying, selling, and trading—although he was already a wealthy man, according to Jack—also made him a tidy profit.

Which gave Daud hope—just a little, just enough. Because it meant that perhaps, if Norcross still had the Knife, then he'd be willing to come to terms of some kind. Daud had left one of the platinum caches on the table in the Suicide Hall back in Dunwall, but another pouch rested in a concealed pocket. If Norcross was interested in money, then money he would get.

And if he wasn't, then Daud would take the Knife anyway.

Daud had expected Eat 'Em Up Jack to come with him, but on that count, he had been disappointed. The woman's attitude was cold, the way she viewed the massacre at Wyrmwood Way with detachment, talking about it with the harbormaster as an unfavorable business situation, rather than the wholesale slaughter of her men and her friends—at least, Daud assumed that some of them had been her friends.

So she was staying in Gristol. She was already planning on regrouping with agents the Sixways still had along their smuggling routes. They may have been driven out of Wyrmwood, but Eat 'Em Up Jack was not so easily put out of business.

Daud admired her resilience. He also appreciated her efforts to arrange a meeting with Norcross. To achieve this, she gave Daud a coded phrase, one that set him up as an interested buyer, and directions on whom to give it to once he arrived in Porterfell. Once the code was accepted, Daud only had to be patient and wait until Norcross himself found him.

The plan suited Daud just fine.

In the meantime, he sat on the boat, watching the two-man crew work, ignoring their passenger completely, even leaving him to prepare his own meals.

That also suited Daud just fine.

The captain and his first mate were highly skilled sailors, and Daud had to admit he was impressed, considering the clipper was a reasonably large vessel, which under normal circumstances would have required a few more crewmen. Daud spent a lot of time on deck, the two-man crew ignoring him, losing himself in the peace and quiet of the voyage. It helped clear his mind.

A little, anyway.

Finally, they reached their destination: Porterfell, a small and unremarkable town, the economy, much like Young Lucy's Grave, based almost entirely on fishing, although here on a much larger, industrial scale. As they approached port, Daud was surprised to find their clipper met by a pilot boat with the harbormaster himself at the helm, until he watched—through his spyglass—the clipper's captain slip the harbormaster a satchel, presumably holding money or something else of value, as the two met inside the pilot boat's tiny cabin. Of course, the Sixways Gang had total control of their smuggling routes and the ports along it.

Clever Jack.

Harbormaster bribed, the two crewmen continued with their almost studious disregard for Daud's presence, and as soon as they were guided into dock, he left, and headed into the town, running the instructions given to him back at Young Lucy's Grave through his head.

Eccentric was how some people described the geography of Porterfell. As he navigated his way through the complex network of ancient streets toward his rendezvous, Daud came up with several other words for the town's layout that were far less polite. Porterfell was not large, certainly in comparison with somewhere like Dunwall, but it seemed to Daud that the town's founders had tried to cram almost as many buildings as the imperial capital into a fraction of the space. The result was a dense municipality, the narrow streets and alleys lined with towering buildings of brick and wood that had an unnerving tendency to lean over the roadways beneath, dimming what little daylight managed to reach the streets. Although it was only late afternoon, the streetlights along the major thoroughfares were already on, casting an orange glow over the town and its inhabitants as they went about their business. The tight alleyways that branched off at intervals remained almost entirely dark, save for the occasional light spilling from a window.

Daud decided he liked Porterfell, even if the whole place did stink of fish.

He continued, following the directions given to him by Jack in his head. Soon enough, he found himself in a part of the town dedicated to the primary industry of the place: fishing. Gone were shops and houses, replaced by warehouses and wholesale markets, the street traffic having changed from citizens and shoppers to those employed by the fishing trade, running with barrows and carts over cobbled streets slick with sea water and slimy effluent running freely from the surrounding processing houses. While the more salubrious part of Porterfell had seemed relatively free of vagrants, Daud noticed the high number in this quarter, huddled in damp blankets around the market and warehouse drains, waiting for whatever scraps were thrown out.

The rendezvous was in a public house, the Empire's End, at the corner of an intersection bounded by the main fish market and two warehouses. As Daud entered, he passed a group of three beggars slouched outside the pub's doors. He felt rather than saw them watching him carefully.

He needed to be wary. While he was perfectly capable of handling himself, he was in unknown territory now.

The plan was simple. According to Eat 'Em Up Jack, Norcross's agent used the Empire's End as base of operations, keeping to a set of regular but rotating hours every other day in order to meet any potential clients of his employer. The pub was famous—locally, anyway— for the interior walls being covered in portraits not only of all the emperors and empresses of the Isles, but of the kings and queens who had ruled the various realms that had existed across the island of Gristol before they were unified. History was not Daud's strong point—nor his interest—but he was to meet the agent under the portrait of Emperor Finlay Morgengaard I. As Daud crossed the pub's threshold, he hoped that the paintings would be labeled.

The Empire's End was very small and very busy, the whole place packed almost to standing room only by workers from the surrounding markets, warehouses and processing houses, the reek of fish covered admirably by the strong tobacco that most of the men—and they were all men, as far as Daud could see—seemed to be enjoying.

Daud approached the bar, where he discovered the selection of liquors on offer was meager, the shelves at the back stacked instead with boxes of tobacco.

The barman paid no attention to Daud, nor did any of

the patrons, all too busy engaged in noisy conversation after a hard shift gutting and packing fish. Jostled on all sides, Daud turned his back to the bar and scanned the walls as best he could, trying to identify the meeting point. With so many people packed inside, he could hardly see any of the portraits, let alone identify one as Finlay Morgengaard I. But after a few minutes, he spotted a patron sitting at a corner table who looked so completely out of place among the muscular fish workers that Daud wondered why he bothered with the specific instructions in the first place.

The man was middle-aged with a thin face and razor-sharp cheekbones, his dark wavy hair crammed under an angled cap made of densely curled wool. He held a long, curved clay pipe—containing the only unlit tobacco in the pub—in his mouth, the bowl of which nearly reached the lowest of three large silver clasps that held his voluminous blue cloak in place.

The man was watching him, and as he and Daud looked at each other, the man extracted a hand from beneath his cloak and lifted a monocle on the end of a long ivory stem to his eye. He peered through the lens, and a moment later a small smile appeared. Lowering the monocle, the man nodded.

Daud got the message and walked over, taking a circuitous route through the unmoving patrons. Before reaching the table he paused and glanced around, but nobody was looking. Nobody cared. Above the man was a portrait with a small brass nameplate attached to the bottom of the frame: *Emperor Finlay Morgengaard I (1626–1651)*.

Daud sat at the table opposite the man in the blue cloak, who didn't acknowledge his presence. He just lifted his pipe and used it to gesture at the portrait.

"Morgengaard the Elder," he said. "A fine ruler, by all accounts."

"The just and noble lord who came to an early end."

"Sad to say."

"Sad to say," repeated Daud. It had worked. He'd found the agent.

The man turned to Daud. "Speaking of early."

"Thought I'd get a drink before getting down to business," said Daud, the corner of his mouth curling up in amusement. "Although the people in this place seem to prefer their tobacco."

The man nodded and put the pipe back between his teeth. "When a town smells as bad as this, you'd take up smoking too," he said. "Have you been to Porterfell before?"

"No," said Daud. "It's one of the few places I haven't."

The man raised his monocle. He looked Daud up and down with it—lingering, Daud thought, on his gloved hands, which were placed on the table. Daud slipped them off into his lap and the monocle disappeared back into the cloak. "One day I think I would like to hear about your travels," said the agent. "You have a story somewhere. I can… sense it."

Daud lifted an eyebrow. Then he leaned in, his voice low. "I'm not here to tell you stories. I'm not here for you at all."

The man frowned, apparently annoyed. Whoever this agent was, he seemed to want to play games. "I need to talk to Maximilian Norcross," said Daud.

The man turned his attention to his pipe, tilting it up so he could look in the bowl. Then the man wrinkled his nose. Still looking into his pipe, he spoke. "Mr. Norcross is a busy man." He glanced up at Daud. "A *very* busy man."

Daud met the other man's glare. "I'm looking for

something," he said. "Something specific. I believe *Mr.* Norcross can help me."

The man hummed and returned his attention to his pipe.

Daud waited. He would wait all day if he had to. He had come this far. His mission was reaching a critical moment and he could feel it.

"Unusual," said the man, not looking up.

"How so?"

"Mr. Norcross doesn't sell to just *anybody*. He trades in certain artifacts, the existence of which need to be, shall we say, kept away from certain official noses. As such, his business needs to be discreet. He only sells to invited tenders." The man turned to Daud and looked him up and down again. "And *you* are not invited."

Daud wanted to grab the man by the shoulders and shake him. But he resisted the urge.

"I understood that Norcross and I have a mutual acquaintance in Dunwall. I'm here with their introduction. That should be plenty for him."

The other man smiled. "Ah yes, the lovely young Jack. A little out of her depth. Bad business, all that." He waved with the pipe. "News travels fast. Some news travels faster than others."

"Do I get to meet Norcross or not?"

The agent opened his mouth to speak, but then there was movement by their table as the mass of bodies in the pub rearranged themselves to accommodate a trio of newcomers.

"Coin for heads, sirs? Coin for fish heads and blood, sirs?"

Daud turned in his chair as the group reached their table. They were an older man with a long greasy gray beard, a younger man, clean-shaven, and a woman of about the same age, her face smeared with greenish muck. He recognized them at once—the vagrants who had watched him enter the Empire's End. If their position outside the pub was a regular one, then they knew Daud was a newcomer—perhaps one worth trying their luck on.

Daud frowned and glanced back at the agent, who waved his pipe.

"Fish heads and blood are considered a delicacy by these... types, I believe," he said. "The bosses around here know it. So, unlike the waste they toss into the street, they have the gall to actually charge these poor unfortunates for it."

The agent's free hand dived back into his cloak, and he appeared to be struggling to extract a purse when the barman pushed his way through the crowd.

"Hey, clear off, the lot of you! I'll have no begging in here!"

The trio ducked as the barman appeared ready to strike them, and the crowd parted to let them escape to the door. The barman looked at Daud and the agent, sniffed loudly, then turned away with a scowl.

Norcross's agent hadn't seemed to notice; by the time he stopped fussing with his purse and looked up, the beggars and barman alike had gone. He gripped the end of his pipe between his teeth.

"Oh, well, nevermi—"

Daud grabbed the man's pipe by the bowl and yanked it out of his mouth.

The agent spluttered, his hand moving to his mouth. "Well, there's really no need for that—"

"Listen to me," said Daud, leaning into the man's face. The agent coughed and cleared his throat, his eyes wide. "I don't care who you are, and I don't care what you do, but I'm tired of playing games and I've spent a lot of time and effort getting here. I need to speak to Norcross. I was led to believe you could arrange this, but if you can't, I need you to tell me, right now."

The agent held his hands up. "All right, all right!" The man glanced around the pub, smiling to the other patrons in case anyone had noticed the altercation. Daud was past caring now. "Your... *insistence*... is noted."

Daud ground his teeth. "I can do more than just insist," he growled.

"Yes, I'm quite sure of it." The man paused. "Very well. You want to see Norcross?"

"Yes. *Now*."

"Now?"

Daud nodded, baring his teeth.

The pipe-smoker cleared his throat, and reached over to the wall, where he had leaned a silver-topped walking cane. "Very well."

"Better," said Daud. He stood and gestured toward the exit. "After you."

The agent motioned in the other direction with the head of his cane. "No, we can go out the back. I have transport waiting." Then he turned and began to weave his way through the crowd.

Daud followed in his wake.

With the burly barman's apparent permission, the agent led Daud out through the back of the pub, the pair emerging into one of the alleyways that crisscrossed between the main streets. The cobbles, already slick with fishy runoff, undulated up and down; together, this made for a treacherous path underfoot. The sunlight was fading fast, throwing the alley into a darkness illuminated only by a lit window high on the rear of the

Empire's End. Daud couldn't see anybody about, and the only sound was the dull roar of the crowd in the tavern.

"Follow me," said the agent. He turned on his heel and strode off up the alley, away from the main street. Daud followed a few paces behind, keeping his senses alert to his surroundings. He frowned, a nagging thought bothering him. He looked over his shoulder. The trio of vagrants had not returned to their spot at the entrance to the pub.

Suddenly he came to a halt. Ahead, the alley was intersected by two others. Norcross's agent walked through the intersection, then, apparently realizing Daud was not with him, stopped and turned around.

"Do you want to meet Norcross or not?" he asked.

That was when they appeared. Two of the vagrants— the younger man and woman—slid out of the alleyways on either side, a gun in each hand now trained on Daud and the agent.

The agent looked around, and his eyes widened as he looked past Daud, back down toward the main street.

Daud turned. The third of the vagrants was walking toward them, gun held aloft. He stopped and cocked back the hammer with his thumb.

"Coin for fish heads and blood, sirs?"

13

"There is little to be said of the notion of strength, because strength is meaningless if you have cunning on your side. Evasion and mystery are your greatest weapons, for one hundred men confused are as one hundred chickens with no heads. Attack when they are unprepared, appear when you are not expected, and if the enemy cannot fathom your tactic, then you have won before the first strike is ever made."

—A BETTER WAY TO DIE
Surviving fragment of an assassin's treatise, author
unknown

Norcross's agent gasped and the clay pipe slipped from his teeth and dropped to the cobbles, where it shattered. Daud turned back to the old vagrant—although he now knew he was anything but a beggar. He also wasn't old; the gray in his beard was real enough, but his bearing was now considerably improved from the hobbling posture he had assumed in the pub.

Something wasn't right. Daud glanced at the gun. "Interesting weapon for a simple mugging."

The vagrant grinned. "That so?"

Daud pointed at the gun with a gloved hand. The vagrant took a step back, the pistol rising in his hand.

"It's well maintained," said Daud. "Recently cleaned and oiled. Replacement strike pin. Your gun is used frequently, but looked after. Almost like it was your job."

The vagrant's face twitched. Daud glanced over his shoulder at the two others. The young man had his firing piece aimed at Daud, while his companion stood to one side, her gun pointed at Norcross's agent, but her eyes flicked periodically over toward the trio's leader.

"I don't know how much coin you collect for fish heads and blood," said Daud, "but unless you know a black marketeer with some *very* good connections, you wouldn't be able to get hold of weapons such as those, even if you could afford them." Daud looked at the agent. "Associates of yours? Given a signal to lie in wait in a dark alley for you to lead your marks in, where they are robbed and murdered before Norcross even knows they're in town?" Daud nodded. "Seems like a good setup."

The agent's jaw went up and down a few times before he found the breath to speak. "What in all the Isles are you talking about?"

Daud gestured back at the leader of the gang. "The guns. They're government issue—military. Well beyond the means of the average backstreet cutthroat. Which means they are not just opportunistic criminals. They're mercenaries and they have an employer. You, for instance."

The leader snarled. "You know your problem?"

Daud glanced at the man. "Enlighten me."

"You talk too much."

"What is going on?" asked Norcross's agent. "Identify yourselves. I demand it!"

The leader scowled and waved his gun at Daud. "You,

we need." Then he waved the gun at the agent. "*Him*, we don't." He flicked his wrist, indicating to his companions. "Throw his body into the harbor when you're finished."

The agent gasped again, and took a step forward before the young man caught him and pushed him back; the agent stumbled, his cane clacking on the cobbles as he fell against the alley wall behind the woman and slid down onto the street.

Daud hissed between his teeth and turned on the gang leader. He was getting close to his goal and he wasn't going to let anybody get in the way.

"You've picked the wrong person to mess with," said Daud. He flexed his hand—he didn't want to use his powers, not again, but it seemed like the universe was conspiring against him, ever since he had stepped back into the rotten city of Dunwall.

Maybe it was the Outsider. Maybe that bastard was watching him, working against him, pushing the events of the world to prevent him from achieving his goal.

But Daud took comfort in that thought, because if it were somehow true, then it meant he was close. The Twin-bladed Knife was near. He knew it.

The two young bandits glanced at their leader, their pistols still aimed squarely at their targets, but their confidence was diminishing, as their quarry seemed immune to their threats.

"They told us to bring you back for questioning," said their leader, baring his teeth. "But they didn't say in how many pieces."

The gun went up again, and as Daud watched, the man's finger squeezed the trigger.

It was now, or never.

Daud gritted his teeth. The Mark of the Outsider flared, enveloping his whole hand in an inferno of pain.

He transversed the gap between himself and the gang leader, appearing behind the man just as he fired. He had been aiming low, trying to cripple Daud rather than mortally wound him, and with the target suddenly gone, the bullet pinged off the cobbles with a bright orange spark and ricocheted up at a shallow angle. The young man cried out and jerked back, blood erupting from his side as the stray round caught him. His companion, to her credit, didn't even flinch—*trained well*, thought Daud—but quickly sidestepped to get a clear shot and lifted her gun.

She was fast, but not fast enough. Even before she could aim, Daud grabbed the leader around the neck with one arm, and, bracing his legs, he leaned back, lifting his opponent clean off the street while reaching around the other side and yanking the man's gun arm down. The leader grunted with effort as he swung an elbow back, catching Daud in the side. Daud didn't stumble, but the jab did make him shift his weight. Sensing this, the leader used it to his advantage, throwing his weight in reverse, causing Daud to lose his balance on the uneven street and topple backward.

They were good. Well trained in close-quarters hand-to-hand combat. There was only one thing they hadn't taken into consideration.

Daud was better.

He let himself fall backward; as gravity took over, the leader, still held tightly in front of him, was suddenly weightless. With the pressure relieved, Daud twisted, swinging them both around so the leader's face crunched into the cobbles. There was an audible crack and the man cried out, rolling to one side. Daud rolled the other way and stood. He was free, but his back was now presented to the other two.

There was a bang. Daud moved without thinking, his

natural instincts guiding him as he pushed off the cobbles, the Mark of the Outsider allowing him to shift to the narrow window ledge of an overlooking building, then, with just enough purchase under the toe of his boot to spin himself around, Daud transversed back down to the alley. He rematerialized behind the young man, who was kneeling on the street with his hands clutching his wounded side. Daud slipped his arm under the young man, gripped the back of his neck and locked his shoulder. He swung the young man's body in front of his and used him as a shield as his companion fired her gun three times before she even knew what was happening. The young man's body shuddered as the bullets impacted. Daud felt hot blood spatter his beard and face and the body became a dead weight in his grip.

He let the man drop, then moved again to the other side of the alley as the last gangster standing swung her gun, searching for her target. Behind her, Daud saw Norcross's agent crouched against the alley wall, holding something small and shiny to his lips, his cheeks ballooning out as he blew into it. Daud couldn't hear anything, and neither, apparently, could the gangster. She was now standing in the middle of the alley, her back to the agent, her gun aimed squarely at Daud. Of their leader, there was no sign—he had fled while Daud skirmished with the others.

Daud braced himself, ready for another move across the Void, cursing the Outsider, silently screaming his rage.

And not just rage at the Outsider—rage at himself. Because the more he used his powers, and the more he fought, a part of him was actually enjoying the action— the thrill of combat, the pleasant, unexpected feeling of nostalgia, the surprised satisfaction that he could still do it. The years of keeping to himself melted away as his muscle memory was rekindled, his skills as sharp as they ever were.

But already he was tiring, his concentration slipping as his muscles began to sing out for rest.

The woman smirked and raised her gun.

All he needed was a couple of seconds to recover, and—

Then the woman's expression vanished. Her eyes darted first to one side and then the other as a long, thin silver blade appeared at her neck, cutting the skin under her chin enough for a line of blood to appear, the liquid quickly running down her throat. She froze on the spot, her gun arm still raised.

Keeping the blade in place, Norcross's agent reached around from where he was positioned behind the woman and pushed her arm down. Then he grabbed her pistol, which she relinquished with only a small struggle.

The agent met Daud's eye, and he smiled.

That was when the others appeared. Six men, three from either end of the alleyway. They were dressed alike, all wearing a uniform of some kind consisting of a long dark-blue coat—the same color as the agent's cloak—with a high square collar, belted, and the matching trousers tucked into high black boots. They were armed with pistols with strangely short barrels, the stocks molded out of metal to form a hollow, weight-saving frame. As the newcomers reached the group, the barrels of their powerful-looking weapons were all aimed at the female gangster.

Norcross's agent lifted his blade away, sliding it back into its scabbard—the black cane. Then he gestured to the uniformed men. "Take her back to the house. We will join you presently."

One of the men, apparently in charge—although Daud could see no insignia that identified him as somehow senior to the others—gave the man a nod. "Sir," he said. "Do you need an escort?"

The agent looked at Daud. "I rather think I am in safe

enough hands." He walked over to the body of the young man and nudged it with his foot. "Take this one as well. There was a third, but he ran."

The officer nodded. "Do you want us to set up a search?"

The agent shook his head. "That won't be necessary. On the contrary, it couldn't be better. Let him report to his superiors." He gave Daud an odd look. "I will be fascinated to learn of their response."

The officer began directing his men. Two of them kept a firm hold on the female prisoner, while two others picked up the body of the young man before they all headed down the alleyway.

Daud watched them, confused. Then he shook his head and stepped up to the agent.

"Look, I don't know what's going on, but you said you would take me to meet Norcross. Whatever this little show was all about, I intend to hold you to that promise."

The agent adjusted his hat, which had managed to stay in place throughout the fight. Then he lifted his monocle again from beneath his cloak and looked at Daud through it. His magnified eye dropped to Daud's left hand, his gaze holding there for a few seconds.

Then he turned away, dropping the monocle on its chain.

"Follow me."

Daud reached forward and grabbed the man's shoulder. He pulled him around and then twisted his fingers in the man's cloak below the neck, pulling his face up to his.

"Take me to Maximilian Norcross, *now*."

The agent just laughed, then coughed as Daud's grip threatened to choke him.

"But my dear fellow," he said, "I *am* Maximilian Norcross. Now, do you want to do business, or not?"

14

"Known for its rolling green hills and foggy meadows, Gristol is the largest of the Isles and is home to half the population of the known world. While most are simple people living in rural areas where sheep, blood oxen and gazelle are raised for their hides and meat, there are also five major cities spread out across the nation."

—THE ISLE OF GRISTOL
Excerpt from a volume on the geography and culture of
Gristol

They traveled by electric road coach; Daud had heard of such vehicles, but had never seen one, let alone traveled in one. The austere, angular vehicle was a cross between a horse-drawn coach and a rail carriage, with large, wide wheels and high suspension, making it look suited to rough terrain.

Norcross hadn't specified their destination, but he'd told his men to take the female captive ahead of them to "the house," so Daud assumed they were going to the collector's residence. But, to Daud's surprise, the journey took the best part of three hours, the coach first piloted through the narrow and winding streets of Porterfell before setting off along the rutted track that passed for an open country road in rural Gristol as they began to wind their way up into the shallow rise of the hills that bordered the town. As they traveled, Daud's gaze remained fixed on the view outside the window to his left, because if he could at least pick out some landmarks, he might have a fair idea of which direction they were going in—and how he might get back to Porterfell alone, if he had to. He abandoned that plan as soon as they left the town, the rough— if regular—purr as the coach's wide tires glided over Porterfell's cobbled streets replaced by an altogether louder rattle as the vehicle's suspension began to compensate for the rough country terrain. At the summit of a hill, Daud could see nothing but moonlit moorland, the flat, virtually featureless landscape stretching to the horizon, covered in almost uniform scrubby vegetation. After several miles of travel along the even, straight road, the landscape began to change again, the moorland now rising and falling as the coach began to weave up and down a series of valleys that grew increasingly steep the farther they went.

Norcross sat facing Daud, his back to the direction of travel. He didn't speak for the whole journey, and Daud, in no mood for conversation, made no attempt to break the silence. Occasionally Norcross yawned and twice as they rumbled along the road, Norcross took his monocle out and stared at Daud through it, lips pursed, his magnified eye moving up and down.

Daud ignored him.

Eventually Norcross leaned forward, looked out the window again, and sat back with a nod. "Nearly there," he said.

Daud leaned forward to get a better look outside, but by now the moon had set and the moorland view was reduced to nothing but a foggy gray halo stretching a few yards from the coach's side lamps.

Then they began to crisscross up another valley hillside, doing nearly a complete loop. Norcross pointed out the window. Daud once again turned for a look, and this time there was something to see.

Norcross's residence wasn't just a house, it was a *castle*, planted against the steep side of the valley. The edifice consisted of one fat, round high tower, capped with battlements, which loomed over the box-like bulk of the main structure, the castellated walls interrupted at intervals by small towers with pointed turrets. As the coach negotiated the curve of the road, Daud could see that same road continued until it crossed a bridge spanning the gap at the narrowest point of the valley, leading directly to the main castle gates, complete with portcullis and drawbridge.

The entire building was lit from within, every window a beacon shining from the sole sign of civilization in who knew how many miles of open countryside.

Norcross sat back in   eat, his hands folded on his lap. "Impressed?"

Daud tore his gaze from the view. "A house is a house."

Norcross barked a laugh and leaned forward, slapping Daud on the knee. "Not just any house, my friend," he said. "This is Morgengaard Castle!"

Daud glanced back at the view. "That supposed to mean something?"

"Mean something? *Mean* something?" Norcross slumped back in his seat. "Oh, I forget, you're from the south, aren't you?" Norcross's nose crinkled in distaste. "Karnaca, perhaps? Serkonos, certainly. Well, I suppose the history of the Empire of the Isles was not a particular strong point of your... *education.*"

Daud said nothing. Norcross frowned, clearly annoyed by the apparent lack of interest and cleared his throat before continuing.

"Yes, well. Morgengaard Castle, I would have you know, is the historical seat of power of the old kings of Gristol, before the unification of the empire after the War of the Four Crowns," said Norcross. "At the conclusion of that conflict, the last king of Gristol, Finlay Morgengaard the Sixth, had himself crowned as the first Emperor of the Isles and became Finlay Morgengaard the First. That was in the year 1626."

Daud grunted and looked out the window as Norcross twittered on about the Morgengaard dynasty, how the first emperor made Dunwall his capital and established a parliament there the same year he was crowned, abandoning his ancestral home. Norcross seemed to know his history, and as Daud listened he wondered how much of that history the Outsider had a hand in.

The electric coach had reached the bridge linking the road to the castle. Leaning forward, Daud looked up at the large building and frowned.

"Looks almost new."

Norcross grinned. "Remarkable, isn't it? It was a ruin when I found it, much farther north, in point of fact, past even Poolwick, near a place called Gracht. I don't suppose you have heard of that, either?"

"I don't suppose I have."

Norcross's grin vanished. "Well, I found it. It took years of research, of course. When old Finlay left for Dunwall he let his ancestral pile fall into ruin, and it was soon forgotten. Do you know, there aren't many interested in Gristol's pre-imperial period? It's almost as though the world didn't exist before the War of the Four Crowns. It's a travesty." Norcross sighed and sank back into his seat.

"So what, you built a replica here?"

Norcross laughed. "You misunderstand. This *is* Morgengaard Castle. I found it, verified it, claimed it, and *moved* it. Brick by brick, stone by stone, the most important historic building in Gristol's history was relocated, right here. Rebuilt, reconstructed, repaired. Oh, and modernized, of course. The home of my personal collection. Ten years of work, but well worth it, as I'm sure you'll agree."

Daud wasn't quite sure what it was he had agreed to, except to accompany a very strange man back to his house. He wondered if he'd even met the real collector yet—oh, he didn't doubt that the man sitting opposite him in the coach *was* Maximilian Norcross, but everything leading up to this point had been strange. The way he had played the part of his own agent in the pub in Porterfell, the way he had pretended to be a cowardly citizen being attacked in the alleyway before becoming the seasoned aristocratic soldier, wielding his swordstick with skill, and summoning guards from some kind of private army. And now, Norcross the historian, the public benefactor, the savior of Gristol's forgotten past.

An eccentric collector? A businessman entertaining a potentially profitable client?

Or was he something else?

Daud didn't know if he was worrying too much, or not enough. He decided on the former. All that mattered was the mission. And if Norcross had the Twin-bladed Knife inside his private kingdom, then all he had to do was take it.

Which meant he had to start making a plan. As the coach drove through the castle's arched gatehouse and into the inner courtyard, Daud began by making a tally of Norcross's men. There had been six of them in the alleyway in Porterfell, plus the two driving their electric carriage.

Eight.

Eight was easy.

The coach stopped, the sudden absence of the electric motor's whine after two hours of travel leaving a dull ringing in Daud's ears. A moment later, the door to the coach's passenger compartment was opened from the outside. Norcross gestured to him.

"Please, after you."

Daud stepped down into the courtyard and looked around. Norcross's castle was indeed huge, the high walls now enclosing them on all sides, and he could see more uniformed men moving within. Of course, a place this size, Norcross would have a large staff, although not all of them would be armed guards like the men in the long blue coats. Glancing around, Daud saw several people inside, but only one dressed like the coach attendants who stood waiting for their master's instruction.

Nine.

Parked ahead of them was another coach, the passenger compartment open, the engine cover steaming in the night air—the carriage that had brought Norcross's six bodyguards, and the female bandit, as well as the body of her companion. Daud wasn't sure what Norcross was going to do with her, and he wasn't going to ask. It was none of his business.

As Daud stood in the courtyard, he felt the Mark of the Outsider flare. He hissed between his teeth, and lifted his hand, flexing his fingers. The burning sensation faded.

Then he looked up, and saw Norcross was looking at him through his monocle again.

Norcross nodded, then dropped the eyepiece. "Follow me. I have a lot to show you."

The interior of the castle was as impressive as the exterior, but clearly little of it was original to the time of Finlay Morgengaard. Instead, Daud found himself in a modern mansion, the double-wide corridors lit with gently humming electric lighting, the floors laid with plush red carpet, making their footfalls silent as Norcross led Daud on a tour of his collection.

And it was, Daud had to admit, impressive. Morgengaard Castle was huge, and Norcross had managed to fill just about every available space with objects, art, and treasure. The collector led Daud through five long galleries of arms and armor, explaining how his collection included artifacts from every part of the Empire. As they walked, Daud looked over strange, twisted spears and highly decorated shields from far-flung islands, articulated suits of armor from Morley and Gristol, heavy, all-weather gear fit for the tundra of Tyvia, lightweight boiled-leather armor from Karnaca. The armory galleries were arranged chronologically, and as they approached the end, Daud was surprised to see modern equipment on display, with complete uniforms from each of the main military units of the Isles from every country in the Empire on display—the Dunwall City Watch, the Grand Serkonan Guard, the Wynnedown Constabulary. There were even Overseer uniforms, complete with silver, gold, and black masks and, Daud noted, among the guns, swords, daggers and batons, a chest-mounted music box. Next to the Overseer cabinets was a full-length, life-size portrait of someone Daud recognized instantly, without needing to read the accompanying plaque: Thaddeus Campbell, the

High Overseer who led the Abbey of the Everyman at the time of the Rat Plague. Seeing his stern features awoke memories that Daud would rather had stayed asleep.

Next came galleries of art, sculpture, gems, and meticulously catalogued cabinets of minerals and rocks. Most impressive were two huge halls with high, vaulted ceilings, from which hung the gigantic, complete skeletons of a whole pod of whales. Daud couldn't even begin to guess the value of Norcross's collection, but he doubted whether all the institutions in all of Gristol—no, in all of the Empire itself—could compete with the grandeur and sheer scale of the castle's contents.

Norcross chatted away as they walked, apparently happy to continue his commentary even though Daud gave no indication he was listening. What Daud was actually doing was trying to map their progress in his head, while counting the guards. After an hour he was surprised that his tally had only reached eighteen. Of course, the castle itself was its own protection—Norcross had spent ten years and who knew how much money relocating and rebuilding it to his own particular specifications, and located as it was in the moorland valley miles away from the nearest settlement, it presented a formidable challenge to any would-be thief.

Another half hour, another five rooms of treasure, and Daud's tally reached twenty-one. It was a lot, but he didn't think they would give him any particular trouble, especially considering how spread out they were. One thing bothered him, however. The collection was impressive—spectacular, even. But so far, everything he saw was… not ordinary, certainly, but… *normal*. Nothing arcane. Nothing heretical.

Daud told himself to be patient. He was close. Norcross was a strange man, clearly proud of his life's work. He was showing off his collection to a prospective buyer—someone he didn't know, and didn't trust. It made sense to be cautious before introducing the darker side of his collection.

At least, that's what Daud told himself.

Then they came to another double-wide corridor, this one ending in a broad staircase that swept up and then began to spiral. There was, bizarrely, a red velvet rope strung from bannister to wall. Daud glanced around, judging them to be at the base of the castle's main tower.

Norcross looked over his shoulder at his guest. "Given the manner of our introduction, I am to understand that you are a collector of the unusual," he said.

Daud nodded. "I'm looking for an artifact. A knife, bronze with twinned blades. I believe it was in Dunwall, and that it came into your possession recently. If this is the case, I hope we can come to some arrangement."

The collector gave a small, if non-committal, nod. "My, my, you are well informed." He gestured to the stairwell, then tapped his nose with a finger. "This is my, ah, *private* collection, shall we say."

Daud had been right. The heretical artifacts that Norcross was apparently famous for collecting were indeed held separately—in the tower.

Norcross reached down and unhooked one end of the rope from the silver loop in the wall when another blue-coated guard—*twenty-two*—appeared from a connecting door. Norcross paused as the guard whispered something into his ear, before retreating to a polite distance. The collector replaced the silver hook of the rope back in its loop.

"Something wrong?" asked Daud.

Norcross spun on his heel, his index finger wagging in the air. "Why would anything be wrong?"

Daud gestured to the stairs. "Shall we get to business? I've come a long way for this, and I would hate to leave disappointed."

Norcross pursed his lips. "Indeed," he said, "but if you will excuse me, there is a certain matter that requires my attention." He turned and looked at an ornate grandfather clock which stood against the far wall. He jumped and clutched his chest, as though the object had given him a fright.

"Oh, my! The time, it flies!" He turned back to Daud. "We can continue in the morning. You will want to rest. I will have chambers prepared for you."

He turned and snapped his fingers at the guard. The guard nodded, and headed back down the corridor the two men had just traveled. He stopped at the midway point, and turned around.

"If you would be so good as to follow me, sir."

The collector waved his fingers at Daud, almost as though he was shooing him away.

Daud took another look at the stairs, then nodded at his host. "I will be waiting," he said.

"Oh, indeed, indeed."

Daud followed the guard away from the stairs— the stairs that led to Norcross's private collection of heretical artifacts.

Heretical artifacts that had to include the Twin-bladed Knife.

15

THE EMPIRE'S END PUBLIC HOUSE, PORTERFELL, GRISTOL
26th Day, Month of Earth, 1852

"Porterfell, Gristol: A pleasant town founded on fishing, for which the traveler will require two items. First, a map to navigate the labyrinthine streets by; and second, a bandanna of sufficient size to cover the entire nose and mouth, as the reliance on the bounty of the sea is, unfortunately, associated with a rather distinctive and somewhat robust odor. The more adventurous may wish to visit the Empire's End public house in the heart of the industrial center, where the emphasis is, unusually yet rather appropriately, on a fine selection of local and important tobacco products as well as the regular libations, both enjoyed freely by local workers to help alleviate the constant aroma of their employment. The main bar also houses a collection of royal portraiture; local legend tells that some of the paintings are original works worth a small fortune."

—PORTS OF CALL
Excerpt from a guide to port cities
across the Empire of the Isles

"Three agents? Three? Against *Daud*? Were you out of your *mind*?"

In the early hours the Empire's End was closed, its patrons long-since turfed out into the smelly street. But the pub was not empty. The back room was a handy meeting spot: private and quiet, particularly when the tavern itself was closed.

The perfect location for a debriefing, with three members of a secret group—including the barman himself, Sal—gathered in the small room to listen to the report given by a man clad in tattered, stinking clothes, his gray beard streaked with blood, one hand gingerly holding a damp cloth against his swelling nose.

The leader of the trio who had attacked Daud and Norcross—Lowry, a loyal agent of more than ten years' service—grimaced, and not just because of the pain of his injuries. Sal was seated at the table, his eyes narrow and filled with ice. Lowry watched the publican, his immediate superior, grind his teeth, the muscles working at the back of his jaw.

Sal was not a person to disappoint. After a few more minutes of quiet seething, the anger almost wafting off him like steam, the publican stood and began to pace, shaking his head, running a hand through his thinning hair, before coming back around to Lowry and slamming both fists down on the table.

"Three agents," said Sal. "Three agents against a man who dismantled a clockwork soldier with his bare hands. Three agents against a man who carries the Outsider's Mark, who wields powers unlike anyone else in the—"

"Oh, how you provincials so love your histrionics."

Sal's lips twisted into a snarl as he turned toward the interruption. The other two members of their secret circle stood by the window, the immaculately dressed couple sharing a thick cigar taken from behind the bar as they viewed the proceedings with almost palpable disdain. The husband-and-wife pair had been at the pub for two days now and it was two days too many. That they weren't agents themselves wasn't Sal's concern. What was a concern was how they still thought they could boss him around.

Sal hissed. Mr. and Mrs. Devlin weren't worth the effort, not now—and besides, they had brought all the information they needed for the operation. An operation now in tatters because of Lowry's failure. He turned back to face the man.

"I certainly counted on the fact that you would follow your orders, not rely on… wait, what did you call it?"

Lowry gulped, unsure of the correct response. He glanced at the Devlins, but they seemed more preoccupied with blowing smoke rings.

"Ah… initiative," said Lowry. "Sir."

Sal grinned. "Oh yes, initiative." His smile vanished as he stepped closer to Lowry, close enough for their noses to almost touch. Lowry dropped his hand holding the cloth and leaned back to try and give himself some room.

"There were only two of them—"

Sal didn't move. Didn't blink. "We took an oath, Lowry. Remember that?"

Lowry grimaced again. "To protect but not to serve whomsoever occupies the Imperial Throne at Dunwall," he said. "To defend against the scourge both from within and without, to safeguard the legacy of the Throne in perpetuity, whatever may be."

"Whatever may be, Lowry, whatever that may be." Sal prodded the man in the chest with his finger. "This is on you. The deaths of two agents is on *you*. And you know what? You're going to have to tell Wyman yourself."

From the window came a quiet chuckle from the

odd couple. Sal glanced over at them. By all the Isles, he *really* didn't like them. They were strange. Creepy. *Arrogant*. Everything was beneath them. Even the failure of their mission.

Then again, what did they care? They weren't members of the League. They were freelancers—mercenaries. Why Wyman had decided to employ them rather than the quite capable agents of Morley, Sal didn't rightly know.

Then again, one of these quite capable agents— Lowry—had just shown himself to be lazy and overconfident, with terrible results. Of course, Sal knew the reason for Lowry's slip, but that didn't excuse him. Even as he regarded the agent, Sal could almost see the words forming on Lowry's lips.

"But, Sal, listen," said Lowry, his voice nearly a whisper. "Magic isn't real. It can't be real." His eyes were wide, like he was struggling to understand what he had seen in the alleyway—a quarry who had possessed remarkable, impossible abilities.

Abilities that Lowry, until now, hadn't thought were possible. Sal knew the man didn't believe in magic, didn't believe the briefing that the Devlins had given them, didn't believe that the Knife of Dunwall was anything other than a legend, an exaggerated fantasy of years past. But those beliefs had gotten one agent killed, and the other carted off by that monster, Norcross.

Sal shook his head and sat down at the table. Not for the first time, he wondered what the League was for, what the point of it—of any of it—was. Because the very thing the League supposedly existed to prevent had happened: the Duke of Serkonos had launched his coup, overthrowing the Empress—an empress the League was pledged to protect. The League had been blindsided, the coup seemingly arising from nowhere. And with the

League's head, Wyman, in Morley—and, Sal thought, as yet unaware of the calamity that had befallen their beloved Emily—it was left to Sal to follow Wyman's last set of orders, issued *before* the coup had taken place.

The League of Protectors' purpose was to protect the Imperial Throne. Before the coup, there was only one obvious threat, one fueled by persistent rumors of his return: Daud. Daud was back, and he was a threat. One that had to be eliminated at all costs. But was Daud really a priority now? Shouldn't the coup take precedence? But Sal knew better than to question orders, whatever his own uncertainties. If Daud was still alive, having disappeared fifteen years ago, then yes, perhaps he did represent a threat. On the other hand, the fact that he had murdered Emily's mother, Empress Jessamine Kaldwin, had perhaps made the matter a little more personal for Wyman.

Sal sighed. Over by the window, the Devlins smoked. Mr. Devlin leaned in and whispered something into his wife's ear, and she threw back her head and laughed. Perhaps Sal *could* understand why the Devlins had been brought in. He didn't know where Wyman had unearthed them from, but they *were* good, there was no doubt about it. They had not only confirmed Daud's survival, they had found him and tracked him across the Isles, their remarkable skills providing the League with solid, actionable intelligence.

Intelligence the League had just squandered. They knew Daud would be coming to Porterfell to meet with Norcross—the collector who was known to pose as his own agent, meeting clients in the Empire's End, where he could vet them anonymously.

And like the intelligence that had told them that, just as the legends had said, Daud was more than just a killer—more than even a man. He possessed magical powers—

witnessed by the Devlins first-hand—that would make him a formidable foe for an *army*, let alone a trio of agents, no matter how well-trained and equipped with small arms supplied—covertly—by the constabulary.

Intelligence that Lowry had failed to act on, risking *everything*.

Sal felt anger begin to boil inside him again. What had Lowry been thinking, sending in his own team like that? To confront Daud and Norcross without backup? There were agents all over Porterfell, just waiting for orders. Maybe it was Sal's fault. He should have taken more direct command.

Mrs. Devlin walked over and stood behind Sal, her long, elegant fingers trailing over his shoulder.

"From the ashes of failure rises opportunity, my dear man. We can either sit here and argue until breakfast, or we can formulate our next course of action. You want Daud dead. At your word, Mr. Devlin and I are happy to oblige." She took a long draw on the cigar, then walked back to the window and handed it to her husband with an elaborate swish of her arm.

Lowry's eyes flicked between the Devlins and Sal, now merely a spectator.

"Very well," Sal said. "What do you propose?"

The Devlins exchanged a glance, then Mr. Devlin looked down his nose not at Sal, but at Lowry.

"Norcross has Daud?"

"He does," said Lowry. "He's taken him to his castle."

"Urgh!" Mrs. Devlin gave a theatrical shiver. "That ridiculous folly of his."

"Oh!" said Mr. Devlin. "Ghastly."

"Absolutely ghastly, my dear. The sheer arrogance of that man."

Mr. Devlin made a face. "Sheer arrogance, my dear."

"If you've quite finished?" Sal frowned at the pair.

Mrs. Devlin turned her smile on. "The solution is simple. The Norcross estate is heavily guarded, and the journey there interminable."

"I asked you what you were proposing to do," said Sal.

"Why, wait, of course," said Mrs. Devlin. "Daud will either come back here or travel to Potterstead. These are the only two ports within easy distance of Morgengaard Castle. Get as many agents as you have here and in Potterstead and have the moorland roads watched. And even if we are wrong—and we are not—and he tries south for Dunwall, or perhaps even north to Poolwick, we shall still see him and we can adjust our plan. He will be back in our sights soon, don't worry."

"And then what?" asked Sal.

"Oh, my dear sir," said Mrs. Devlin. "Have a little faith. Mr. Devlin and I have never failed a contract." Her smile tightened.

The publican sighed. The sooner he was back out on the streets, organizing the agents—out of this bloody *room* and away from the Devlins—the better.

16

THE NORCROSS ESTATE,
SOMEWHERE IN SOUTH-CENTRAL GRISTOL
26th Day, Month of Earth, 1852

"Know this: in pain, there is truth. In pain, all barriers fall, all masks are cast asunder. In pain, we are naked, each of us. Our very being exposed, our very minds open for anyone to read. The ability of pain to equalize all men cannot be overstated.

Pain, then, is a tool. But it is not an iron hammer or a steel saw. It is a fine brush, feather-light, to be wielded not by a laborer but by an artist.

In war, we may be warriors, but we must be artists also."

—A BETTER WAY TO DIE
Surviving fragment of an assassin's treatise, author
unknown

Norcross yawned, and pulled a fob watch from his waistcoat pocket. It was late. No, it was *early*. Replacing the watch, he arched his back. Not time to retire yet. Far from it.

Things were just starting to get interesting.

He leaned back against the stone wall and folded his

arms as, in front of him, the blue-jacketed guard grabbed the prisoner's blood-matted hair and yanked her head back. The female bandit from Porterfell was chained to the wall by both wrists, stripped to her underclothes to allow the interrogator access to her bare skin, which bled from the dozens of straight cuts. She hadn't spoken—or screamed, for that matter—in quite a while, and as Norcross watched he wondered if the interrogator had gone a little too far. But a moment later, the woman opened her eyes and took in a great gulp of air.

The interrogator turned to his boss, long razor in his free hand, the front of his blue coat splattered with dark stains. Norcross nodded, and the interrogator turned back to the prisoner, sizing her up as he prepared to make another cut. He was an *artist*, Norcross could see that. It was always enjoyable to watch someone who really *loved* their work, and this man really was a master. Norcross got the same thrill as when he watched a sculptor at work. And here, in a bare stone room under Morgengaard Castle, the interrogator was shaping his own work of art, not out of stone, but out of flesh.

The interrogator cut with mathematical precision. The woman moaned, her head rolling against the stone. She was disappointingly quiet. But, still, that was to be expected. She wasn't going to last much longer, despite the skills of the interrogator.

Norcross scratched his chin. As much as he was enjoying the performance, perhaps it was time to actually ask some questions, even though it would mean interrupting proceedings.

Such is life.

The interrogator took a step back, looking down the edge of his razor as he planned his next cut, but Norcross held up a hand and, at the man's quizzical expression, gave a slight shake of the head. The interrogator gave a small bow and moved back, cleaning his blade with a cloth.

Norcross stepped up to the woman as she sagged in the chains, her feet dragging on the floor. He glanced down, taking care not to step in too much blood, then folded his arms and leaned over the woman. Her eyes were open and for a moment they settled on his, but her gaze was clouded, her pupils without focus.

No matter. She didn't have to *see* him.

"Perhaps now you will be a little more cooperative," said Norcross. "So we'll try again. What is his name?"

The woman stared at him. Her lips moved, her jaw worked, but nothing emerged from her throat but a croaky hiss.

Norcross tutted. "Now, you can do better than that, surely? All I want to know is who he is. Well, actually, that's not quite true. I also want to know why he is here and what your interest in him is, not to mention the small matter of who you are and who you work for, but let's not get ahead of ourselves. We can start with a name, and maybe move on from there, hmm?"

"I…"

Norcross turned to the interrogator. "She *can* speak, can't she?"

The interrogator shrugged. "For now, yes."

"Hmm," said Norcross, turning back to the prisoner. "Let's try that again, shall we? What. Is. His. Name?"

"Daaa… Daaa…"

Norcross laughed. "Oh, you really do need to try harder. You see, I know that this man is… special, let's put it that way. He carries the Mark of the Outsider. Now, I suspect you know what that means as much as I do. We are not like the ignorant masses who so boldly deny the existence of magic even as they feverishly pray every night that the Abbey of the Everyman will deliver them from evil. You and I know that evil is real, and it walks among us, the symbol of heresy burned into its very flesh, don't we?"

Norcross snarled and grabbed the woman's face, squeezing her cheeks between thumb and fingers. "So, let's make a deal. You tell me his name, and I let Alonso here put you out of your misery. What do you say?"

The woman's lips moved. Norcross released his hold, and her head fell against her chest. Then he leaned in, turning his ear toward her mouth as she whispered.

"Daaa… Daaa…"

"Come along. Once more, with conviction, if you please."

"Daa… Daud. His… name… his name… is… Daud."

Norcross straightened up and clapped his hands. "Excellent! Now then…"

The interrogator stepped forward, still cleaning his razor with the cloth. The man looked over the prisoner's body, then pushed her head with his finger. The woman's eyes were open, but they were glazed. The interrogator sighed, then flicked his razor across her cheek. Blood welled immediately, but there was no movement or sound from the prisoner.

The interrogator stepped back and shook his head at Norcross. "Too late, I'm afraid. She didn't last as long as I thought she would."

Norcross frowned, his hands laced in front of him. "A pity. We are cheated of our entertainment." He paused and pursed his lips. "'Daud'. Unusual name."

"There's only one person I know who went by that name, sir."

"Oh? Do tell."

The interrogator folded his arms. "When I worked in

Dunwall, for the City Watch. Oh, fifteen years ago now. No, maybe more. There was a gang, they used to dress up like whalers—you know, masks and everything. They weren't like the other street gangs. They were mercenaries—assassins. If you had the coin, their services were yours."

"Interesting. This Daud was one of them?"

"Oh, no, more than that, sir. Daud was their leader. We had a name for him—the Knife of Dunwall. Cold and ruthless, he was. A master of his craft, too. Must say, I admired that."

"But of course," said Norcross. "There is much to admire in the work of others." He gestured to the prisoner.

The interrogator smiled and gave a bow. "I believe there is an account of Daud and the Whalers held in your library—among the Overseer field reports, from the cache of Abbey documents I brought with me."

"Ah, excellent." Norcross clapped his hands. "The Knife of Dunwall, eh? I knew our friend had a story. The Dunwall City Watch was right to think him special."

"This Mark you mentioned?"

Norcross lifted his left hand. "Branded on his flesh, the symbol of the Outsider, signifying a connection to the Void."

The interrogator nodded. "If your guest really is the Knife of Dunwall, he would make an excellent addition to the collection."

"What a wonderful suggestion."

The interrogator gestured to the body chained to the wall. "What about her?"

Norcross reached forward and lifted the woman's head by her hair. Norcross grimaced as he saw white foam begin to bubble on the woman's lips. He let the head fall, then he stood back and carefully extracted a handkerchief from his pocket and began wiping his hands with meticulous care. Then he looked down, noticing he had her blood on his jacket.

"Gah! I shall have to get changed."

"The girl, sir?"

"Take her to the preparation room. Once she has been processed she can go up in gallery ten, with her erstwhile colleague. I'll compose a display card for them in the morning." Norcross gave the interrogator a small bow. "With full credit to the work of the artist, of course."

"Most kind, sir."

There was a knock on the torture chamber's door, then it opened and a guard ran in.

"Sir!"

Norcross turned to him. "Yes?"

"Your guest, sir. He has left his room."

"Impatient sort of fellow, isn't he?"

"Orders, sir? Do you want us to apprehend him?"

"No, that won't be necessary. I know exactly where he is going. I will meet him personally."

"Is that wise, sir?" asked the interrogator. "Daud is a dangerous man."

"I don't think our guest is here for a fight, but your point is noted." Norcross turned to the guard. "Have him followed, but at a distance. I want you ready to assist me, should I call for it."

"Sir."

"In the meantime, take another guard and go to the Whitecliff gallery."

"Whitecliff gallery, sir?"

Norcross nodded. "There is something I need you to bring with you."

17

THE NORCROSS ESTATE,
SOMEWHERE IN SOUTH-CENTRAL GRISTOL
26th Day, Month of Earth, 1852

"The earliest stories tell of a gang-killer without mercy, moving among the shop keepers and City Watch officers of Dunwall like a reaper through wheat. Then a period of silence followed; years we now believe he spent traveling the Isles, studying anatomy and the occult in the great halls of learning and in hidden basements frequented by fellow dabblers in the forbidden arts. Daud is even purported to have spent a winter in the Academy of Natural Philosophy itself. And for a time, before a schism developed, he counted the Brigmore Witches among his allies. All the while, he honed his craft, and it is during this time that we believe he began to consort with the Outsider."

—RUMORS AND SIGHTINGS: DAUD
Excerpt from an Overseer's covert field report

Daud moved through the galleries in silence, and while the entire building was well lit, he found plenty of places to hide—behind cabinets, around corners, behind doors. He made good progress, easily avoiding the blue-coated guards as he made his way back to the roped-off staircase that led up to the main tower.

That had to be the place, it *had* to be. Norcross had called it his "private" collection. He had a reputation for collecting and trading in the arcane and heretical. Daud had seen no such objects on his tour of the galleries. And while he hadn't explored the entire castle, all signs pointed to the tower as being where the collector locked away his special treasures.

He stepped over the low velvet rope, and crept up the stairs. The steps themselves were stone and thickly carpeted, but as they began to spiral, his forward vision became obscured. Taking no chances, Daud kept to the edge of the staircase, pausing every few steps to listen for any movement before continuing.

So far, so good. This part of the castle seemed to be empty.

The stairs continued up without interruption, the floors only counted by narrow windows that Daud passed on his left—four, five, six, seven, each offering a view of nothing but deep blackness beyond, the desolate moorland lost in the night.

On the eighth turn of the spiral, Daud came out onto a landing. In front of him was an arched double door of shiny black wood, two great silver rings for handles. Daud moved to the door, listening for any signs of life beyond.

The tower was silent.

And the doors unlocked.

Daud stepped through.

The vaulted chamber beyond was large and circular, occupying the entire top level of the castle's tall tower. The room was well lit—like all the other galleries in Morgengaard Castle—by numerous electric globes hanging from golden chains. Glass-fronted cabinets lined the curved wall of the chamber and stretched from floor to ceiling. And behind the glass—bonecharms and runes and other carvings of ivory and metal, their surfaces crawling with arcane inscriptions. Daud could feel the Mark of the Outsider pulse softly on the back of his hand as he approached the heretical, powerful objects. He couldn't begin to count the number of artifacts—there were hundreds of charms and runes, each one immaculate, as though they had just been fashioned from fresh whale bone.

He had guessed right. He was in the right place.

But what captured Daud's attention, what made his breath catch in his throat and his head buzz with excitement, was the object directly ahead, on the other side of the room. There, standing clear of the curved cabinets behind, were two plinths of glossy black stone. On each was an artifact resting on a glass stand, itself an elaborate work of art that would not have looked out of place elsewhere in Norcross's collection. On the left-hand plinth was a mirror, or at least a part of one; the jagged shard roughly square and about the size of a large dinner plate. It looked like it was made of glass, but the surface was dark, as if smoked. Sitting at an angle in its frame, Daud could only see the reflection of the light globes and the vaulted ceiling above the chamber's arched doorway.

On the other plinth was a weapon. It was a bronze knife with two parallel blades, each long enough to be more like a short sword than a dagger. The weapon was plain and unadorned, and while its surface was dull and unpolished, the metal of the blades seemed to flash as Daud blinked, reflecting a light that wasn't in the room but which seemed to be moving, like firelight, like the light of an inferno, trapped in the metal and echoing down the millennia.

Daud was drawn in by the light, the blades almost pulling him physically toward them, like the artifact had a gravity all of its own. As he got closer, he heard whispering, far away at the edge of sound—music, or a song, perhaps. A cold feeling began to swim up his arm, radiating from the Mark of the Outsider.

The Twin-bladed Knife. It was real, and it was here.

He took another step toward it, his hand reaching out for the weapon, almost moving of its own accord.

"Interesting, isn't it?"

Daud stopped, rocking on his heels. Then he turned to look over his shoulder. Behind him, Maximilian Norcross was walking through the arched doorway, dressed in a long robe of green silk, a loose-bound folio of papers in one hand.

Norcross joined Daud at the plinth and looked down at the Knife. "It's almost like you *know* it, isn't it? As if it once belonged to you, a relic from another life."

The blades flashed.

The Knife had power. Purpose. Daud could sense it.

Norcross bent down, his nose an inch from the Knife. "The condition is most remarkable," he said. "This is easily the most ancient artifact in my entire collection, and yet it looks like it was forged today. Quite a fascinating mystery." He stood tall. "Legend tells that this is the very knife that was used, four thousand years ago, by a cult to sacrifice what they called the 'perfect victim,' giving the life of a street urchin to the power of the Void."

Norcross turned to Daud. "A young man," he continued, "who was reborn as the Outsider."

Daud met the collector's gaze and held it. The Knife was within reach. He didn't have time to play games, not now.

He let out a breath. "The Outsider is a legend. A story

for dark nights and naughty children."

Norcross lifted a finger. "Says the man who appears rather desperate to acquire the Knife. Please, I expected better of you. You are talking to the man who owns the greatest collection of heretical artifacts in the entire Empire. You know, as well as I do, that the Outsider is no myth."

"I don't know what you're talking about."

Norcross cleared his throat and opened the folio of papers. He began to read, tracing the lines with a finger.

"*New reports emerged of a dusky-skinned assassin, paid by the elite to eliminate their rivals in Dunwall and in the other major cities across the Isles. Those who saw him and lived numbered in the handful, but all of them reported something strange.*"

"What is that?" Daud took a step toward Norcross, reaching out for the folio, but Norcross moved out of the way and began to stroll along the curve of the cabinets as he continued.

"I like this bit—listen. '*He appeared and vanished like smoke. From a nearby rooftop, he gestured and a noble woman stumbled from her balcony, falling to her doom on the cobblestones below.*'"

"I'm not here to listen to bog-spirit tales."

Norcross still had his nose in the folio. As Daud spoke, he held up his finger again.

"*Most recently, as this new threat of plague has risen in Dunwall, Daud has been seen leading a gang of men in dark leather, dressed as factory whalers in their vapor masks. They seem loyal beyond comprehension for one so unworthy, leading me to wonder if some of his magic is dedicated to lulling their minds, enslaving them.*" Norcross snapped the folio shut and pressed it against his chest. "So ends the report of a covert operative from the Abbey of the Everyman." Norcross cocked his head. "And he was talking about you, wasn't he? Daud, the Knife of Dunwall, leader of the Whalers. At one time the most hunted man in the whole Empire. I have an entire gallery of wanted posters collected from nearly every city in the Isles. Of course, that was a long time ago, and I must admit I didn't recognize you. I like the beard. Suits you."

Daud shook his head and spread his hands. "All I want is the Knife. I was telling the truth when I said I was a buyer—name your price."

"And what happens after that?"

"Nothing happens."

"Nothing? You're seriously trying to tell me that you'll take the Knife and leave and nothing will happen?"

Daud shrugged. "You'll be richer. I'll be gone. Never to be heard or seen again."

"And what if the Knife is not for sale?"

"I'm not looking for trouble. Either we reach an agreement or we don't. Either way, I'm leaving with the Knife." Daud pointed at the folio. "If you know so much about me, then you'll know what I'm capable of."

Norcross bowed to Daud. "I don't doubt it." Then he reached inside the fold of his green robe and extracted the monocle again. He held it to his eye, and pointed toward Daud's clenched fist. "Tell me, the Mark of the Outsider— does it hurt?"

Daud glanced down at his hand, flexing the fingers underneath the leather. "You can see the Mark?"

"Oh, yes," said Norcross. He lifted the monocle to the lights above, and turned the ivory stem between his fingers. "Another artifact of the arcane and magical. The lens is a ground crystal from the Pandyssian continent. It is possessed of certain properties that are quite remarkable." He gestured to the cabinets and their contents. "Useful for seeing whether a bonecharm or rune is the real thing or a fake. And, it seems, for seeing the Mark of the Outsider, no matter how you try to hide it."

Daud frowned at Norcross. His eyes darted from the collector, to the Twin-bladed Knife, and back.

"Ah, yes," said Norcross. "The Knife. The pride of my collection. You really want it, don't you?" He stopped his pacing and tapped his chin with a finger. "But what for, I wonder? Something to do with the Outsider." Norcross began to pace again, his eyes scanning the floor as he thought, ignoring Daud. "He's an interesting… phenomenon, shall we say? For the last four thousand years, every child in the world has been scared by their mother by tales of this strange being. Belief in him comes and goes, waxes and wanes over the centuries, but never completely fades. Cults rise, shrines are built, superstitions flare. The Abbey of the Everyman call him out as their divine enemy, the Overseers tasked with driving belief in him back into the darkness."

Daud looked at the Knife. He could hear it—*feel* it, like it was… singing to him. Music, from beyond time, from beyond the Void.

"Of course," said Norcross, "there are other stories, other legends, about the Outsider. Some say that, far from being a distant observer, he takes a keen interest in the affairs of the world, and that as ages creep ever onward, he reaches toward us, choosing people, putting his Mark on them, and using them to act out his will."

Daud almost didn't hear him, so loud was the song in his head. The blades of the Knife flashed orange and red.

He lifted his hand, the Mark burning.

"The Mark of the Outsider would make a fine addition to my collection," said Norcross. "As would the infamous Knife of Dunwall himself."

It was now, or never.

Daud lunged for the plinth.

And then he froze, his hand inches from the weapon's grip. Every muscle in his body seized as the tower chamber was filled with a harsh, metallic roaring sound, an awful cacophony that Daud could feel pushing all conscious thought from his mind.

He dropped to his knees. He leaned over, his forehead touching the black plinth on which the artifact sat, his curled knuckles pressed hard into his temples as the ancient music soared.

He saw movement out of the corner of his eye. Daud tried to turn his head, but only managed to move his neck a little. He saw the trailing edge of a long green robe and matching green slippers as Norcross stood next to him.

Daud fought to draw breath. He tried to scream but only managed a croak. With a colossal effort he looked up.

The Twin-bladed Knife was there. Within reach. He lifted his hand. It felt like it was made of lead and his head full of cotton wool. He pushed his arm forward. It was like moving through whale oil.

He yelled, louder this time. His throat was on fire, spit flew from his open mouth, but he couldn't hear himself. All he could hear was the terrible music.

He fell back, the room spinning. The last two things he saw were the guard with the Overseer's music box strapped to his chest, the barrel-like mechanism on the front of the thing turning as the guard cranked the handle.

And Norcross, in his green robe, laughing, staring down at him with the folio clutched to his chest.

And then everything went black and Daud sank into a blissful and infinite silence.

18

"Maximilian Norcross is a strange one. A self-made man, there is no record of his arrival in Gristol, although he has at various times claimed to have been born in no fewer than a dozen different cities from Wei-Ghon to Tyvia to Serkonos. Our investigations suggest that he may, in fact, be a native of Morley or northern Gristol, and that certainly Maximilian Norcross is a new identity, one adopted relatively recently.

Whatever his true past is, we have yet to ascertain. It is possible that he is hiding something. It is just as likely he is a supreme fantasist. His collection, by all accounts, is certainly fantastical. How he acquired it—and his wealth—remains the subject of ongoing investigations, in cooperation with our brothers in Wynnedown. However, we have evidence to suggest that he is in possession of a great number of heretical artifacts, although as yet no first-hand reports that his collection actually contains any. Indeed, it is unclear whether Norcross is interested in witchcraft or magic, and so far there is no evidence to suggest he is a student of such black arts, but I end this report with a recommendation that this man be watched carefully."

—REPORT ON THE ACTIVITIES OF
MAXIMILIAN NORCROSS
Excerpt from an Overseer's covert field report

Daud awoke in a small, brightly lit stone room. The air was damp and smelled sharply of chemicals. He was lying at an angle on a table; when he tried to move, he found he couldn't, and as his senses finally came back he looked down and saw the metal cuffs that secured his ankles and wrists.

He growled, pulling on the restraints, but this just made him feel dizzy. He slumped back against the table and closed his eyes, waiting for the ringing in his head to subside.

When it didn't, he forced his head up again, the room rolling slowly in his vision as he tried to focus on the source of the sound.

It was the Overseer's music box, strapped to the front of, not one of Norcross's guards, but a wooden mannequin, similar to the ones modelling the collection of arms and armor in the main galleries. Only thing about this one that was different was its right arm. It was metal, and moved smoothly on oiled joints as it turned the music box handle. Fighting against the nauseating effects of the ancient music, Daud looked down, and saw a fat cable running out of the back of the mannequin and down into a port in the wall. The mannequin was automatic, the mechanical arm electric.

Daud lowered his head back to the table. The ancient music—he'd forgotten what it was like. Had it always been this bad? The music not only prevented him from drawing on the power of the Mark of the Outsider, it also drained his energy, both physical and mental, and dulled his senses, leaving his head throbbing.

"Relax, Daud, relax," said a voice. "You must forgive the noise, but I'm afraid I had to take out a little insurance. You are quite a remarkable specimen and I really don't want you trying to escape. If I understand it correctly, so long as this terrible racket persists, you are quite incapable of anything at all, so just lie back and don't wear yourself out trying. The process you are about to undergo will be taxing enough, even as it kills you. I would recommend you conserve your strength. It will make your death less… traumatic, shall we say."

Daud opened his eyes and he managed a hard-won lungful of the acrid air.

Norcross moved in front of him, his arms folded across his green silk robe. Behind, Daud now saw there was a blue-coated guard watching while another fussed with a large machine. The room itself had walls of smooth white stone, like the rest of Morgengaard Castle, but there were stainless-steel panels at intervals, on which hung equipment on racks—saws, scalpels, clamps, forceps. Surgical equipment, and lots of it. Hanging on a hook on the wall beside the automatic mannequin was also an old-fashioned speaking tube with a contoured mouthpiece of brass, the kind of device you might find on an old whaling ship for the captain to shout down orders to the engine room.

Daud grimaced and forced his head to turn back to Norcross, the collector still smiling calmly. Daud's eyes flicked to the machine next to him.

"What are you planning?"

The machine consisted of four large steel cylinders

with curved caps topped with complex valves—tanks of some kind, sitting on a wheeled steel trolley, in the base of which a whale oil tank was installed to provide power. A multitude of rubber hoses connected the valves to each other, and to another device at the end of the trolley, closest to the angled steel table to which Daud was held. The device had a smaller tank, and a mechanism with a large off-center wheel, which slowly turned, and a bellows, expanding and contracting, like the machine was breathing. There were six bolted ports on the end, from which came six more rubber hoses—far thinner than the tank hoses, each one ending in a cap, from which protruded a long silver needle.

Three of these hoses were held against the side of the trolley with clips. The other three trailed off to Daud's left. He turned his head to see where they went, and he felt the heat of anger rise within him as he saw, for the first time, that there was another steel table next to his, also occupied.

It was a woman, her skin covered in small, deep cuts. Her eyes were open, but she was clearly dead. The three other hoses from the machine trailed over her body, a needle deeply embedded in her neck, her left side, and the calf of her right leg. Daud recognized her as one of the three vagrants from Porterfell who had ambushed him and Norcross behind the Empire's End.

Daud had seen all kinds of horror in his life—and had been responsible for a good deal of it himself. He had seen people tortured by the more vicious street gangs of Dunwall, back in the day. He had seen others torn apart by hounds for sport. He had encountered cannibals in the wilds of northern Tyvia, catching and eating travelers in the harsh tundra just to survive.

But this? This was something else entirely.

Norcross stepped over to the woman's body and looked her up and down. "A remarkable process," said the collector, "and one which, I am rather proud to say, is of my own devising." He looked over at Daud. "As an admirer of the natural world, I had long sought a method of preserving specimens for my collection that was beyond mere taxidermy, which is effective, but results in exhibits that are somewhat… well, artificial. So I developed my own technique."

He turned and walked over to the machine, gesturing to it like an academic giving a lecture. "The exact methodology is complex, and I won't bore you with the precise details. But with this system, we can extract the water from any organic specimen, and replace it with a mineral solution. This solution—again, of my own invention, after many years of experimentation—then hardens, perfectly preserving the specimen in a manner that leaves them exactly as they were in life."

Daud took a deep breath, trying to organize his thoughts amidst the terrible roar of the ancient music. He tensed his muscles, pulling just a little on his restraints, testing them rather than trying to free himself. The cuffs were heavy, but the metal was thin—they weren't, he realized, designed to restrain a prisoner. They were merely designed to hold a body in place while Norcross used his process on them.

A human body. Daud closed his eyes, his efforts rewarded with a deep, rolling nausea. Norcross spoke of collecting specimens like he was a zoologist, hunting exotic animals to mount in his private museum. But the tables were designed for people.

Daud opened his eyes. "How many?"

Norcross frowned. "How many what? Really, you are a man of intelligence. I was expecting a little more interest."

"How many people have you... collected?"

"Ah. Well, I must admit my catalogue is somewhat incomplete. But it would be close to a hundred."

"And now you want to add me."

Norcross clapped his hands. "Why, yes, of course! What better addition than the Knife of Dunwall himself! Daud, once the most wanted man in all the Isles! Not only a notorious criminal and assassin but a magician, marked by the Outsider himself, wielder of remarkable abilities gifted by the Void."

Norcross stepped closer to Daud and pointed at his face with an elegant ringed finger. "*You*, my friend, will be the centerpiece of a whole new display. Yes! I can see the scene now!" He turned and swept a hand in the air, his gaze fixed somewhere in the middle distance. "The dark streets of Dunwall! The year 1835! An assassin stalks the night, creeping up on his latest victim, knife held ready, the Mark of the Outsider already glowing on his flesh—"

"You're moonstruck," said Daud.

Norcross dropped his hand, his mouth twitching with annoyance. "I am a *curator* of history. The life and times of the entire Empire are represented in my collection." He pointed at Daud again. "And that history includes *you*."

That was when the lights went out, the preparation room plunged into darkness, lit only by the blue glow of the whale oil tank under the trolley.

The chamber was also silent. Instantly, Daud felt better—more awake, the fogginess in his head clearing. He craned his neck and saw that the automatic mannequin had stopped working. The music box was silent.

Norcross gestured angrily at a guard, waving his hand toward the speaking tube.

"Well, don't just stand there! Find out what—"

He was interrupted by a shrill whistle—someone was

trying to contact *them*. The guard picked up the end of the speaking tube, pulling the stopper out before bellowing into it.

"Yes?" Then he pressed the tube to his ear.

Norcross joined him, waving his hands. "Well? Well?"

The guard shook his head, then spoke again into the tube, alternating the mouthpiece between his mouth and his ear as he awkwardly received the report from elsewhere in the castle.

"Are you sure you... Well, have you checked... Send patrols five and six... Yes, he's here... Yes, sir... right away, sir... Understood."

Recapping the tube, the guard looked at Norcross. "Intruders, sir. They've disabled the house's whale oil tanks and have entered the main galleries."

Norcross looked at Daud, as though his prisoner had something to do with it. Daud narrowed his eyes as he watched the almost cheerful demeanor of the collector crumble and his eyes glinting with an altogether different set of emotions.

Among them, fear.

Norcross turned back to the guard. "Seal the galleries. Have the patrols flush the intruders out—"

The guard shook his head. "No, you don't understand, sir. The intruders have already taken out four guard patrols. It's a large group, on the loose in the galleries." He gently took Norcross by the arm. "Now, if you'll come with me, sir, the guard captain has ordered you to the safe room."

Norcross blinked as if he was coming out of some kind of trance.

"Very well." Norcross turned to Daud, but the way his eyes moved over him and the body of the woman on the other table, Daud wasn't entirely sure he was really seeing what was in the room. "We will resume this… ah, later."

The two men left Daud alone in the preparation room. Next to him, the motionless body of the woman was pumped full of chemicals as the machine on the trolley continued to whirr.

Intruders? Thieves… or assassins? Daud didn't care about the latter. But the former was a different proposition. There was plenty to steal in Norcross's collection. The guard had said it was a large group—an organized gang, perhaps.

Daud didn't care who they were, so long as they didn't take the Twin-bladed Knife. That was his.

And now it was time to get it.

With the music box deactivated, he felt his powers returning, although the sustained broadside of ancient music had drained him and he knew it would take a while to recover fully. He pulled against his bonds again. The cuffs shifted but remained firm, strapped to the table.

He felt the Mark of the Outsider catch fire, but he dampened the urge to draw on it—it was too soon, and he was simply too weak.

And he didn't need supernatural power to get free from the processing table.

Daud counted to three, then wrenched his right arm, tearing the metal cuff from the table. With one arm free, he made short work of the other bonds. Then, with one last look at the horrific remains on the other table, Daud drove his fist into the side of the preservation machine in anger, punching a hole clean through it, then tore the wheel off.

Daud left the room, heading toward the tower chamber and Norcross's private collection.

Toward the Twin-bladed Knife.

19

THE NORCROSS ESTATE, SOMEWHERE IN SOUTH-CENTRAL GRISTOL
26th Day, Month of Earth, 1852

"So, heed my warning, gentle reader. Should you or anyone you love witness some misshapen shadow fall across your path, or should you hear the slightest rumor of dark words whispered from rooftops, then flee. Flee with all haste."

—THE KNIFE OF DUNWALL: A SURVIVOR'S TALE
From a street pamphlet containing a sensationalized
sighting of the assassin Daud

Morgengaard Castle was quiet as Daud came up out of the cellars and back into the entrance hall, emerging from a set of stone steps hidden behind a small service door underneath the grand staircase that swept up from the huge double doors of Norcross's castle.

The rest of the castle was also dark, thanks to the reported sabotage of the house's whale oil tanks. However long Daud had been unconscious, it was still night, the great windows letting in nothing but dim, grayish moonlight.

Daud paused by the service door, cocking his head

as he listened for something, *anything.* But there was nothing except the sound of his own quiet breath and the distant ticking of a grandfather clock.

The guard had reported a large group of intruders; but Daud had no idea how many or where they were, but as he listened, he could hear no movement.

But he wasn't planning on taking the intruders on. They could help themselves—which was exactly what *he* was planning on doing.

Getting his bearings, he headed in the direction of the tower stairs, sticking close to the walls where the shadows were darkest, the master of stealth once more in action.

He saw the blood first. Daud paused, scanning the stairs, the landing above, and the wide open doorways that led out of the entrance hall. All were clear. He waited, counting, but after one minute, two minutes, there was still no sound. He crabbed along the wall, then ducked down and across to the other doorway, across which lay the body of the guard.

The man was face down on the floor, his head turned to one side, his eyes open. A prodigious amount of blood was pooling beneath the body, the thick carpet soaking it up like a sponge and shining wetly in the moonlight. Daud glanced up, looking in the direction the man had fallen, and saw a line of blood traveling up the wall in a cone-shaped spray. The guard had had his throat cut with some violence, his back to his assailant. He hadn't seen it coming.

Daud moved on, alert. His progress was slow but sure, his senses alive to any movement or sound. He wondered where all the guards were—the intruders had come in, yes, and they had taken out some of Norcross's men. But someone had sounded the alarm. Had they all rushed to fight? If so, where exactly *was* the fight? Daud still couldn't hear a thing.

He stalked through several dark galleries. Then he found the next body.

And then the next. Soon he had counted twelve dead guards with their throats cut. One of them was still holding the brass end of a speaking tube in his hand, the torn end of the rubberized pipe hanging uselessly from the wall above him.

Daud paused and took stock of the situation. Whoever had come in had not only been vicious, but highly capable, carefully staking out each target before silently dispatching them. Oh, they were good. Daud's lips curled into a silent snarl. It was just what he would have done, back in the day. Take out the lights, stalk the targets, eliminate them one by one. Efficient. Ruthless. Professional.

He proceeded with the utmost caution. He kept a count of the bodies he discovered on his path, and soon had tallied more guards than he had seen on his grand tour with Norcross. There were occasional signs of a struggle, as the intruders had penetrated further into the house after the alarm had been sounded. But the quiet of the building was unnerving. It was like walking through a mausoleum. Somewhere below, in his secure room, Norcross and his bodyguard hid. Daud began to wonder if they were the only three people left alive.

That none of the exhibits showed any sign of damage was worrying. As far as he could tell, nothing had been opened or smashed—every display case was intact, the treasures within undisturbed.

The intruders had come to steal from Norcross but Daud began to formulate a theory he didn't much like; they weren't just after treasure or art. No, they were here for something else.

Daud's blood ran cold.

Norcross's private collection. That was their target.

The tower room, where the heretical artifacts were kept—those were worth a fortune on the black market.

That was, if you even *wanted* to sell them.

But what they wanted wasn't his concern. The only thing that mattered was the Twin-bladed Knife.

With no sign of the intruders and nobody in the galleries except dead guards, Daud threw caution to the wind. He sprinted through the remaining galleries and reached the tower stairs, pausing only to judge distance, angle and height before clenching his fist and summoning the power of the Void. He transversed onto the bottom step from across the passage, then he traveled up, his power carrying him up the curves of the wide spiral. He arrived in the lobby of Norcross's private vault in just three seconds.

There he stopped, the Mark of the Outsider burning on his hand, his own reserves of energy sapped by the sudden effort. He craved a vial or two of Piero's Spiritual Remedy, but even as he wondered if Norcross had any in his collection, he saw that the black metal doors of the vault were open, two bloodied bodies—castle guards, both dead—lying on the floor in front of them.

Daud's eyes were on the black plinths at the far end of the tower room. He felt the tight grip of panic close around his chest, and without thinking he moved forward into the room, crossing the distance in a heartbeat. In his haste he came to halt a fraction too close to the plinth, his sudden reappearance knocking the ornate glass framework off the top. He watched it fall, moving almost in slow motion as it hit the floor and shattered. As the shards bounced around his feet, his heart thundered, a thousand thoughts screaming for attention in his mind.

The Twin-bladed Knife was gone. The intruders, the

thieves—whoever they were—had come in and taken it while he had been strapped to the table, ready for Norcross's obscene entertainment. They'd left everything else exactly where it was. The cases that circled the room, filled with runes and bonecharms and other heretical artifacts, were sealed, their contents secure. They had wanted just one particular object.

He had been close—so very, *very* close—to his goal. The Knife had been here. And now it was gone, the opportunity to acquire the weapon he had been chasing for months taken from him.

He cursed himself for being so cautious, so slow to act. He had denied his instincts, his experience, even his training. He had been an assassin, a murderer, ruthless in the pursuit of his missions. And now he was on the most important mission of his life, and his own desire to flee from his past had resulted in failure. He had allowed Norcross to play his twisted games when he could have— no, *should* have—taken the Knife as soon as he'd set eyes on it, even if he'd had to kill everyone in the building on the way out.

The one thing—the *only* thing—that could do the Outsider harm, that could *kill* that immortal bastard, the single essential tool he had spent so much time following whispers and rumors, tracking from island to island, country to country, was gone.

Gone.

Daud yelled in frustration. He kicked at the fragments of the shattered glass stand at his feet, sending razor-sharp pieces flying across the room. He curled his left hand into a fist, then spun around and punched through the glass-fronted cabinet behind him. The door shattered, the runes inside the case jumping on their shelves as the whole unit shook under Daud's anger.

Daud yelled again, feeling the power already swelling into a wave that threatened to crash down upon him. He didn't even know what he was doing as he reached forward and grabbed the first rune he touched. The scrimshaw artifact began to glow in his hand—he could feel the heat of it through his glove, feel the power locked within the whalebone, and for a moment he knew he could take that power, use it to augment his own abilities. He hadn't done it in years, but he still knew how, and with the object of his quest stolen right from under him, perhaps he needed more power now than ever.

But as Daud drew on the rune's power, the artifact grew hotter and hotter, the glow from within the whalebone soon a blinding white light.

He fell to his knees, screaming in rage. It was a terrible roar from the very depths of his being. He felt the pain of the Outsider's Mark flood over him like boiling oil, until he felt like he was enveloped in a cloak of fire.

The rune in his hand exploded. The shockwave shattered the glass cabinets and knocked Daud back to the floor. The tower room was filled with exploding glass; Daud rolled onto his front, shielding himself as the debris rained down. His eyes were screwed shut, but he could see a blue light, so bright it was blinding, and all he could hear was the guttural roar of his own voice as he screamed and screamed again until his throat felt shredded.

What had gone wrong? Had he forgotten how to use runes? Or had it been too long—had something changed as he had aged? Or had he simply lost control? Rather than channeling the power of the rune into himself, perhaps he had reversed the process, diminishing his own power and overloading the artifact?

That thought did not sit well. If he needed power, then he couldn't risk trying another rune. Norcross's special collection housed dozens of them, and there were none he dared touch now.

Finally, there was silence, save for the tinkle of broken glass. Daud opened his eyes.

And found himself staring at his own face.

He blinked, his breath catching in his throat even as his chest heaved. He stared at the face—the dark hair, streaked with gray, hanging across the brow. The beard, long and thick and black, the gray stripe down the middle; the whiskers caked in dust and wet with spit. The scar, running down the right side of the face, skirted the eye before vanishing into the beard.

It was the face of an obsessive. A loner, standing apart from the world, years of running from his own history culminating in a new monomania, the all-consuming reason for his being.

He blinked again, and reached for the large shard of black mirror that lay on the floor in front of him. He recognized it—the artifact from the other pedestal, some kind of heretical object worthy of displaying next to the Twin-bladed Knife. Despite the carnage of the tower room, the object was undamaged, and as he looked at his own image in its pure, metallic surface, Daud felt as though he could almost reach through the glass and the liquid surface would part for him, allowing him access to the Void itself.

As he knelt on the floor, he found himself doing just that, his right hand creeping closer toward it, fingers outstretched, reaching for the shadow world beyond the mirror's horizon. In the mirror he saw something— some*one*—moving, far away, walking toward him across a desolate landscape of metal and ash. It was a young man: dark hair, dark eyes, his arms folded, his very *being* radiating sheer, unbridled arrogance—

That was when he heard the sound. Footsteps, running, and relatively close. Daud looked up, ready to see Norcross and his bodyguard arrive from their secret panic room.

What he saw instead was a figure dressed in a black suit, the tail of his coat flying as he bounded across the tower lobby and raced down the stairs.

It must be one of the intruders—disturbed by Daud, and now taking their window of escape.

Daud stood and reached out with a roar, transversing the gap between where he was kneeling and the top of the tower stairs in the blink of an eye. Ahead, he could hear the intruder leaping down the stairs as he fled. Daud wasted no time. He moved down the stairs, bouncing from the curved exterior wall of the tower as he rematerialized in split-second intervals down the side of the staircase. He traveled past the man in black, arrived at the bottom of the tower and quickly turned and transversed back up into his quarry's path.

His forearm connected with the man's throat, throwing him backward onto the stone stairs. Before the intruder had even touched the stairs, Daud grabbed the man under the armpit and shifted back up and around the tower staircase three times, reappearing in the tower room in a hurricane of debris. He felt a shard of glass pierce his face, the blood running down his beard and into the corner of his mouth. He licked at it, tasted copper, and then with one arm threw the intruder up into the air. Daud moved forward, traveling just a couple of feet, and caught the man's suspended body by the neck once more before throwing him into one of the shattered display cabinets. The man rolled his head, blinking away dust. He was battered, but alive.

Just as Daud intended.

He transversed the short distance across to the man

and grabbed him by the lapels of his coat. Daud's tight grip tore the man's shirt, revealing a large tattoo on his exposed chest—a hollow triangle, with a cross emerging from one side. Daud peered at it with a frown. The symbol was unusual, perhaps marking the intruder as part of a gang. Daud ignored it and pulled the man's face up to his own.

"Where have you taken it?" he roared.

The man screwed up his face, his arms swimming uselessly as he struggled to get away. Daud did nothing but tighten his grip.

"Listen to me," Daud snarled. "You've taken something I need. The Knife. *Where. Is. It?*"

The man squinted at his attacker and began to laugh, which sounded like more of a choking cough as his fingers feebly pulled on Daud's hand.

Daud snarled and relented, letting go. The intruder dropped back into the ruined cabinet and rolled onto his side, feeling his neck as he sucked in great lungfuls of air.

Grabbing him by the jacket again, Daud drove his fist into the man's stomach, then as his victim wheezed for breath, he pulled him up until they were nose to nose.

The man tried to focus on Daud's face. He laughed. "You'll never find it."

Daud's lips curled into a snarl. "I can make your death fast or I can make it slow. You choose."

The man laughed again, and Daud let him drop to the floor. This was getting him nowhere. He needed the information, and he was going to get it—and he knew *how* to get it. All he needed was something sharp.

He reached down and picked up the largest shard of glass he could see—the fragment of black mirror. Although it was large and awkward to hold in one hand, the edges were wickedly sharp.

Good enough.

Hefting the makeshift weapon in one hand he moved back to the fallen man. He could extract a great deal of information out of a person with a blade. He knew a thousand ways of keeping the man alive while cutting the answers out of him, one by one.

He could have given Alonso a few pointers downstairs.

Daud stood over the man—and then stopped. His interrogation subject was staring, not at him, but at the mirror, his eyes wide, his forehead creased in apparent concentration. Then he began shaking his head, slowly at first, then with more and more energy, all the while his eyes locked on what Daud assumed was the man's own reflection in the mirror.

Wasn't it? He remembered the feeling he had when he looked into it: the sense of depth, the spinning giddiness of vertigo that threatened to overwhelm him, like he was about to plunge into an abyss.

Daud crouched down, adjusting his grip on the shard to hold it like the object it was—a mirror. He tilted it this way and that, pointing it toward the man's face. In the gloom the mirror reflected what little light there was, forming a dull spotlight on the man's face—a spotlight that was reddish orange, that couldn't possibly be the reflection of the bluish glow of the room.

Could it?

The man sucked in a breath, tears gathering at the corners of his eyes. His lips moved and thick ropes of saliva dripped down onto his chin and his chest.

"No, no, no…"

Daud tilted the mirror; the light moved, the man's eyes followed. He repeated the motion, and the man's eyes moved with it again, like he was mesmerized.

Daud whispered, "Where is the Knife?"

The man shook his head, frowning like he was trying to remember. Then he lifted a hand, reaching slowly for the mirror.

Daud moved the glass out of the man's reach, and the man flinched. Then he shook his head again, his mouth forming something. Daud wondered what it was the man could see in the glass. He had no idea what the mirror was, or where it had come from, but Norcross had clearly placed some value on it, putting it on a plinth next to the Twin-bladed Knife. Was it something else salvaged from the factory in Dunwall? Perhaps another kind of artifact— one, like the Knife, that was linked to the Void?

Or even to the Outsider?

Daud returned his attention to his questions. "Where is the Knife?" he asked again, his voice calm and level.

Finally the man managed to speak properly. "Karnaca," he said. "Serkonos, Karnaca. It will be kept in a safe place."

Daud fell into a crouch, careful to keep the mirror pointed at his victim.

Daud wracked his brains. Why Karnaca? Who were these people? What did they want with the Knife? They'd known that Norcross had it—more than that, they'd known exactly where to go, ignoring the rest of his collection and heading straight for the tower room. Not only that, they were a formidable gang, having overcome all of Norcross's guards with apparent ease.

He frowned, every possibility that came to mind was troubling.

Then the intruder cried out, his eyes wide. "No, I'm sorry, I'm sorry, I… no, keep back! Keep away!"

He fainted, slumping back into the cabinet, his head rolling against his chest. Daud clicked his tongue, and reached forward to check the man's pulse. It was there, slow but steady.

Daud's gloved fingers curled around the edge of the mirror shard in his other hand. He held it low, out of his range of sight, but even now, he felt the urge to lift it, to stare into it, to try to see what the man had seen.

He glanced down and caught a glance of something orange, like flames, as the surface of the mirror flashed in his peripheral vision. He stood, quickly stuffing the shard into his tunic.

Karnaca. The thieves were already ahead of him and that advantage would only grow with each passing hour— Daud wasn't entirely sure where Morgengaard Castle was, and he could spend a week wandering the countryside, trying to pick up the gang's trail.

No, he would have to go to Karnaca directly. If the Knife was there, then that is where he would find it. But there was still unfinished business to attend to within the walls of the castle. If he was going to cleanse the world of the Outsider, he might as well cleanse it of another brand of evil.

He had to kill Maximilian Norcross.

It wouldn't take long.

20

GALLERY TEN, THE NORCROSS ESTATE, SOMEWHERE IN SOUTH-CENTRAL GRISTOL
26th Day, Month of Earth, 1852

"Sometimes I ask myself, without these gifts, would I be a man to fear? Would I be called the Knife of Dunwall, with my name whispered through the markets and the alleyways, the high towers and drawing rooms? I'd like to think so, but it really doesn't matter. As long as I bear this Mark, I'll use whatever craft I have to force my will on the world. The harder trick is undoing what I've done."

—COBBLED BITS OF BONE
Excerpt from a journal covering various occult artifacts

Daud headed back down to the entrance hall of Morgengaard Castle, through the service door and down the stairs into the passage that led to the processing room. He didn't know where Norcross's safe room was, but he'd seen the collector and his bodyguard take the left-hand path from the preparation room, so that was a start.

Things were not as he had left them. The processing machine had been rolled against the far wall and the three-needled hoses that had been pumping chemicals into the body of the woman now dragged on the floor. The woman was gone, the steel table on which she had been shackled sticky with dark, thick blood.

He had no interest in the woman—she had tried to kill him, after all—but there was something about Norcross's design for her that didn't sit well with Daud. Despite his past actions, he had lived almost his entire life by a code of discipline. True enough, it was the code of death, that of a trained killer. But even so, a desire stirred within him.

He needed to kill the monster of Morgengaard Castle.

The left-hand passage was pitch black. Daud looked around the preparation room, lit only by the processing machine's whale oil tank.

He yanked the tank free of its moorings and held it in front of him as he exited the room. Its blue glow was bright but the light didn't travel far. But, paired with Daud's preternaturally acute eyesight, it was enough.

The passage curved back and forth and soon split into other paths, all featureless, identical, service tunnels beneath Norcross's reconstructed fortress. Fortunately, Daud had a trail to follow: blood, and lots of it, streaked across the white stone floor, shining and black in the blue glow of the whale oil tank.

Eventually he came to a large vaulted chamber, the ceiling disappearing up into darkness. Ahead of him were two arched black doors. They were not quite closed— through a half-inch gap, a yellowish light shone.

Daud pushed the door open, and froze in his tracks.

The room was a basement gallery, windowless, lit by the ever-present light globes that hung from the high ceiling—more here, perhaps, to compensate for the total lack of natural light. But now the globes were dark, the yellowish light instead coming from the two square lanterns on the floor in the middle of the room.

Daud looked around, his jaw set.

The gallery was full of people. Most of them were on metal racks, their limbs pinned in place. Daud counted ten bodies on each side, with another two rows fixed to the walls above. Sixty corpses in total, hanging on display. They were all dressed, they all had their eyes open, and their skin shone with a waxy quality.

But that wasn't the true horror of Norcross's secret gallery. In the space between the racks, occupying the central display area of the gallery, were a series of low daises. On each stood the rest of Norcross's collection of people. Like the ones in the racks, these subjects were clothed, but they were also *posed*, the bodies arranged in groups as scenes, frozen in time. Three members of the City Watch took aim at a fleeing thief. A gangster—a Hatter—slit the throat of a victim. An aristocratic couple gave each other a loving look as they walked hand-in-hand. A mother handed her two children to their governess.

The people, they were real. Daud knew that. He walked toward the nearest, drawn to the hideous tableau. This one showed two factory workers—whalers—wiping the sweat from their brow as they worked on something that wasn't there. They looked like they could just spring to life at any moment. The low angle of the yellow light from the lanterns illuminated the display from below, if anything making the corpses look even more lifelike.

The dark secret of Norcross's collection—the *real* secret—wasn't the heretical artifacts in the tower room. It was this.

This was an altogether different sort of crime.

"I knew you would like it."

Daud turned and walked to the center of the chamber,

where the two lanterns had been placed. Sitting cross-legged between them was Norcross, and draped across his lap was the stiff and bloodied body from the preparation room, her dead eyes staring up at the collector as he stroked her cheek.

The collector was smiling, his eyes glittering in the lantern light as he looked around. "Do you know, I have examples from every corner of our fair Isles here. Of course, it took a long time to complete the collection—well, I say complete, but is a collection *ever* complete, hmm?"

Daud said nothing. He just clenched his fists by his sides, the leather of his gloves creaking loudly.

Norcross looked down at the head in his lap. He traced the line of the woman's jaw with a finger. "They're all dead, you know. Every last one. And it is such trouble getting the right kind of staff. You can't just hire any mercenary. I have certain secrets that must be kept from prying eyes, and sometimes money isn't enough to keep mouths shut. Do you know what they took?"

Daud nodded, but still he didn't speak. Norcross returned his attention to the body in his lap. He began to hum something—a lullaby, one Daud recognized from his own childhood in Serkonos.

Daud left the hidden gallery with the flames from the smashed whale oil tank licking at his heels. When he closed the great double doors, the last thing he saw was Norcross's lifeless eyes staring at him, from where the infamous collector lay, next to his final victim.

21

"They met in secret and spoke in whispers, their huddled forms cloaked against the night, their heads bowed low, so as almost to touch.

But then there was betrayal, as terrible and as cold as the snows of Tyvia. Each man had a dagger— the blades long and silver and hidden no longer! Together, the instruments of death were raised. Together they fell, as did the men, their bodies sliding to the earth in a silence that was befitting their craft. The men would not move again, their secrets safe to the very grave!"

—THE NIGHT OF DARK SHADOWS
Extract from a popular penny novel

"Unusual, perhaps a little heavy, but not without some, shall we say, *primitive* charm."

"I think the word you are looking for, my dearest Mrs. Devlin, is naiveté."

"Ah, yes, Mr. Devlin, how right you are. Unusual, perhaps a little heavy, but with a certain kind of—" she waved her cigar in the air, drawing a figure of eight in blue smoke over the table "—*naiveté.*"

Sal walked over to the Devlins as they sat at a corner table in the Empire's End, underneath a portrait of Emperor Alexy Olaskir, two tankards of ale in front of them. Immaculate as ever, the husband and wife were clad in matching suits woven out of dense Morley wool cloth, the fabric patterned with an alarming red-and-green plaid. They looked entirely out of place, two aristocrats slumming it for their own pleasure. Sal gritted his teeth as he joined them, half-heartedly wiping the table with a cloth in case anyone was paying attention. The pub was as busy as always, the shifts of the fishing warehouses and markets around the establishment staggered, providing Sal with a steady stream of customers.

Mr. Devlin pointed at his tankard. "Don't look so unhappy, landlord. I'd suggest you have a drink, but this 'ale,' as they call it, is not entirely to be recommended. I can see why your establishment leans more toward the smokable. Quite commendable, actually, given the outrageous olfactory assault of this horrid little town."

Sal ignored them, as he had been ignoring them for days now. Then he turned as a woman entered the pub, glanced around, and headed straight for him. "Daud. He's been sighted."

Sal nodded. "Go on."

"He's got passage to Karnaca, aboard a whaling trawler, the *Bear of Tamarak*. It left Potterstead this morning."

Mrs. Devlin raised one eyebrow. "A whaling trawler? How quaint. I didn't think many were still running these days."

Her husband blew a smoke ring. "I've heard tell that pods of the creatures have returned to the seas near Pandyssia. It would be a lengthy expedition, one final roll of the dice for the oil trade perhaps." He nodded at the messenger. "But you say it is going to Karnaca?"

"To pick up more crew, yes."

Mr. Devlin winked at Sal. "So our quarry scuttles back to his nest, eh?"

Sal considered the options. Karnaca was a long way away—what was Daud doing? Had he acquired the artifact from Norcross? Or did the search continue?

Mrs. Devlin glanced at the messenger, the distaste obvious on her face, then she looked at Sal. "I suggest we leave at once."

Sal nodded. "If he's on a whaler, the journey will be slow. Take a clipper to Bastillian. You'll find plenty of transport there. You should reach Karnaca before him."

"Oh, you're not coming?"

"Wyman hired you, not me. I took an oath out of my love for the Empire. Which means I have a pub to run."

Mr. Devlin smirked. "How quaint."

Sal managed to control his annoyance. "Just find him," he said. "And kill him."

Mrs. Devlin raised her tankard. "To the death of the enemy!"

Sal returned to the comfort of the bar, happy at least that the unpleasant pair would be out from under his roof soon enough.

INTERLUDE

THE ROYAL CONSERVATORY, KARNACA
2nd Day, Month of Timber, 1841,
Eleven Years before the Dunwall Coup

"It was suddenly obvious to me that at this rate of attrition we would not only fail to sufficiently research the continent, but we might soon lack enough crew to make the return voyage! Something had to be done to save the venture! And so I immediately declared myself Captain. On my orders the remaining crew kept to the relative safety of the beach for the duration of the week."

—A REFLECTION ON MY JOURNEY TO
THE PANDYSSIAN CONTINENT
Anton Sokolov, excerpt from the Introduction
to the second edition, 1822

The two men lay on the couches while Sokolov fussed around the machinery between them.

Finally, thought Stilton. Sokolov's lecture had been far too long but, perhaps sensing the restlessness of the audience, the natural philosopher had finally ended his talk and called for two volunteers.

The man on the couch farthest from Stilton was an older gentleman in a gray suit with long tails, the ends of which he now clutched with white-gloved hands as he lay back and stared into the high ceiling of the Royal Conservatory's entrance hall. On the other couch was a much younger volunteer, a dandy of perhaps twenty, his evening attire a far more flamboyant affair of green-and-red velvets. This man was grinning, his attention torn between watching Sokolov at the machine and someone he clearly knew down in the front of the audience, whom he kept waving to.

Stilton's head buzzed a little with the drink, and he swayed as he sat on the tall stool. As he looked at the young volunteer, admiring his handsome features—not to mention his elegant fashion sense—he smiled, feeling his heart kick up just a little. The way the man's skin glowed with sweat in the spotlights made a chill run up Stilton's spine. Ah, if only he were ten years younger. He took a swig of his drink. No, make it *twenty* years younger. A youth like that would see nothing but an overweight oaf with ruddy skin from too much drink.

Ah, but once upon a time.

The youthful volunteer waved again. Stilton frowned and slipped off the stool, somehow managing to stop it from tipping over as he did so, and peered around the edge of the wings, trying not to be seen by the audience but desperate to see who the young man's friend was.

Ah, there. Second row, near the aisle. A young woman with dark skin and dark hair wound tightly on her head and held in place with a wide-brimmed bonnet—much to the clear inconvenience of the gentleman sitting behind her, who was leaning out into the aisle to see around her elaborate headgear.

Stilton settled back into the wings. Well, there you are. Another lost cause. He went to take a swig of his hipflask and was surprised to discover it was empty.

Out on the stage, Sokolov rose from the machine and nodded, apparently to himself, then turned to the audience.

"As I have already related, my investigations into the electro-potential properties of the Pandyssian minerals—" he paused, tugged at his beard, and laughed to himself "—let us call them *sokolites*, for the sake of convenience— the electro-potential properties of the sokolites, came to a head when they were cut into twenty-sided polyhedra and subjected to a concentrated charge delivered by the standard whale oil transformer." He gestured at the base of the machine where the tank—the machine's power source—glowed.

"Now, as magnets have poles described as north and south, so the crystal structure of the sokolites have two additional dimensions, which I describe as *east* and *west*.

When these linearities are aligned with the negative and positive terminals of the electro-potential source, so the crystal structure itself becomes permeable to other kinds of force entirely."

Stilton swayed on his feet. He didn't understand a word of it, and neither did the audience. This evening of natural philosophy was a mistake. He would be a laughing stock, his folly at the Royal Conservatory would be the talk of the season. Back into the mines, they'll say. He was amazed the audience hadn't gotten up and left already.

Sokolov slipped the two stones—*sokolites, was it? Really, the sheer ego of the man!*—into the claws on the end of the machine's articulated arms, then he gently pressed the young volunteer back onto the couch.

"Try to relax and close your eyes. You will be able to see your good lady friend very soon, don't worry."

The audience tittered, but Stilton only frowned again. They were bored. Maybe he should have booked some dancers to open for the lecture. Let them get an eyeful of Churners from Morley, maybe.

The young volunteer complied, shuffling himself to get comfortable on the couch, while over on the other side, the older gentleman first turned to watch, then gave the audience a shrug. The audience laughed again, causing Sokolov to look up, casting a stern glance at his other volunteer.

"I shan't keep you a moment, sir."

More laughter.

Sokolov then pulled down the machine arm, adjusting the joints and the claw until the clasped sokolite was about six inches above the young volunteer's head. Standing back, and apparently satisfied, Sokolov moved to the other couch and made the same arrangements. Then he clapped his hands and walked back to the machine.

"Now, I shall require the assistance of a third volunteer." He turned to the wings. "May I request the presence of our most generous host, Mr. Aramis Stilton?"

Stilton jumped, like he'd got an electric shock. *Him?* Sokolov laughed and waved him over encouragingly.

Well, he hadn't said anything about this. He wanted his help? Stilton shook his head, his jowls flapping.

Oh, to hang with it.

Stilton stepped out onto the stage, acknowledging the applause with a wave, trying very hard to walk a straight line toward Sokolov. When he arrived at the machine he realized he had been holding his breath, and he let it out in a great exhalation. If Sokolov noticed, he ignored it. Instead, the natural philosopher reached into his inside pocket and drew out a stack of thin cards. Stilton frowned as they were handed over and he fanned them out in his hand. There were maybe a dozen of them: each card was about six inches by three, one side was blank, and the other featured one of a series of symbols—a square, a five-pointed star, the outline of a stylized fish, a wine glass. Stilton shuffled through them, unsure what he was looking at.

"When the crystals are charged and aligned with the poles of electro-potential," said Sokolov, once more addressing the audience, "I have discovered that they exert their own electro-potential field, which acts upon the fields around it—in our demonstration, that field being the human mind itself. The charged crystal will draw the poles of the mind into alignment with its own poles." He turned to Stilton. "Mr. Stilton, if you would be so kind, please select a card."

Stilton pursed his lips and concentrated; suddenly his fingers felt fat and uncooperative. He managed to pull a card before the entire pack slipped from his grasp. Stilton felt his face go red.

"Now," said Sokolov, "if you would please show the card to the audience."

Stilton moved to the footlights and held the card up. Members of the audience in the front couple of rows leaned forward in their seats to get a better look as Stilton walked from one side of the stage to the other, while farther back, several pairs of opera glasses glinted in the darkness.

"Thank you," said Sokolov, moving to the machine. He flicked four switches in sequence, and the whine of power increased in volume, the glow of the whale oil tank becoming slightly brighter. After making a final check of the two crystals in their articulated arms, Sokolov moved to the older volunteer.

"Now, Mr. Stilton, if you will, please move to my young friend on the other couch, and show him the card. Please ensure that neither I nor my gentleman friend here can see you."

Stilton laughed and waved at the machine. "Bit of a contraption for a simple parlor trick!" he said, mostly to the audience. They laughed, and Stilton felt the weight slowly lift from his shoulders. Yes, this was the way to do it. Get the audience on his side, and perhaps they'll forgive him for the evening of utter boredom for which he was responsible.

Stilton arranged himself by the couch, his back to Sokolov. With a flourish, he lifted the selected card and adjusted his cuffs, then held it in front of the young man's deliciously sharp features.

"Just relax, my boy," he said, "let old Aramis guide you through the mysteries of the universe!"

"And... now!"

Sokolov pulled a lever, and the whine of the machine went up in pitch. The whale oil tank glowed and then, with a crack that made Stilton jump, a tendril of blue energy arced from the silver sphere at the top of the machine to the crystal held over Stilton's subject. Then there was another crack, and a similar arc snapped to the crystal opposite. Stilton watched over his shoulder, unable to prevent himself from wincing every time the power spat across the air from terminal to terminal.

"Please pay attention, Mr. Stilton!" called Sokolov. Stilton turned back to the young volunteer.

"Now," said Sokolov, gesturing to the audience, "we begin." He turned to the older man. "Tell me what you can see."

The volunteer screwed his eyes tight, and wrinkled his nose. He shook his head slightly, and then the power snapped again and he seemed to relax.

"Oh, a… water. Something small. A… fish. A fish!"

Stilton met his own subject's wide-eyed glance, then turned the card over to double-check. He held it up again for the audience.

"It is a fish!"

The audience made an appreciative noise, and there was another smattering of applause, but the increasing crackling of the contraption drowned it out and there was another murmur, this time of unease.

"Relax, ladies and gentlemen, relax," said Sokolov. "The power flow is quite safe. Now, again, Mr. Stilton."

Stilton complied, as did his subject. The fish card was followed by the wine glass, an open book, a square. Each time the volunteer on Sokolov's side got it right, and with increasing speed, his hesitations replaced by merely a tight breath and a nod as he listed the symbols almost as soon as Stilton had presented them to his subject.

The power crackled. Stilton was enjoying himself. He was part of the show, part of the spectacle, and while it was a neat trick, using the impressive equipment, there was a simplicity to it that was a kind of strange relief after the tedium of the lecture.

Perhaps the evening was not yet lost.

The power cracked again. Stilton could feel the hairs on the back of his neck go up. He was standing *very* near to the device, after all.

"A… light. A … a blue light."

Stilton turned as Sokolov's subject spoke. Sokolov was looking down at the man, who was still reposed, apparently relaxed, his fingers curled around the tails of his coat.

With his back to the audience, Stilton saw Sokolov's eyes narrow, one hand smoothing down his moustache.

"Ah… no, that's not right," said the older volunteer. He frowned, his eyes tightly shut. "It's… a… I can't quite… there's something—"

"There's something in the way."

Stilton spun on his heel, his head suddenly clear, the dank air of the theatre suddenly cold. His young subject now had his eyes closed, his forehead creased in concentration as he struggled to see something with his mind's eye.

"There's something… I can't see it… there's a light, but there's a shadow. Something is in the way. A… man…"

Stilton looked down at the cards in his hand. The next one was a simple triangle. He shuffled through them. Spoked wheel. Knife. Square. Circle. Horse. Another fish. Another wheel. There wasn't anything that looked like a man.

"The blue light," said Sokolov's subject. "It's too bright." And then the two subjects spoke as one.

"The blue glow is bright. I feel cold."

The steady murmuring of the audience was growing in

volume. Stilton glanced over his shoulder at Sokolov, but the natural philosopher still had his back to the audience, his attention on the crystal held in the claw over his subject's head. Power arced from the silver sphere to the crystal, Sokolov's beard illuminated in bright blue flashes. But still he didn't move.

"A man... I see a man... he's... he's..."

Stilton's subject gasped, his eyes still shut, his chest rising and falling as he gulped for breath. His hands were clenched fists by his sides, and as Stilton watched, he started hammering the couch.

A few people in the audience rose from their seats. Stilton summoned up the voice he used to address his mine crews, and quickly moved to the front of the stage.

"Ladies, gentlemen, please, do not be alarmed. As our illustrious guest has already told us, the power flow is quite safe. What you are witnessing is merely a wonder of our natural world, harnessed by the amazing intellect of Anton Sokolov, renowned thinker and—"

"A knife! I see a knife! There is a man holding a knife! A knife!"

Sokolov's subject sat up, knocking his head against the crystal frame above him. His eyes were still closed, but his upper body shook. He reached out with his hands, still holding onto the tails of his coat.

"No! No!"

He screamed in terror. Stilton felt the bile rise in his throat as a sizeable portion of the audience also cried out, the sound of the crackling machine this time drowned out by the thunderous roar of feet on wood as the audience panicked and started for the exit.

"The blue light burns, the blue light burns!"

Stilton ignored the ravings of the subject on his couch, and rushed across to Sokolov. He grabbed the natural philosopher by the shoulders, spinning the man around. Sokolov didn't resist, his expression one of curious bewilderment rather than fear.

"Sokolov! What's happening? Stop this! Stop this at once!"

He shook Sokolov by the shoulders until, finally, he seemed to snap out of it. The natural philosopher looked around, as if seeing the theatre for the first time, then nodded.

"Most fascinating… Oh yes, of course, of course," he said, moving quickly to the machine. His fingers flew over the switches, and he looked up at the silver sphere at the machine's apex, but nothing happened. The power still arced, and the two subjects continued to rave about the light, the man, and the knife.

Sokolov stood back, looking up at his machine. "I don't understand, if the electro-potential squared equals charge to the third power, then surely it should be—"

Stilton's young volunteer screamed. There was blood trickling from the youth's nose and from under his closed eyelids.

Stilton shoved Sokolov to one side, sending him tumbling to the boards. Then he ducked down, his fingers closing around something heavy and cold. He stood tall.

"No! Don't! What do you think you're doing?" cried Sokolov from the floor.

Stilton ignored him. He swung the crowbar sideways with all his might, smashing the gem hanging over his subject. There was a bang and a bright-blue flash that left Stilton with purple spots floating in his vision; he blinked rapidly and saw the brass claw hanging from a broken joint. Of the crystal—the sokolite—there was no sign. He had succeeded in knocking it out of the machine and that was all that mattered. As the ringing in his ears began to clear, the theatre sounded quiet.

Glancing down, he saw the whale oil tank in the base of the machine was dark.

"You stupid, stupid—"

Sokolov's eyes went wide as he looked at the crowbar in Stilton's hand. Stilton dropped it and it hit the stage with a thud.

The hall was half-empty, but those audience members who remained had turned back to the stage. With the danger apparently over, they were now curious to witness the aftermath of the disastrous performance.

Yes… a performance. Stilton nodded to himself. A performance. That's what it was. Parlor tricks in the guise of a lecture. Yes, it was perfect. All he needed to do was pay for the story to run in the newspaper the following morning, celebrating the audacious, nay, scandalous spectacular at the Royal Conservatory. That would cover the real story, and the editor was not only a greedy little man, but he also owed Stilton a favor.

Stilton glanced at the royal box, and with some relief saw it was empty. The Duke and his entourage had left.

He moved to the front of the stage—stepping *over* Sokolov—to address the remnants of the crowd.

"Of course," he said, "full refunds will be issued. Please retain your tickets and present them to the box office at your earliest convenience. Thank you!"

He gave a bow, finishing with a flourish of the arm. When he stood up, he found the crowd just staring at him.

And then, a single person started clapping. Stilton squinted, standing on his toes as he peered into the back of the hall. A young man, rail-thin with a pencil moustache, was sitting in the center block, a grin plastered on his face. He clapped, either unaware or unconcerned that he was the only one.

Stilton thought he recognized him, but he wasn't sure.

Was he one of the special invitations? Perhaps. He would have it checked.

From the Royal Conservatory's main doors, new arrivals began pushing their way past the exiting crowd. Stilton caught sight of their tall white helmets and blue-green tunics and sighed. The Grand Guard. Precisely what he needed. His pockets were deep, but not limitless, and to avoid any scandal he would have to pay them off. The expense account of the Stilton Mining Corporation was going to need some very creative accounting this month.

"You, Aramis Stilton, are a fatuous ignoramus."

Stilton glanced down at Sokolov, who had propped himself up on his elbow.

"Oh, do shut up," said Stilton, as he headed to the wings. He had to gather the Grand Guard up and move them away from the stage. As he passed Toberman, the assistant grabbed his sleeve.

"The subjects, sir!"

Stilton hissed in annoyance. "Blast it all, lad, can't you see I'm busy? I have one of several crises to avert. Now, if you would kindly unhand me—"

"No, sir, listen! They're dead. That bloody machine of Sokolov's has killed them."

Stilton felt himself deflate. "Dead? What, both of them?"

"Dead, sir!" Toberman shivered and swept the cap off his head. "And them things they were saying. Horrible things, sir! Heretical, I'll wager."

Stilton twisted his arm out of Toberman's grip and pushed the young man against the wall, sliding his arm up under Toberman's chin and pinning his head back.

"Now you look here, my young lad, whatever you think you've seen, you just forget it now. This was a marvelous evening of supernatural entertainment, nothing more. A show, my young lad, a *show*. Now, do you understand me?"

"Please, Mr. Stilton, you're hurting me."

Stilton hissed and leaned harder against Toberman. He wasn't a strong man and Toberman was a good deal younger, but he had sheer bulk on his side. "Take fifty coin from my office and get rid of the bodies."

"I… what?"

Stilton glanced back toward the stage. "And don't worry about our friend Sokolov, I'll handle him. Now go, get a move on."

He released Toberman, who collapsed, gasping for breath.

That was when two red-jacketed officers of the Grand Guard appeared. Seeing Stilton and the puffing Toberman, they immediately headed toward them.

"Good lad," said Stilton, patting Toberman's back. "Off you go."

Toberman shook his head, then headed off, squeezing past the guard officers as he ducked down a corridor.

Stilton thrust his chest out and looped his thumbs into the pockets of his waistcoat. As the guards got closer, he felt his hands shaking and his heart pounding in his chest. Sokolov's experiment was a disaster. Two men were dead—and it was all his fault. If he hadn't organized the event in the first place, hadn't been so preoccupied with raising his standing among the elite of the city, none of this would have happened.

He only hoped that one day he would be able to forgive himself.

Sitting at the back of the auditorium, the young man with the pencil moustache leaned back. He lifted his feet and placed them on the back of the chair in front of him, then leaned forward and brushed a speck of dirt from his brilliant white spats. In front of him, the empty seats had been thrown into disarray as the crowd had scampered for escape, while on the stage the curtain was now down, with a couple of stagehands standing in front of it as they spoke to a member of the Grand Guard.

The man leaned back and placed his hands behind his head as he thought back over the evening's events. Sokolov's machine was remarkable, even seen from afar—the man was glad to have brought his telescopic opera glasses, a little invention of his own that improved upon those commonly available. As he had sat and watched the theatrics of the performance, he had begun to sketch a schematic of the machine on the back of an old envelope. Or, at least as much of it as he had been able to see over the heads of those seated in front of him—Stilton's temporary theater was an impressive piece of dressing, but the Royal Conservatory's grand entrance hall made for a poor auditorium.

He regarded his sketch. Many of the core components were not, in and of themselves, especially exotic. But the machine was ingenious… no, it was more than that. It was… well, *easy*, that was the only word to describe it. He considered himself an inventor and an engineer, but what he did was hard work. He slaved over his devices. But the work was worth it.

Sokolov's machine, however? It had an elegance that could only come from years of experience, knowledge so finely honed as to become pure intuition.

Of course, the machine was only part of it. Now, those crystals—what had he called them? Sokolites? Ha, of course he had. Now, *they* were interesting. A natural mineral formation that was able not just to conduct power but also transform it, without any apparent loss of energy.

He knew a great deal about crystallography, but the properties of the minerals from Pandyssia were unique.

The results were intriguing, certainly. But inconclusive. The hall was hardly a controlled environment, and while Sokolov had spoken with authority and confidence, the man knew—from attending Sokolov's past lectures—that this was merely his natural demeanor. Ten years of work on the machine and there was a flaw to the design, a mere fraction of the unimaginable power of the crystals tapped to enact a simple parlor trick.

Now, what if that power could be amplified? What if you could not just see what someone else saw—what if you could see and *hear*? What if you could do that not just across a room but across a country? Could the transmitter be in Tyvia and the receiver in Karnaca?

And... what if you could reverse the process? Rather than merely observe through the senses of another, what if you could *project* your own thoughts into the mind of another.

What if you could do it without the recipient even being aware of it?

Now *there* was an interesting theory. The applications were limitless. It would herald a new era of natural philosophy, giving rise to a new age of espionage.

Perhaps even a new generation of warfare.

The man could see that there was work to be done. The machine was adequate, but Sokolov treated his crystals with kid gloves, afraid to tap their potential. Cutting them into polyhedra was a good first step, but the effect could be amplified—could be *focused*—if the minerals were sectioned, those sections then polished into lenses.

Yes, lenses. That was good. That was *interesting*.

He needed to speak to Sokolov about it. Fortunately, they were acquainted, despite the matter of their past disagreements. The man had once been Sokolov's student at the academy in Dunwall—that is, until he was thrown out after that little accident. But that was history. Even if Sokolov remained the bad-tempered buffoon the man remembered him as, he also knew that the natural philosopher wouldn't be able to resist discussing his research with someone who actually knew what he was talking about.

As the Grand Guard moved around the stage, the red-jacketed officers having a heated conversation with Aramis Stilton on stage left, Kirin Jindosh lifted his feet from the chair and, gathering his fur shawl around his shoulders, made his exit.

PART THREE
THE HOMECOMING

22

THE *BEAR OF TAMARAK*, SAILING FROM POTTERSTEAD TO KARNACA
5th to 22nd Day, Month of Harvest, 1852

"Whale oil. Liquid power! How astonishing that within those beasts, inside the oil harvested along with their flesh, was enough power to see the Isles through these tumultuous years! And it all seemed limitless, but now the lights begin to dim. Our fisher folk say the great beasts are increasingly rare!

Not all places will suffer this loss equally, fellow natural philosophers! Karnaca has a unique feature—the cleft in Shindaerey Peak, through which the winds are channeled and amplified.

As whale oil begins to run short, with the cost of finding the remaining leviathans escalating beyond the worth of the oil itself, Karnaca will find itself ascendant among the Isles."

—THE SHINDAEREY GIFT
A Study, by Emora Clipswitch

The journey from southwestern Gristol to Serkonos aboard the Tyvian whaler *Bear of Tamarak* took eighteen days, and it was time Daud relished.

Before leaving Morgengaard Castle in flames, he had searched Norcross's private chambers and taken a set of maps. The moorland in which Morgengaard Castle was situated was many miles southeast of the port city of Potterstead. Daud knew that was his best bet—Dunwall was too far to travel, and the ports there were likely in lockdown thanks to the coup. If he was to get to Karnaca he needed fast transport. Potterstead was a good gamble, being a waypoint for Tyvian ships taking advantage of the favorable ocean currents down the western coast of the Isles. It was certainly a better option than returning to Porterfell. From Potterstead he wouldn't have much trouble getting passage south.

The journey to Potterstead had been long, as Daud was forced to make his way on foot, the two electric road coaches that had been parked in the courtyard of Norcross's castle absent, perhaps stolen by the strange intruders to prevent any fast pursuit. Daud had traveled by both day and night, taking as direct a route as possible across the desolate, scrubby landscape, avoiding the roads and always ready to take cover in the rich purple heather should he need to hide quickly.

He needn't have worried. He didn't see anyone on his entire journey.

Along the way, he thought back to the events at Norcross's castle, his mind racing as he tried to put the pieces of the puzzle together. Who were the intruders? How had they known the Twin-bladed Knife was there? And why did they even want it? Did they know—as Daud did—what the Knife was capable of, the powers the artifact possessed?

Questions without answers. They continued to plague Daud as, finally, he sought shelter the second night in an old farmstead, the slate buildings nothing more than empty shells leaning precariously against the side of a shallow cliff, the only inhabitants the rats that scurried quickly away from Daud's footsteps as he searched the property. He didn't know what he was looking for, but he had an urge to look, the Mark of the Outsider a dull ache on the back of his hand.

The shrine was in the back of the barn up on what was left of the hayloft. It was built out of a stack of flat slate blocks that had been salvaged from the collapsing structure of the main farmhouse. The stubby remains of ancient, rotten candles littered the haphazard construction, and on the largest slate block, which formed a sort of altar, there was the mummified remains of something organic—dried leaves and sticks and something else equally desiccated— and scratched into the dark surface of the stone was a refrain that brought memories rushing back to Daud's mind.

THE OUTSIDER WALKS AMONG US!

Daud spent the night in front of the altar. At first he kneeled in front of it, then, realizing what he was doing, he turned his back on the shrine and sat on some of the slate stacks. As the hours slowly slipped by, Daud found himself calling into the night, asking the bastard Outsider to show himself and admit what he had done.

If the Outsider heard him, there was no reply.

After another hour, Daud took the shard of black mirror from his tunic and, taking a deep breath, turned and balanced it on the altar. He stared into the glass, willing the Outsider to show himself, but all he saw was his own reflection in the moonlight that shone in through the barn's broken roof.

Daud pocketed the mirror, destroyed the altar, and left before dawn.

Arriving in Potterstead, he first went to one of his caches, long hidden in the years spent wandering the Isles aimlessly after Corvo had exiled him from Dunwall. The cache, secreted in a bricked-up culvert underneath a bridge, had remained undetected, and included another pouch of Overseer platinum ingots, twelve in total. It was a lot of money to carry, but he wanted to make sure that nobody asked him any questions about the next part of his journey.

Then he scouted Potterstead harbor, and saw it—a huge whaling ship of the kind that he had thought retired years ago. It was an expensive hulk, a relic from the earlier days of the whale trade. It had been patched up, and the crew was still in the process of cleaning and repair when Daud found the captain discussing business with the harbormaster. The ship had been exhumed from dry dock in the Tyvian city of Tamarak and had set off from the northern isles to hunt whales off the Pandyssian Continent. But first it was scheduled for a shakedown run, which included the maintenance stop at Potterstead after the first leg of the journey, and another stop at Karnaca, where it would pick up more crew.

Daud paid the captain one ingot, and the harbormaster another—probably a half- or even a full-year's wages for each, Daud thought. Neither asked any questions after that, and the *Bear of Tamarak* steamed out of Potterstead harbor that afternoon, with one extra crewman whose name didn't appear on the roster.

During the nearly three-week journey south, Daud worked alongside the others. There were seven crew plus the captain, the bare minimum required to pilot the ship and begin the laborious task of cleaning and repairing the tools of the ship's primary function—the harpoon guns, the winches, the whale frames and their complex crane and gantry systems. Daud and the crew worked hard, stripping chain and cable, disassembling mechanisms and reassembling them. It was laborious, but Daud felt invigorated, alive with his purpose, his determination to complete his mission more acute than ever.

While the crew slept, Daud trained. The ship was gigantic, and with a skeleton crew working mostly on deck, the vast innards of the vessel became Daud's private domain. In one of the cargo holds he began to build a gymnasium for himself out of scrap and bits of broken machinery removed during the repairs. He built four makeshift mannequins, with multiple arms and panels Daud could punch and kick, the combat practice sharpening his already formidable skills. He built multi-level scaffolds and platforms, towering frames holding horizontal bars. At night he leapt, and ran, swinging from poles and bars, jumping, rolling, jumping again from platform to platform.

The sound of his training echoed in the huge hollow chambers of the *Bear of Tamarak*. Once—just once—he saw the captain appear through a bulkhead door high up in the wall of the cargo hold, watching him work. When Daud stopped and looked up at him, the captain nodded, and then disappeared.

When he wasn't training or working, Daud spent much of his time in the cabin the captain had allocated him, an officer's room, away from the bunks of the main crew. Here Daud slept deeply, his body tired from his work aboard the ship, or he practiced various meditation techniques he had learned across the Isles, focusing his mind, readying himself for the tasks ahead.

It was all time well spent. As the ship neared its destination, Daud felt calm and rested, despite his exertions.

The ship skirted the west coast of Serkonos, riding the

fast ocean current that arced around the southernmost landmass of the Empire of the Isles, and as the city of Karnaca came into distant view, Daud deemed himself ready to face the Outsider. He wondered if the Outsider felt it too, if he was watching him and somehow nudging events toward their conclusion. In moments of doubt, it felt as though Daud had no free will but was merely following the contours of the universe, his life hurtling with inevitable finality toward the ultimate confrontation.

In his cabin, Daud cut his hair with a cut-throat razor and slicked it back with a smear of grease made of beeswax and Tyvian bear fat, taken from one of the harpoon guns on deck. Then he shaved his beard, slowly revealing a face he hadn't seen in years, a face that felt like it belonged not just to another person, but another world. When he was finished he washed his face and stood in front of the small mirror, staring at an old man with an old scar running down the right side of his face from temple to jaw.

He got dressed in a long-sleeved undershirt, then a pale, long-sleeved tunic with a high buttoned collar. On top of that, a protective brown leather jerkin, and then, finally, a short-sleeved red coat that fell to mid-thigh. He fastened a heavy brown belt around his waist, then pulled on a long coat he had liberated from one of the crewmen, a fine garment with a deep hood, crafted for the climate of Tyvia.

Then he turned and looked in the mirror again, and he didn't seem himself. He saw a man he thought was dead. A man exiled from Dunwall fifteen years ago, never to return to the life of violence and darkness he'd left behind.

When the *Bear of Tamarak* docked in Karnaca, Daud,

former leader of the Whalers, master assassin, the Knife of Dunwall—and puppet of the Outsider—slipped from the vessel silently and vanished into the city.

23

"Hush-a-bye, and don't be affright,
Mama will sing through all the night,
Many an hour before morning sun,
Don't dream of horror yet to come."

—TRADITIONAL SERKONAN SONGS
Extract from a popular melody

The two witches watched the *Bear of Tamarak* as it sat out in the harbor, the hulk dominating the view, larger than most of the buildings that crowded this part of Karnaca's shoreline. The pair sat high up on top of a billboard, their legs dangling in the air, the advertisement beneath them having long since faded to a shadowy palimpsest of indistinct images.

Lucinda cocked her head, her eyes on the horizon. "He has returned. As our mistress foresaw."

Her companion, Caitlin, frowned. The warm evening breeze ruffled her shorn black hair, and she ran a hand over her scalp.

"We can't expect the plan to continue, can we?"

Lucinda smiled. "And why not, oh sister of mine?" She

shrugged. "All is prepared. We need but the last items from the Royal Conservatory. Then the trap will be set. All we need is for our quarry to walk into it."

"But Breanna is powerless, she—"

Lucinda pushed Caitlin's shoulder, forcing the witch to grab hold of the top of the billboard to stop herself from losing her balance. "Breanna has no magic, but she is far from powerless."

Caitlin shook her head. "I don't understand."

Lucinda leaned in toward her companion, and as Caitlin watched, her eyes turned black, becoming two deep pools. Caitlin gasped.

"You still have power? But how?"

Lucinda's eyes returned to normal. "Our mistress was cut off from the Void, but some of her magic remained in the world. Her black bonecharms still sing. And some of that power remained in me, and a few of the others. See?" She slipped her shirt down to reveal an ink-covered shoulder. The lines of the tattoo swam as Caitlin studied it. "This, one of her last special undertakings, a final experiment, persists, though even now I can feel it fading. But there is enough. The plan proceeds as before. Breanna needs us now more than ever."

Caitlin turned back to watch the *Bear of Tamarak*. She felt breathless, excited—exhilarated. So it was not over, not yet. The grand plan, the one Lucinda had hatched as soon as she had learned that Daud still walked the world, would go ahead. Originally, they had planned to present Daud to their mistress, Breanna, to curry favor—Breanna was powerful, untouchable, and Lucinda had wanted to share more of her power, using the gift to demonstrate their worthiness to her.

And then something had gone wrong, something with the Oraculum. It had stripped Breanna of her powers, leaving her helpless as a babe. Now she was hiding somewhere in the city—maybe Lucinda knew where, although if she did, she hadn't said yet.

But… was she speaking the truth? Was there hope yet? Did some vestige of Breanna's power still exist—and had some of it entered Lucinda? And was she able to wield it?

If so…

Caitlin turned to Lucinda, who nodded.

"It makes the mind reel with the possibilities, doesn't it, sister?"

Lucinda laughed, and Caitlin laughed with her, their voices echoing over the dockyard.

Then Lucinda stood and held her hand out to Caitlin. She took it and the two witches balanced on the top edge of the billboard.

"The final pieces?" asked Caitlin.

Lucinda nodded. "They are still in the Royal Conservatory. Come, let us go back to the hideout. I have called the others to join us. It is only a matter of time."

Hand in hand, the two witches of Karnaca tiptoed along the billboard, before jumping down to the roof of the building behind.

And as they headed for their hideout, Caitlin's mind sang with anticipation. The plan was going ahead. The plan was going to work. Daud would be theirs, along with the secrets of his magic.

And with him in their grasp—and his powers now theirs—the coven would rise once more.

24

THE ROYAL CONSERVATORY, KARNACA
23rd Day, Month of Harvest, 1852

"Investigations continue into the ongoing closure of the Royal Conservatory, which had already been shut to the public for some time before the Grand Serkonan Guard closed off the area last week. Although the Office of Grand Guard Command has stated repeatedly that an official statement is forthcoming, no such proclamation has yet been received by this publication.

Meanwhile, rumors continue to circulate that the closure of Karnaca's premier cultural and natural philosophy establishments—the Royal Conservatory and the Addermire Institute—are connected with the actions of a masked criminal, reports of whom have reached this reporter despite attempts by the Grand Guard to issue a classified notice. Speaking on a condition of anonymity, one inside source said that something unusual had happened to Breanna Ashworth, Curator of the Royal Conservatory, who has not been seen in some time, and that her private chambers within the institute are now an active crime scene.

The Office of the Grand Guard Command declined our invitation to comment.

—GRAND GUARD PRESENCE AT THE ROYAL
CONSERVATORY: UNEXPLAINED CLOSURE
BECOMES "OFFICIAL INVESTIGATION"
Newspaper report from the *Karnaca Gazette*

It took Daud just one day to get word to his contact in Karnaca; he could have done it faster, but he needed to play it safe, moving only at night, sticking to the darkness and the rooftops. He needed to be master of the situation and have every aspect of his mission under his control. The Twin-bladed Knife had been brought to Karnaca by the strange gang who had managed to infiltrate Norcross's collection and steal the artifact from under Daud's nose. But to find the gang, he needed to know more about them.

And to know more about them, he went to a woman who, he hoped, would be able to furnish him with all the information he needed.

Sierra Esquivel. Or, to be more specific, *Officer* Sierra Esquivel. Daughter of one of Daud's former—now deceased—lieutenants in the Whalers, Sierra had been born in Dunwall and smuggled out with her mother during the inter-gang war that had cost her father his life. In the years that had followed, Daud had kept an eye on Sierra herself, watching as the child became a woman and the woman became an officer of the Grand Serkonan Guard. Daud knew that having a contact in her position would be useful one day, and the trust Sierra's father had had in Daud had been passed down to his daughter.

While he waited for their meeting—arranged for the next night in a place they were guaranteed not to be disturbed—Daud caught up with local news, reading about recent mysterious events in the *Karnaca Gazette*. While the affairs of the world were not his concern, Daud had much still to do in the city, and felt it wise to at least be as informed as the rest of the populace. He had to admit the reports—if in any way accurate—were strange. Disappearances of prominent citizens, sightings of a masked criminal, and rumors that the Grand Serkonan Guard had sustained heavy losses in fights with this miscreant; losses they were denying to the press.

Daud wondered if it had anything to do with Luca Abele's coup in Dunwall. It couldn't be a coincidence. Daud thought back to his sighting of the Empress, Emily Kaldwin, as she fled Dunwall Tower.

Not for the first time, Daud wondered if the Outsider had been watching too.

At the appointed time, Daud made his way across Karnaca to the rendezvous, stopping first to visit another of his caches, hidden in a small cave in the rocky cliff face of Shindaerey Peak, the mouth of which could only be accessed by the most foolhardy of climbers—or by the power of transversal. Kneeling in the cave, Daud unwrapped a long object—a short sword with a black-and-gold grip and a blade with a flat, straight spine and a cutting edge, which tapered to a wicked point. It was his sword from his days with the Whalers, crafted from Tyvian meteorite metal. He hadn't thought he would ever wield it again, yet something had compelled him, years ago, to keep it rather than throw it into the sea.

He slid it into its scabbard, hung it from his belt, and continued on his journey.

The Royal Conservatory was traditionally open to the public, the complex consisting of a cluster of connecting buildings, within which were housed rooms for public performances, lectures and exhibitions, smaller spaces where academics conducted private tuition or research, and an extensive library—the largest outside of Dunwall—available to all.

At least, that *had* been the case. Daud had learned that over the last few months, the Royal Conservatory had been closed to the public on the orders of the institute's curator, Breanna Ashworth—much to the disconcertment of the academic aristocracy of the city, as they had been promised an exhibition of items from the Roseburrow Collection, taken from the personal collection of renowned natural philosopher Esmond Roseburrow.

Breanna Ashworth. The name rang a bell, but there had been so many names, so many faces, over the decades. Most were underground now, so if Daud *had* known her, she was either lucky or tough. He narrowed his eyes, looking out across the moonlit city as he thought about how much was lost to memory and to time. The building certainly looked like it had been closed for months. The library was in the worst shape, the shelves covered with dust and some of the precious volumes already sagging in the humid air of the city as they were left with no air circulation by the building's apparent lack of power. The fans were off and most of the windows were closed.

Daud admired Sierra's choice of meeting place. The Royal Conservatory was huge, accessible only, at the moment, to senior members of the Grand Guard. Here, in the heart of Karnaca, the echoing halls were the most secluded and secret place in the whole city.

He made his way to the mezzanine floor, an extension of the library that wrapped around a large central atrium. Here, the debris was even worse; there were books thrown onto the floor in great heaps, and some of the shelves had collapsed. Moving around the left-hand side of the mezzanine, the bright Serkonan moonlight streaming through the high windows lit a wide, empty space, highlighting gouges in the woodwork that suggested something large and heavy had once occupied the spot before being torn out.

Daud was early. He had gained access through an upper level, expecting guard patrols inside as well as on the street. He'd been wrong. So now he had reached the rendezvous, all he could do was wait.

He moved to the railing and looked down at the floor below. A great ironwork chandelier had fallen from the ceiling, crushing several work desks below. Whatever had gone on in here, it had been quite some accident.

"You have two minutes," said the voice from the other end of the room, "starting… *now.*"

Daud turned as Sierra walked in. She was dressed in the red jacket of a guard captain. The distinctive white helmet of the Grand Guard was tucked under one arm, her long black hair braided into cornrows that vanished against her equally dark skin in the gloomy interior of the Royal Conservatory. In one hand she held a pocket fob, her thumb hovering over the watch's crown.

"I knew the Guard was corrupt," he said, "but I didn't expect it to charge by the hour."

"One minute, fifty-five seconds."

Daud rubbed his chin, surprised for a moment to find the skin clean-shaven. "I'm looking for a group—a gang. Don't know who they are but they might be identifiable by a tattoo."

Sierra pulled a pencil from her jacket. She turned to the nearby shelf and tore out the blank front page of a book, scrawled something on it, and handed it over.

"Like this?"

Daud cast his eye over the page. Sierra had drawn a

symbol on it—a hollow triangle and a cross. It was the same symbol he had seen tattooed onto the intruder's chest back at Norcross's castle.

"That's it."

Sierra nodded. "The Eyeless."

"Never heard of them."

Sierra pursed her lips. "They're relatively quiet. Local to some parts of the Empire. Got stronger in Karnaca about a year ago. The Grand Guard got word from a couple of informants in the Butcher Brothers and the Howlers. Seems the Eyeless had appeared in their territory, but when challenged, they cleared out, set up somewhere in one of the outer districts. Didn't bother them again. One minute fifteen seconds."

Daud frowned. "And the other gangs just accepted that?"

"Accepted isn't the right word. Tolerated, maybe. At least for now."

"Interesting," said Daud, and then he paused, considering.

"One minute."

"Base of operations?"

"Unclear."

"I need more than that."

"The Howlers think the Eyeless have some kind of fortified facility, hidden in plain sight, but we haven't been able to confirm that. The Grand Guard has been a little… preoccupied, lately." Her eyes returned to the fob. "Forty seconds."

"Leader?"

"Don't know. Thirty-five seconds."

"Numbers?"

"Small. We've counted a few dozen individuals, but it's hard to tell. Could be a lot more. They're bigger than the

Sly Eyes. Smaller than the Howlers. We haven't crossed swords with them yet, so official reports are hazy at best."

"Okay."

"Ten seconds." Sierra sighed and thumbed the crown on the fob watch. "Piece of advice. I'm not going to ask what you're planning to do, but you're on your own with this one. The Grand Guard has enough on its plate at the moment. You get yourself in trouble, you get yourself out of it. If you're planning on taking out the Eyeless, you do that on your own. I can't help you, and once I walk out of this building, you don't see me again. Understand?"

Daud nodded. Sierra held his gaze for a moment, then left.

Daud leaned back against the bookcase and listened to her heavy-booted footsteps as they faded away. So, they were called the Eyeless. He still didn't know what they wanted with the Knife, but that didn't matter. The Twin-bladed Knife was here, in Karnaca.

He was one small step closer.

Daud waited in the shadows, counting time in his head to allow Sierra to exit the building, then he pushed off the bookcase and prepared to make his own departure.

That was when he heard the sound of a book falling. Daud stopped and looked over his shoulder, but the case against which he had been leaning had not been disturbed by his movement. As he examined the tomes, he heard more sounds—shuffling, like someone going through papers, then another thud as a second book was pulled off a shelf and tossed to the floor.

The sounds continued as Daud moved over to the atrium and peered down into the depths of the Royal Conservatory library. The noise echoed up from somewhere far below, and it was too loud for rats. Daud doubted it was the Grand Guard either—they may have had the place under lockdown, but Daud had seen no evidence that they were actually working inside the building.

No, someone else was here. And Daud wanted to find out who.

Daud made his way down to the lower floors of the Royal Conservatory, gliding silently across the polished floorboards as he followed the sounds of the mystery intruders. Away from the library atrium it was darker, the windows smaller, the moonlight dimmer.

The rooms on this level were less ornate, more functional, than the rest of the building, and consisted mostly of offices, storerooms, and workshops. Daud crept forward, the sounds growing in volume as he got closer. If he had been able to hear them up in the library, echoing through the cavernous space of the building, then the intruders must have been listening in to his conversation with Sierra. And if they were the Eyeless, they would report back to their leader. That they'd been at Norcross's castle was a coincidence. That they were here, at the Royal Conservatory, was too much. They must have been following him.

Perfect. Now was the chance to grab one and extract the information he needed.

Daud turned a corner, his fists clenched, ready to confront the intruders. There was another thump as a heavy book hit the floor.

The room beyond was a large office, acres of carpet leading up to a huge desk in front of a wide bookcase. Stairs curved up around either side of the bookcase, leading up to another railed mezzanine. The desk was covered with papers, as was the floor around it, along with a good many books that had been pulled off the case.

Two women were searching for something. Their hair was shaved to the scalp, their skin pale, almost translucent, covered with a tracery of black veins. As one half-turned to deposit another book on the desk, Daud could see there were arcane marks across her face and the exposed skin of her arms.

Witches!

Daud backed away, adrenaline rising, as he decided what to do—fight or flight were his options, and the latter seemed most prudent. Whatever they were doing here, it had nothing to do with him. More than that, witches were a complication he did not wish to get involved with. Not now.

He turned. Behind him was a third witch, heading toward the office, a cloth-wrapped bundle held under one arm. Daud froze—as did the witch. The two stared at each other for a moment, then the witch turned on her heel and vanished in a puff of inky black nothing.

Daud spun around. Flight was no longer an option.

The first two witches, disturbed by their sister, had now seen him. They stalked around either side of the desk, slowly, one foot carefully placed in front of the other, their eyes fixed on Daud.

He felt the Mark of the Outsider burn on his hand. Unsure of what magic they had access to, he might well need to use his own now. Two witches against one of him wasn't bad odds—he'd faced far worse, although right now that time at Brigmore Manor felt like a lifetime ago—but even a single witch was a formidable opponent.

Then the witches shrieked in unison, and vanished from the end of the office, reappearing almost within touching distance.

Daud lunged forward, his whaling knife already slicing toward the closest witch. She snarled, her eyes glowing fiercely as thick black ichor began to run from them, coursing down her face. She vanished in a puff of sticky smoke, Daud's blade sweeping through thin air.

But he was prepared. He knew what witches could do—and he knew how to fight them. Allowing his momentum to carry him forward, he curled his knife arm around, ducking the outstretched grasp of the other witch and, aiming low, he swiped the blade across her leg. The witch screamed and fell backward, then in a swirl of black fog she was gone, her sister switching positions with her.

The witch reached forward, screeching, her razor-sharp fingernails an inch away from Daud's face. The Mark of the Outsider blazed and he transversed away, materializing on top of one of the bookcases. Below, the two witches turned to look before vanishing from the floor and appearing on the top of the bookcase opposite. In unison, the pair threw their hands out, from which grew twisting, writhing black-and-green tendrils of vegetation, the blood briars magically soaring outward to ensnare the assassin.

Daud reacted, transversing up to their bookcase and appearing behind them. His blade sank into the first witch's back, piercing her squarely between the shoulder blades. Screaming in agony, she groped behind her, but Daud twisted the knife and yanked it out, before moving away, kicking as he did so. The witch toppled to the ground, dead. Burning lines began to run along her skin, blackening her clothing—the remains of some occult tattoo that Daud did not quite understand, though he'd seen other sorcerers employ similar tricks.

Her sister stared up at Daud as he crouched on the black iron chandelier that swung high from the ceiling. He saw her tense, ready to make an impossible leap, ready to ensnare the light fitting in more blood briars.

That was when the shot rang out. The witch jerked to one side, a spray of black-red blood erupting from her shoulder. She howled and dematerialized, the sooty black residue of her power quickly evaporating as two newcomers entered the room.

They were not Grand Guards, but a man and a woman, dressed in matching khaki-green suits and elaborate cravats held in place with jeweled pins. She had blonde hair that rose in a pompadour, while the man's hair and moustache were black, his bangs falling over his face as he ducked for cover by a low, glass-topped cabinet of curios.

Daud was exposed on the chandelier; but he wasn't sure the newcomers had seen him yet, their attention now on the remaining witch who was zig-zagging around the room, her shrieks bouncing from the walls. Daud glanced up—at the far end of the office, over the main doors, was a large stained-glass window, the ledge large enough to stand on. Summoning his power, Daud moved onto it, then flattened himself against the narrow space and crawled forward, looking over the edge and directly down on the newcomers.

He had no idea who they were. He had no interest in finding out. A more urgent issue was the remaining witches—the one with the bundle he hadn't seen again, but the other, while injured, would now be even more dangerous as her anger took hold. From his high position, Daud watched as the witch darted around the room, then vanished altogether, while the strange pair paused, scanning the office.

Daud let out a breath he hadn't realized he'd been holding. Witches, here, in Karnaca? Linked to Delilah Copperspoon, or someone else? Covens and sorcery-cults had existed as long as the Outsider had been around, for thousands of years, their numbers rising and falling, but never fading completely. They were part of a disease spread by that black-eyed bastard.

But they were a symptom of the sickness, and not the contagion itself. And they were also not his problem.

The two newcomers weren't either, although he wondered who they were. They weren't witches, certainly. Nor were they Grand Guards. Members of the Eyeless? That seemed more likely; their attire was of the highest quality, and some of the gangs Daud knew certainly prided themselves in their appearance, in some instances crafting a mocking approximation of aristocratic fashion.

But… no, these two were different. They almost seemed like they *were* aristocrats, apart from the fact that they were armed and they moved with stealth, now splitting up to cover both sides of the office, signaling to each other with hand gestures while they scanned the room.

They were agents then. Of what, Daud could only begin to guess. Part of Corvo Attano's retinue of spies? He was the Royal Spymaster as well as Royal Protector. Had he escaped the coup, like Emily? Perhaps these were his agents, investigating the strange occurrences in Karnaca and hunting down the culprits, including witches.

Including the Eyeless? Did the agents have more information on the gang than the Grand Guard?

Then Daud saw the injured witch appear *behind* the man and the woman, who seemed oblivious to her presence.

No! Daud needed to question them, find out anything they might know about the Eyeless and their hideout.

And that meant saving their lives.

Daud stood, counting his own heartbeats until the witch was directly below him, and stepped off the ledge. He transversed without thinking, rematerializing directly on top of the witch. She screamed as he drove his blade into her neck and pulled it to one side, nearly decapitating her. Thick, viscous black blood poured out of the wound, coating his heavy leather gloves. Again, lines of fire streaked along her back and shoulders as the strange marks burned away. Daud grimaced as the stench of rotten, decaying vegetation assailed his senses. He sidestepped, swinging her body in front of him as he saw the two agents spin around and raise their guns.

Multiple shots rang out and the witch's body shuddered as the bullets hit. Ammunition spent, Daud dropped the smoking body and moved toward the agents, materializing close enough to grab their gun arms and yank them down. The man yelped in surprise and with his free hand reached for another pistol holstered on his right hip—only for that arm to be suddenly grabbed and pulled away by some unknown force. Daud dived to the other side, dragging the woman with him, as her companion was flung into the air, caught in the thorned tendrils of blood briar. Looking up, Daud saw a figure standing on the left-side stairs behind the desk—the third witch, the blood briars streaming out from her outstretched arms.

The woman pushed Daud aside and stood, pulling two fresh pistols from inside her jacket. She strode forward, firing at the blood briar that held her companion as she moved, her expression one of icy determination. The tendril exploded, sending wet, rank plant material flying, but no sooner had the bullets torn the putrid flesh than it resealed itself, the shredded fibers re-weaving back into the main structure.

The witch—the third one, with the bundle? No, this was another—vanished from the stairs and reappeared within striking distance of the woman, who was completely unaware of the danger. Daud pushed himself to his feet and transversed across the space, appearing behind the witch. Sensing his presence, she spun around fast, her claws already slicing the air.

But he was faster. He ducked and, anticipating her next move, turned and moved just a few yards backward as the witch did the same. She disappeared in a puff of nothing and reappeared right in front of Daud, rematerializing *around* the blade he held out.

The witch wailed, staring down at the knife she had impaled herself on. Daud pushed the blade home, lifting the witch off her feet and shoving her back until she hit one of the bookcases that lined the office walls.

He stared into her eyes, his fingers wrapped tight around the knife's grip, until they went dull. Then he stepped back, leaving her lifeless body skewered against the wood, the witch's feet dangling inches from the floor. He staggered, exhausted, the Mark of the Outsider on fire on his hand, his muscles and mind robbed of energy.

Oh, for a vial of Piero's Spiritual Remedy.

He heard a safety catch pull back, and he turned around. The woman's twin silver guns were both pointed at his face.

Daud spread his hands. He had no energy to escape, not anymore. He focused on his breathing, began calculating the odds and planning his next move. He couldn't draw on the Mark of the Outsider for a while, but he could still fight.

The woman's face was a dark scowl. And then she reset the safety catch on both guns, and lowered them. She and Daud stared at each other for a moment, then the woman spoke.

"Daud," she said, "we've been looking for you."

He frowned. "Why?"

The woman turned, heading back to the man, who was now lying on the floor, pulling the dead, sticky mess of the blood briar off himself.

"Because we know you've been looking for the Twin-bladed Knife. And we can help you find it."

Daud's breath caught in his throat.

"But first," said the woman as she knelt by her companion and looked over her shoulder, "a little help, if you would be so kind?"

25

"And I say to you, brothers, it is here that we make our stand as a righteous force against the growing darkness. It is here that we unite against the spirits of the unknown that would drag us screaming into the night, never to return to our homes, to our families! Together we will serve as a rod to those who would stray from the herd, to the foggy gray wastes of the Outsider. We will burn a bright fire with our virtuous actions so that others will not lose their way. And to those who choose to wander, beyond the walls of our homes, in far places, we will strike at them swiftly before they whisper to their neighbors, filling their hearts with strangeness and doubt."

—LITANY ON THE WHITE CLIFF
Extract from the primary text of the
Abbey of the Everyman

Daud followed the strange couple as they led him across Karnaca, heading west through alleyways and backstreets that even he didn't know existed. The pair did not appear to be natives of the city, or even of the country, but then Daud knew you didn't need to be born in a place to learn its secrets. He had known Dunwall better than most of its inhabitants, after all.

Their destination was a long, low building in the Aventa District, the structure perched on the edge of the mountainous slopes that rose up above the city. Quite what the box-like building was, Daud could only guess—while the area was residential, there were commercial properties here too, and the building to which he was led could have been the offices of a minor shipping company, their profits spent on one of the best views of the harbor before sliding into bankruptcy, because the block was clearly abandoned, like so much of this quarter of the city.

Abandoned, but not disused. The pair of strangers stopped by the main entrance, the man's chest heaving as he fought to catch his breath, his arms wrapped around his middle—he had been hurt by the blood briar, and only now was he allowing the pain to show. The woman, meanwhile, extracted a large set of keys and began the lengthy process of unlocking the four steel bars that were placed across the main doors, each with its own, different mechanism. When she was done, she unlocked the door itself, and helped her partner inside. Daud followed.

The interior was dark, the row of windows looking out to the harbor firmly shuttered. The woman helped the man to a nearby chair, then moved over to the wall and flipped a large lever to turn on the lights.

Daud looked around, but there was nothing much to see. He was right about it being offices—the main door opened right into the middle of a kind of bullpen, with two rows of desks stretching down a central aisle, which led to a set of enclosed offices at the back. Each desk had a typewriter and a small set of shelves that were still laden with yellowing, decaying paperwork. The desk the male agent was sitting in front of was larger than the others, and as well as a typewriter, had an audiograph machine.

The woman walked back down the aisle and crouched by her companion. He winced in pain again, but nodded at her before looking up at Daud.

Daud said nothing. Not yet.

Apparently satisfied, the woman stood and gave a small bow. "Mrs. Margot Devlin, at your service. The temporarily incapacitated gentleman is my husband, Mr. Miles Devlin."

"Delighted, my dear fellow," said Mr. Devlin with a cough. He began feeling for something in the pockets of his jacket. He paused, winced, and caught his wife's eye. "Despite the odds, I suspect I will live."

Mrs. Devlin's mouth twitched into a smile. "How very convenient."

"Indeed," said Mr. Devlin. "I believe there is some axiom or other that tells about how it is more difficult than you imagine to get rid of a problem." As he spoke, he continued to gingerly search his pockets. He paused, frowning, then shook his head. "Well, needless to say, if I could remember what said axiom actually was, I would at this point insert it into the conversation and we would all laugh heartily, for together we have beaten the odds and live to fight another day, and so on, and so forth." The man waved a hand in the air, then winced again in pain. A moment later his eyes lit up. "Aha!" He pulled a pouch out from an inside pocket and extracted a tightly rolled black cigarillo with his teeth. Mrs. Devlin lit her husband's tobacco and the man took a deep drag, then handed it to his wife, who did the same.

Daud watched the pair. "Time for you to answer my questions," he said. "What do you know about the Eyeless and the Twin-bladed Knife?"

Mr. Devlin sighed. "Oh, after all that effort, how positively charmless."

Mrs. Devlin put a hand on her husband's shoulder. "Ignore Mr. Devlin. He's always like this when he's in pain." She turned and stepped toward Daud. "We have much to discuss. But perhaps that can wait, until I have tended to my husband's wounds. Suffice to say that we would like your consideration and your time. I believe we can come to a mutually beneficial agreement, if you will hear us out."

Daud drew breath to speak again, then bit his tongue, willing himself to be patient. He needed to be cautious, and not let the obsession with his mission cloud his judgement.

Mrs. Devlin gestured to the back of the room. "Please, this way," she said, heading toward the offices on the other side of the room. Daud followed her as they went past a series of doors, then through another and down a long passage. It was darker here, the bulbs weaker, their faint orange glow struggling to illuminate the space. The corridor was lined with more doors, each with a square window; most of the doors were open and led to yet more offices, some of which were interconnected to form a rabbit warren typical of such buildings in the city.

She stopped at one of the closed doors toward the end of the corridor. Here there were no windows, and in the hot, wet air, Daud could see condensation running down the wall paneling in rivulets.

Mrs. Devlin opened the door and gestured inside. "If you would please wait in here. I must attend to my husband. I shan't be long, and then we can talk."

Daud stepped into the room—another office, but far larger than the others, furnished in not insignificant luxury. There was a huge rug atop the carpet, the walls were lined with paintings, all of which showed different men in the same kind of pose, each standing beside a tall globe, the real version of which stood over on the other side of the room, next to a huge, elaborately carved desk. It was the office of the company director, perhaps, his illustrious predecessors looking down at the current incumbent as he pored over his ledgers.

The door closed behind him, and there was a click. Daud didn't bother reaching for the handle. Of course, he was locked in. It was more symbolic than practical—the strange Mrs. Devlin had seen what he was capable of. The room he was in now was just an office, not a prison cell. It would take more than a locked wooden door to hold him. The Devlins were just making a point that everything that would happen next would be on their terms.

Fair enough, thought Daud. He would do the same.

The room was lit by one fizzing light globe on the far wall, the only working survivor of a series that were spaced between the portraits. The light flickered annoyingly. With a frown, Daud went over and tapped it, then he walked to the desk. There was a table lamp there, and as he peered down into the shade he saw it was more or less intact. He fumbled around for the switch, but the lamp was a delicate thing, an antique with a stained-glass shade that wouldn't have looked out of place in the drawing room of one of the city's old mansions. Unable to activate the lamp, Daud pulled his glove off so he could feel for the switch. Once located, he turned it on. The desk lamp flared bright white, then went out with a pop, taking the wall lamp with it—but as the wall lamp went out, there was a blue flash that seemed to fill the room. Daud, temporarily blinded, screwed his eyes shut and cursed to himself. The entire building was rotting away—electrics included.

And then he realized he wasn't alone. He could sense

it, the feeling of presence like a sudden pressure on his eardrums.

She stepped out of the shadows and into the cone of light that came in through the window in the door. She was tall, dressed in a short red leather tunic with a wide round collar and heavy brown shoulder panels. Her pants were a dark brown that matched her skin, and were tucked into high boots. Her hair was shorter than he remembered, but she was wearing a scowl Daud knew all too well.

He stared at her, not sure whether to believe his own senses. There was a shard of some dark matter embedded where her right eye should have been, its center a glowing red. Her right arm was also strange—artificial, from the elbow down at least, a complex latticed framework of metal and wood and what looked almost like *stone*.

Despite her changed appearance, despite the years that had kept them apart, Daud recognized her in an instant. He exhaled, suddenly—surprisingly—relieved, like a weight had lifted from his shoulders. He shook his head in amazement.

"Billie Lurk, as I live and breathe."

Billie moved toward her former mentor, a smile appearing across her stern features. As she got closer, Daud's gaze was drawn to her artificial arm, and he saw it wasn't a mechanical prosthesis, it was something else entirely, a collection of mineral shards, the pieces sliding around each other, magically, moving fluidly like no machine could.

Then he looked up at her face, and saw that she wasn't wearing an eyepiece, the glowing red ember *was* her eye, embedded in the socket, framed with dark metals.

Daud shook his head in wonder. "What happened to you?"

Billie's smile vanished. "I'm afraid I can't tell you that

now," she said, "but I can tell you something else."

Daud frowned. "What?"

"That you, Daud, are in great danger. The mission you've undertaken has consequences you can't even imagine. So I've come back to try and fix things, before it's too late."

26

PROTECTORS' LEAGUE SAFE HOUSE, AVENTA DISTRICT, KARNACA
23rd Day, Month of Harvest, 1852

"Well, it was pure luck, but I managed to get myself passage to Morley aboard a decent ship. *The Dreadful Wale*, it's called. Is that a mistake? Shouldn't it be *The Dreadful Whale*, like the sea beast? I didn't want to risk pointing something like that out to the captain, that Foster lady. She looks like the sort to dump a disagreeable passenger overboard without a second thought."

—GOODBYE KARNACA: A MUSICIAN'S FAREWELL
Excerpt from a personal diary, author unknown

Mr. Devlin sat on the edge of the desk, his naked torso glistening with sweat. He winced as his wife tightened the bandage around his ribs and took a swig from the bottle of old King Street brandy, which had been stowed in the hideout along with a basic field-dressing kit.

"How's that?" asked Mrs. Devlin, standing back to admire her handiwork.

Mr. Devlin glanced down. "A work of art, my dear. It's always been a thing of wonder that your exquisite eye for fashion sees into the medical arts as well." He frowned. "Although I would have preferred something a little more... colorful."

Mrs. Devlin dumped the surgical shears onto the tray behind her, wiping her bloody hands with a cloth as her husband eased himself off the desk and reached for his shirt. Fortunately his wounds were limited to bruised ribs and a gash on his abdomen that had bled far more than it looked like it should have.

As he gingerly buttoned himself up, he glanced at his wife. "Do you think he believed you?"

Mrs. Devlin shrugged. "Does it matter?"

"That, my dearest Mrs. Devlin, depends very much upon your point of view," said her husband, settling himself back into the chair.

Mrs. Devlin started packing up the medical supplies. "He is driven to complete his quest for the artifact, and while we dangle the possibility of its easy recovery in front of his nose like a carrot leading a bloodox, he will be sufficiently distracted."

"That distraction, my dearest heart, will change into something rather more alarming if he begins to suspect we are lying to him."

"But even if it reaches that point, my darling husband, we shall by then be making our exit from this dreadfully moist city."

Mr. Devlin winked at his wife. "You are a sly one, my dear."

"But of course, Mr. Devlin. Have you ever known me to be otherwise? Wyman has paid half of our agreed fee already. Ample funds."

"So we send in the troops then skip out before things get sticky?"

"Precisely so. Either the men are successful and Daud

is eliminated—and our contract is completed—or Daud kills them all. And, my dear husband, I have a distinct feeling the latter possibility is all the more likely. Hence a material change in our assignment—specifically, a pressing need to survive."

Mr. Devlin eased himself into a more comfortable position in the office chair. "Hence a small army of our own employ. Poor Wyman is going to be disappointed."

Mrs. Devlin barked a laugh. "I'm sure Empress Emily will find a way to console Wyman."

"Well, if you are sure…"

"You know what your problem is, my darling heart?"

"I have the strangest feeling, my very dearest, that you are about to elucidate the matter further."

"You know me so well, Mr. Devlin."

"Indeed I have that honor, Mrs. Devlin."

"You," she said, pointing a finger at his face, "worry too much."

Mr. Devlin laughed, then pushed himself off the chair, his hand dragging the bottle of brandy off the desk with him. He swigged from it, then offered it to his wife. She looked at it and grimaced, practically recoiling in horror.

"Without ice, in this humidity? You are an animal, Mr. Devlin."

Her husband shrugged and took another sip. "You know what they say, my dear."

"No, what *do* they say, my dear?"

"When in Karnaca…" He swirled the liquid in the bottle, regarding its movement.

Mrs. Devlin suppressed a shudder. "The sooner we are away from this frightful city, the better. I will need to soak in a bath of milk and honey for a week, my dear."

"I do so hope you will have a vacancy for a back scrubber."

She smiled and took a fresh cigarillo from the pouch on the desk. As she lit it, she said, "So, are you ready?"

Mr. Devlin raised the half-empty bottle of King Street. "I believe I am."

"Very well," said Mrs. Devlin. "Time to light the blue touch paper and retire ourselves to a safe distance."

With that, the pair left the office. The main doors opened onto a small intersection, a large boulevard crossing with a smaller street. Mrs. Devlin helped her husband limp through the door, then she gave a nod.

The men loitering in the intersection peeled out of doorways and lifted themselves from stoops, twenty elite mercenaries, late of the Royal Morley Constabulary, dressed in civilian clothes, all here illegally—all employed by the Devlins themselves.

The men filed into the building as Mr. and Mrs. Devlin made a hasty departure.

27

"The greatest victories may be won with the smallest numbers."

—A BETTER WAY TO DIE
Surviving fragment of an assassin's treatise,
author unknown

"I don't understand," said Daud. "Consequences? What are you talking about? And how do you know, anyway?"

Billie held up a hand. "No questions. Not yet, anyway. First I have to get you out of danger. Then we can talk."

"Danger?"

"That couple," said Billie. "The Devlins. They didn't track you across the Isles to help you. They tracked you to *kill* you."

Daud hissed between his teeth. "I'd like to see them try," he said.

"They're not the ones you need to worry about."

Billie moved to the door. She placed her ear against it, listening.

Daud joined her, watching her every move, watching

the pulse in her neck as she strained to hear what was going on in the corridor.

How many years had it been? Fifteen? She had been his protégé among the Whalers, his most promising student, and he had handled her training himself, watching her rise rapidly through the ranks of his mercenary band of killers. In Billie, Daud had seen his successor, seeing the potential that was so tightly wound within her right from that first night, when he had allowed her to follow him back to the Whalers' hideout, offering her a choice— to die, or to join him. And even, years later, when she betrayed him to Delilah, he had spared her life, sending her into exile.

As he had been, by Corvo Attano.

Fifteen years. Daud had changed in that time. He had become someone else entirely, and deliberately. But even without that self-determined quest to escape his past, the years had softened him.

Perhaps Billie would be no different. She was older, certainly. And, physically, had changed more than he had... Daud still didn't know what her glowing red eye was, or her magical arm.

Or how she had appeared in the empty room in the first place—

"They're here," she said.

Daud broke from his reverie as Billie turned from the door, motioning him to stand back.

"Who's here?"

Billie stepped toward him. "Listen, and listen good. Once we're out of this, I'll explain everything, but right now, I need you to follow my lead." She glanced back to the door. "I've *seen* this. If this is like last time, those two out there have run to save their own necks."

Daud frowned. "Like last time? What does that mean—"

"No, Daud, you *listen* to me. Right now, there are people out there who think you are the biggest threat to the stability of the Empire and that you must be eliminated at any cost. Behind that door is a small army. They're here to kill you in order to assure the safety of Emily... of the Empress."

Daud ran his fingers through his hair as he regarded Billie. She was more poised than before, changed, but she was still Billie. He knew she was telling the truth. Questions could wait—including the question of how she knew what was going on. In the meantime—

Billie pointed to the other side of the room. "Stay here," she said. "Let me handle this. I'll get you when it's safe."

"You might have been my best," said Daud, "but I don't need you to fight for me."

"No, this time you do. Trust me. I've seen it more times than I care to remember."

Daud was perplexed but... well, despite everything, despite their past—he had faith in her. He had no idea where she had come from—but clearly Billie knew what had to be done.

She waited until Daud had backed away, then Billie nodded—perhaps more to herself than him—and opened the door, slipping out into the sickly yellow light beyond.

The corridor was empty and quiet, the only sound the soft creak of Billie's boots on the decaying floorboards and the faint buzz of the weak light. They flickered, making the shadows dance down the passageway as she stalked toward the door at the end. The air was hot and heavy and smelled of mold and earth.

She made it as far as the middle of the corridor when it happened. It was sooner than she remembered, but then every time she came back to save him—to save the world—things were different.

They came out of the doors on both sides of the passageway. Six men in total; less than half of the mercenaries, Billie knew, but the passageway was tight and combat was going to be difficult. This was merely the first wave.

They were armed with blackjacks, knives, and pistols, but in the close quarters of the narrow passage their primary tools were their fists, encased in heavy protective gloves, the knuckles studded with brass.

That was the same every time, and for that fact, Billie was grateful. Because, as big as the men were, they were no match for her.

As they moved in to crush her from all sides, Billie raised the odd artifact that had replaced her right arm, and a weapon materialized in it, coalescing out of mineral shards and metallic slivers—a knife, the grip square and heavy, the two parallel blades straight and sharp and sparking with a light from another place, another time.

The Twin-bladed Knife, but from days to come, from a time that had not yet transpired.

Billie hefted the weapon and attacked—the best defense was, of course, to go on the offense. And she was ready for them—more ready than her opponents could ever be. Because she had fought this battle before. In fact, she had almost lost count of the number of times she had seen this fight, had *fought* this fight. Every time was a little different, but the elite team stuck to their training.

This gave Billie the advantage. She knew this, and was determined not to waste the opportunity again.

Despite her experience with this very fight, she couldn't allow her concentration to falter. Each time she had come back, she had failed. Each time she had learned, she had remembered, but each time the fight had been different, and it had taken her far too long to realize that fact.

Something was interfering with time, working against her, preventing her from completing her own mission to stop Daud. Because his quest to kill the Outsider was going to ruin *everything*.

How and why things kept changing, she didn't know—maybe she was doing it herself, her repeated re-visits to this single point in time pushing at the fabric of the world, causing it to crease and ripple. So while she learned about her attackers at each encounter, learning their moves, their tactics, their decisions, their *instincts*, each and every time she returned, something was off. And each and every time, that change, however small, led to failure.

All she could do was fight, hoping that this time—*this time!*—she would succeed. That she would get Daud out, away from Karnaca, away from his quest, and that when she returned to her own time, the world would be fixed.

The men swarmed around her, their combat dance expertly synchronized. Billie ducked and weaved, parrying blows, riposting with her own. In such close quarters, the fight was little more than a brawl, bodies crushing together between the paneled walls, Billie and the men bouncing off one another as they struggled.

One man swung high; Billie ducked, spinning on her toes, slicing out with the Knife. Since the fall of the Outsider, the weapon was no longer capable of striking with the power of the Void, but it was still a masterwork of blacksmithing and a formidable blade when wielded by her expert hand. The parallel blades caught two attackers in the calf, the knife slicing through flesh and bone like it wasn't there. They screamed and collapsed—not dead, but incapacitated. Billie stood and pushed through the gap now formed in the pack, then turned, ducking left and right as armored gloves ploughed through the air toward her face.

Remembering what the man on the left would do next, Billie countered, almost too soon. He swung a fist, then swung his other arm, the blade of his dagger held tight against his forearm. Billie parried, the Twin-bladed Knife sliding off the dagger with a flash of sparks, causing her to lose her footing as her body lurched forward.

Seeing a window of opportunity, one of the other men punched her in the gut. The air left her lungs in one explosive gasp, and Billie staggered, the fingers of her mystical arm suddenly grasping at air. She watched as the Twin-bladed Knife spun down the passageway, coming to rest by the door of the big office.

No! It had happened again. No matter the differences, no matter how long or short this fight, this was the one thing that never failed to occur. And no matter how many times she came back, she seemed to be powerless to prevent it.

Billie lunged forward, throwing herself toward the Knife, but she was immediately grabbed from behind, one arm around her middle, others taking hold of her by the shoulders. She thrashed against them, but it was no use. The four men left standing were joined by others, the elite force now packing the passageway as reinforcements poured out of the adjoining offices.

The fight was over, the combatants standing, chests heaving, looking at Billie.

Then, almost as one, they turned to face the other end of the corridor. After all, Billie was not their target.

Daud was.

One of the men, perhaps the leader, stepped forward, heading toward the closed office door.

The door opened. Daud stepped out, rolling his neck, cracking his knuckles.

The group froze. Billie could sense their hesitation—it wasn't fear. These men were trained soldiers, the best Morley had to offer. They weren't afraid, but they were cautious.

The closest men charged. Billie watched as Daud bent down, scooping up the Twin-bladed Knife.

She screamed his name. Screamed her warning, as she had time and time again, not to pick up the Knife.

But it was too late. Always too late.

Daud froze, his hand on the hilt, his jaw clenched. Billie saw his eyes narrow, the sweat break out in beads on his forehead.

And then, as soon as the men were in range, Daud screamed in rage and flung himself forward, the Twin-bladed Knife flashing before him, three men cut to ribbons before they could even reach him.

Billie slumped to the floor as she was released, her captors rushing to help the others as Daud churned through his opponents. Billie could only watch as Daud moved with impossible speed, his form blurring, stretching as he transversed from target to target, the knife cutting, slashing, thrusting. Soon the wood panels of the passageway were covered in blood as Daud got closer to Billie, men and body parts falling before him.

There was something else about him. Billie, kneeling at the end of the passage, saw a blue light whenever she closed her human eye, the bright flashes almost rendering the scene in front of her in a series of still images, the raging monster that was her former mentor demolishing the men from Morley.

It happened as it always happened. There was nothing she could do about it. Maybe you couldn't change the past. And maybe it was time she realized that.

As Billie dragged herself to her feet, the last man

dropped, lifeless, to the floor. Daud moved again, crossing the remaining space between him and Billie in a second. He stood in front of her, his chest heaving, head bowed, his greased hair dropping across his forehead. In his right hand he held the Twin-bladed Knife, and Billie could see the Mark of the Outsider glowing on the skin of his left— glowing *through* the leather of his glove.

She reached out for him.

And then he fell, the Twin-bladed Knife clattering to the floorboards as his body hit the ground.

28

THE (FORMER) RESIDENCE
OF KIRIN JINDOSH,
UPPER AVENTA DISTRICT, KARNACA
24th Day, Month of Harvest, 1852

"It was late in the evening, and, may I say, a great
many cigars and rum drinks had been shared
among my fellow guests when our host, Mr.
Jindosh, took us into his private study. Fortunate
and few were we, to see the very spot where, as Mr.
Humphries was apt to put, 'the magic happens!'
Mr. Gallant, his senses perhaps dulled more than
a little while his naturally temperamental nature
had been stoked by Mr. Jindosh's fine collection
of liquors collected from every country in the
Isles, provided at least some amusement. He cast
a disparaging comment at our host, and was then
himself cast on his not insubstantial behind when
Mr. Jindosh activated a lever and Mr. Gallant
found the portion of the room in which he was
leering suddenly transformed into an altogether
small accommodation, the very walls and floor of
the place swinging into an entirely new form in a
matter of mere moments.

Mr. Jindosh may be an odd bird, but there is no

doubting that peculiar house of his is a true labor of love."

—AN ACCOUNT OF AN EVENING
WITH KIRIN JINDOSH
Extract from an aristocrat's private journal

Daud woke up on a wide couch, the red leather heavily padded and studded with buttons. The room he was in was large but dark, the only light coming from the lantern on the long, low table beside him. He glanced around, trying to remember where he was, what had happened, but nothing came to him.

Then, with a start, he remembered. The Twin-bladed Knife. Billie had it—somehow she had found it. And he had wielded it himself, and fought with it, and—

Then he remembered something else. The nausea, great rolling waves of it, clouding his mind, making the world swim around him. He remembered the feel of the Knife in his hand, the deep cold that radiated from the metal, penetrating his flesh, making every bone in his arm ache with it.

The artifact. The object of his search—of his *obsession*. It was Billie's. Somehow, the Twin-bladed Knife was hers.

Daud closed his eyes as the nausea returned. He took a breath, feeling his heart rate kick up as he both heard and felt a wheeze in his chest. He took another breath, slowly, and found it was shallower than he expected, despite the extra effort. He rubbed his chest with his hands, unsure of what was happening. His arms felt heavy.

Something was different. Something had happened to him. He felt… tired.

He felt *sick*.

As he focused on his breathing, he finally took note of

his surroundings. Where in all the Isles was he? The room was… strange. Wrecked, certainly, furniture overturned, tables and chairs and more couches on their sides, even the floor had been pulled up and—

He pushed himself up onto his elbows, then paused, surprised at the effort it took. He stared around the room. No, it wasn't wrecked, it was… well, he didn't know what it was. Part of the floor over by the wall *was* pulled up, but it sat at an angle, like it was a long, wide trapdoor, propped up by the… were those *hydraulic* pistons, underneath?

Daud looked down at the floor next to the couch. It was carpeted, the fabric covered in an ornate swirling pattern. The couch on which he lay was comfortable, extravagant. But over by the section of floor that was open, in the weak light he could see metal, and rivets, and toothed wheels running along the edge of the raised panel.

"You need to rest."

Daud started. Billie moved around from the head of the couch, into his eye line. She stood with her hands on her hips, her red eye unblinking as she looked down at him. She shook her head.

"You'll feel better soon enough, but I'm sorry, I couldn't stop it happening again."

"*What* happened?" asked Daud. "Where are we?" He looked her up and down, but she appeared to be unarmed. There was no scabbard hanging from her belt, or any other sign she was carrying a weapon. "The Twin-bladed Knife—where is it? How did you get it from the Eyeless?"

Billie pushed her tongue into her cheek, regarding Daud silently for a moment. Then she began to pace around the room. As Daud watched her, he took in more of the room—it was huge, some kind of dining room, but it was… deconstructed. The furniture was fixed to the floor, and parts of the floor were lifted at an angle.

The walls were wood paneled, but along the far one, the paneling seemed to have slipped, revealing more of the metal superstructure beyond it. The ceiling there was lower, too—a great rectangular block seemed to have come partially down. There was a gap between it and the ceiling; Daud could see the gap led to another room, more furniture and expensive decor just visible. "We're in the home of Kirin Jindosh," said Billie, looking around, ignoring his question about the Knife. "Well, former home. The owner was an inventor, loyal to the Duke of Serkonos and his coup against the Empress, but someone—" here she let her lips curl upward, one part wry, one part sad "—a friend of mine, that is, changed his fortunes. Jindosh doesn't live here anymore. Don't worry, we'll be safe."

Daud grunted in acknowledgement and tried to pull himself up off the couch, but as soon as he put weight on his left hand, he felt a deep, cold sensation—not the burning of the Mark of the Outsider, but something deeper, something that wasn't in itself pain as such, but a strange, creeping ache that immediately made him feel ill. Light-headed, he fell back and shook his head.

"What's happening to me?"

Billie came over to him and crouched by his side. "I'm sorry, Daud. It's my fault. You're sick. In fact, you're—" She stopped herself and shook her head. "It's always my fault," she said, her voice a whisper.

Daud sat up a little more, then waited for the room to stop spinning in his vision before he spoke. "Listen, I don't know what's going on," he said, "and I don't understand what you're talking about, but the Twin-bladed Knife—I need it. You have to give it to me."

Billie stood back up. "I'm sorry, I can't do that."

"Billie, you *have* to. It's important. I've been looking for it."

"I know," said Billie. "And I know what you plan to do with it. But I can't give it to you. It's not time. It doesn't belong here, and neither do I."

"What are you talking about?"

Billie sighed. "I mean I don't belong here. I've come back, to try and fix everything, but it doesn't work. I've tried and tried, but it always ends this way. No matter what I do."

"Come back from where?"

"From the future—your future, anyway. About three years from now, give or take. Things aren't good where I'm from, so I've come back to try and fix it. Except it doesn't look like I can."

Billie paused, her eye—her human eye—locked onto Daud's. He stared at her, then flicked his gaze to the glowing red ember embedded in her right socket.

Finally, he spoke. "Is this something to do with the Outsider? Did he do this to you? Did he mark you, allow you to travel into the past somehow?"

Billie frowned. "You know I can't tell you."

"What does it matter? If nothing works, why not tell me everything? Do I succeed? Do I kill the Outsider?"

Billie said nothing. Daud sighed and sat back on the couch, one arm wrapped around his middle. It hurt to breathe, although it at least felt like he could get a proper lungful now. He still felt tired, more than he ever thought possible, but his head was clearing. Billie watched him, apparently content to keep her secrets, grateful perhaps that he wasn't asking any more questions.

He had plenty, of course. But he believed her story. She was Billie Lurk. She had no reason to lie to him. Where the Outsider was concerned, anything was possible. She certainly looked older, and as for the eye, and the arm...

He closed his eyes and thought back to the fight in

the abandoned office. He remembered opening the door, seeing the Twin-bladed Knife on the floor, right by his boot. He remembered bending down, picking it up.

And he remembered the cold, and the pain.

He opened his eyes.

"It was the Knife, wasn't it?"

Billie tilted her head.

"You said I'm sick," said Daud. "But it's worse than that, isn't it? I can feel it." Billie frowned at that and Daud chuckled. "I'm dying, aren't I? It was the Knife. It did something to me when I picked it up."

Billie paused, then nodded.

"All this time," said Daud, "I've been looking for the Twin-bladed Knife, and even if I'd found it, I couldn't have wielded it." Billie watched him in silence. "I know," he said. "You can't tell me anything. You're from my future." He paused, narrowing his eyes. "You came to help me, only you've killed me, haven't you? Because if you hadn't come back with the Knife, I would never have touched it." Daud laughed again, louder this time.

"I'm sorry," said Billie. "It's my fault and I can't fix it. When I came back the first time, it crystalized this moment, making it part of history. Now, no matter what I do, no matter how many times I try, I can't change it. I can't."

The pair locked eyes, then Billie looked away. Finally, Daud spoke. "I guess I'm going to have to get someone to help me with the mission. Someone I would trust with my life—or what there is left of it."

Billie stood. "I wish I could show you the future," she said. "I wish I could show you what happens. But I've tried that too." She sighed. "Nothing can change what is happening—what will happen. Nothing. I'm sorry for what comes next, but don't worry. We will meet again, very soon. Trust me."

Daud nodded. "I do trust you. And you can trust me. I won't say anything."

The cold ache continued to spread up his arm. He lifted his hand and flexed the fingers. The bones of his hand felt like dry twigs. Something was broken. Wincing with effort, he propped himself up again and he carefully pulled his heavy glove off with his other hand. Then he turned his naked hand over, rolling his knuckles as he examined his skin.

The Mark of the Outsider was there, the familiar dull black symbol. But that wasn't the only mark. His skin was covered with a tracery of black lines, as though his veins were filled with ink. He turned his hand over, the fingers of his other hand running over the marks as he traced them up his wrist. He pulled back his sleeve as far as it would go. The marks went up his arm. It looked like the skeletal structure of a leaf tattooed into his flesh.

Billie pulled at the pouch on her belt. She extracted a vial of light-blue liquid and handed it to Daud. "Here."

Daud took it from her and examined the vial. "Piero's?"

"Addermire Solution. Does the same. More, even. Take it, and rest. No one will disturb you here for a while. Your strength will return, in time."

"But not completely."

Billie looked at the floor.

"Where will you go now?" asked Daud. "Back to your own time?"

She looked up and nodded. "I have a lot of work to do," she said, then she turned around and moved to the center of the room.

A blue light appeared, small at first, then growing larger, until a swirling elliptical vortex formed in the room. Daud could only stare as Billie looked over her shoulder at him, then turned and stepped into the vortex.

And then she was gone, and the room was dark, and Daud was alone.

Alone… and sick. It was a strange feeling—the Mark of the Outsider granted him a supernatural constitution, sparing him illness. This new feeling was disconcerting. Alarming.

Feeling the panic build, he screwed his eyes shut and concentrated to center himself.

Then he opened his eyes, twisted the cap off the vial of Addermire Solution, and drained it in a single draft. It tasted sweet and clean, and he felt his mind clear and the strange, cold creep along his arm fade.

He lay back on the couch and let his fatigue claim him. Before he closed his eyes, he felt inside his tunic and pulled out the black mirror shard. He held it in front of his face, and looked at his own reflection in the lantern light. He looked old and tired. As he tilted the mirror, he thought he saw a light, orange and red, and heard the roar of a fire, echoing down the ages.

And then he was asleep.

29

"Spending two years in the company of heretics, the insane, and those rare, black-hearted villains who were truly practitioners of magic, I can say with truth that I have seen such things as to break the minds of most. While the trials and burnings weigh heavily upon my heart, I must chronicle what has been a unique opportunity to witness the multifarious perversions that the Outsider bestows upon those who seek his black council."

—THE GREAT TRIALS
Excerpt from an Overseer's findings,
by High Overseer Tynan Wallace

"Is it ready?"

The witch's servant turned to his mistress, Lucinda, and bowed low to the ground, his ragged black cloak pooling out around him. Still bent over, he looked up into her face. He hesitated, afraid perhaps that he had somehow displeased her. He wrung his hands and nodded vigorously.

"All is prepared, my lady," he said. Almost crawling on the ground, he turned around and pointed toward the mansion that clung to the edge of the mountain on the other side of the chasm. "Daud sleeps in the old house. We have but to wake him and the trap is set."

Lucinda cocked her head, looking at the mansion. The sun was rising, the sky above bruised purple and orange.

A new day. A new beginning.

"I hope it was worth it," said Caitlin. She was leaning against a low white wall, her arms folded. She stared at her feet, not willing to meet Lucinda's gaze.

Lucinda padded over to her, then reached down and lifted her head with a finger. Caitlin tried to keep her eyes away from her sister's, but then she looked up.

"I regret their deaths as much as you do," said Lucinda.

Caitlin's lips were pressed firmly together. Lucinda knew the pain she felt—they'd lost two of their number at the Royal Conservatory, a substantial loss considering the coven had scattered after the capture of Breanna Ashworth. Caitlin had fled—Lucinda knew her sister felt guilt over that, but it had been a wise decision. Because yes, it had been worth it. Caitlin had found and recovered some of the lenses of the Oraculum, the Void-touched machine crafted by Breanna, working alongside none other than Kirin Jindosh.

And two fewer witches actually made things easier. With each hour, Lucinda could feel the power slipping away from her. Sharing what little remained among the others was a serious drain, but now she felt she could hold onto the power just a little longer. The lines of ink across her body—more of Breanna's work—burned and pulsed.

She would need to. The trap would require every last scintilla of power she could summon.

But she didn't say that to Caitlin. She had not only lost two friends, but a lover, too. Killed by the man who was sleeping so close.

She pointed at the mansion. "But we will have our revenge, believe me. When Daud wakes, he will be ours. It is only a matter of time."

Caitlin stared up at Lucinda, and then she smiled. She glanced at the prostrate form of Lucinda's familiar, the twisted little man nothing more than a bundle of rags on the ground.

"What about the final part?"

Lucinda turned to follow her sister's gaze. Then she moved over to her servant. She reached down to the cowering man—he looked up at her and jumped back, startled... and then, slowly, he reached out with his emaciated arm, the look on his face a mix of surprise and rapture.

Lucinda pulled him up, stepping close, so close her body pressed against his.

"Challis, you have served me well."

"Yes, mistress."

"You have done all I have asked of you."

"Yes, mistress."

"Without question."

"Yes, mistress."

"Then hear me, Challis. I have but one final task for you."

"Anything, mistress! Anything at all."

Lucinda looked down at him. Caitlin joined her side.

"I was hoping you would say that," said Lucinda. She lifted her hands, her nails growing into long, curved claws as Caitlin did the same.

Challis's dying scream echoed across the chasm and bounced off the towering walls of Kirin Jindosh's mansion, before fading out over the city in the early morning.

30

THE VOID
Time immaterial

"You ask what the Void looks and feels like, if it can be measured like a real place. Here's my answer: Don't concern yourself with such matters. It is as real as anything I've ever experienced, but if you understood it, you'd know that such a statement makes as little sense as saying that I have been dead.

The Void is unspeakable. It is infinite and it is nowhere, ever-changing and perpetual. There are more things in the endless black Void, Kirin Jindosh, than are dreamt of in your natural philosophy.

Leave aside things beyond your reach, and be content that you are gifted with more insight than the common man."

—LETTER FROM DELILAH TO KIRIN JINDOSH
Surviving fragment, date unknown

Stone, and ash, and the cold dark.

Daud looks around. He smells rust and corrosion. He tastes metal and the sharp sour tang of electricity.

He is standing on rock, gray and dark and ancient. Gray clouds swirl above in an infinite nothing that surrounds him, surrounds everything. This nowhere, this no place.

This Void.

"Tell me, Daud, is this really how you thought it would be? Is this how you thought your story would end?"

Daud turns and looks at him, the young man, his hair dark and short, his eyes small and black. The young man stands with his arms folded, his back to a rising glow, like an early morning sunrise. Except in the Void there is no sun, there is no morning, and the light is cold and bright and blue.

The Outsider watches Daud, his expression unreadable, as he paces, circling Daud like a painter circling his easel.

Daud stands, watching. He says nothing.

"You think you are alone, Daud? You think you are the only one who is in pain? Running from a past you cannot forget, the memory of evil deeds a fire inside your mind—a fire that, no matter how hard you try, you cannot extinguish, not fully. The embers will always be with you, burning in the eternal night of your being."

Daud clenches his fists. He begins to walk, turning a circle, following the Outsider, keeping pace.

"I have watched the world for four thousand years," the Outsider says. "Can you even imagine that length of time? If you could, it would drive you from your senses."

Daud lifts his chin and speaks. "Is that why you do it, then?"

The Outsider stops walking and stares at Daud, his arms tight around his body, his black eyes reflecting an orange light from long ago. He cocks his head.

"Perhaps I have underestimated you."

Daud takes a step closer to the monster, to the source of so much turmoil, so many sadistic acts. But then the stones of the Void move, the architecture of the nothingness shifting, and the Outsider stands farther away, on a slab of rock that floats in the blue-black expanse.

"You call yourself the Outsider," Daud says, "but that's not the truth, is it? You don't observe. You meddle."

Daud holds up his hand, presenting the back to the Outsider. On his skin, the Mark flashes blue and white.

Daud thinks he sees the Outsider flinch, but he is not certain.

"How many have there been? How many have you branded with your mark? How many have become your tools—your *property*? How many have done your work for you, interfering with the world for your entertainment? How many have lived and died for you?"

"You still do not understand."

Daud takes another step forward. His hand is still raised.

"What's it all for? Tell me that much. What do you want—what do you *really* want?"

The Outsider cocks his head once more, and then he is there, in front of Daud, just an arm's reach away.

"You know, you were always one of my favorites," he says, and he begins his pacing again. "You're right. There have been many—so many names, so many lives. But lives that are so brief, fluttering out like a dying flame even before you realize how very short the time you have is."

He turns and steps toward Daud, who feels the Outsider's black eyes boring into his own.

"But you, Daud. You were different. I thought maybe you were the one. But perhaps I was wrong. Doubtful, but possible. In four millennia anything is possible, I suppose."

Daud grinds his teeth. He pulls in air through his nose—impossible air in this impossible place. He feels the Mark glow on his skin.

The Outsider's eyes flash, his expression flickers again.

This time Daud is sure of it.

The Outsider is afraid.

Afraid of him.

"You weren't wrong," says Daud, and now the Outsider frowns, and he moves, as though to take a step back before reconsidering and holding his ground.

"I'm the one," Daud says. "The one who's going to kill you. Of that, I'm certain."

The Outsider turns back to Daud.

"Daud, the Knife of Dunwall, one of the greatest assassins of his age. It is true that I will die, but it will not be by your hand."

Daud rolls his neck.

"We'll see about that."

He leaps forward, arms outstretched, a growl emerging from deep in his chest.

The Outsider shrinks back, stumbles.

Daud falls.

He sees a light.

A blue light, shining, bright, as bright as the rising sun, as bright as—

Daud hit the floor with a heavy thud, waking him. He opened his eyes, blinking into the light of the lantern next to him, then rolled onto his side, bumping into the side of the red leather couch.

A dream. It was just a dream, nothing more.

He rolled again, his hand scrabbling for purchase as he pulled himself upright. The windows of the weird house were dark—night had fallen again.

How long have I been asleep?

Daud rubbed the back of his neck with his right hand. It felt stiff, but not sore—looking at it, the tracery of black lines was still there, but fainter. He was feeling better, too. Tired, certainly, but definitely better.

Turning on the floor, he noticed something flash on the couch—the black mirror shard. From the angle on the floor, the shard should have been reflecting the strange, segmented ceiling of the room, but all Daud could see were gray clouds scudding across a dark expanse of nothingness.

He looked up, but the ceiling was there, intact. Looking back in the mirror, the image—the image of the Void— had gone. The mirror was just a mirror once more.

Daud pulled himself up on the couch and sank back into the soft leather.

He closed his eyes.

He slept.

When Daud woke again it was still dark. Was it the same night? He had no way of telling.

Daud swung his feet to the floor, then pushed himself up. He stood for a moment, getting a sense of his condition, judging his current state of being. He felt stiff, but there was no pain or discomfort. Just a nagging tiredness—nothing much, but enough to remind him that he was now marked in a different way.

Marked for death. How long he had, he didn't know. He only hoped it was long enough.

He lifted his hand again and stared at the Mark of the Outsider. He flexed his fingers and pulled on the power of the Void, just a little. Immediately the Mark grew warm, but… it felt different. He was still marked, and the Outsider's brand allowed him to draw power from the Void, but it was, well, harder. It took more effort, and as Daud concentrated, closing his eyes, it almost felt like the power was erratic, less controllable, like his connection to the Void was slipping away.

Daud opened his eyes. He looked at his hand again, then shook his head and picked up his discarded glove and pulled it back on.

Time to leave.

The room Billie had brought him to wasn't the only one with strange angled panels; as he explored the building, searching for an exit, it felt like he was moving more through the inside of a machine than a house. Some doors led to other rooms and hallways. Others led to dead ends that were nothing but steel boxes, and in other rooms the floors were uneven, the panels stuck at odd angles, revealing more mechanisms beneath.

The whole interior of the house was clearly designed to *move*, to be reconfigured. Why, Daud didn't know, and he cared even less, but certainly the bizarre clockwork mansion of Kirin Jindosh was like nothing he had ever seen before.

He moved on, his route to the main doors—or at least the *direction* of the main doors, going by what he could see out the windows—circuitous, thanks to the jammed machinery of the building blocking his way. As he walked, he noted the levers that were scattered all around the place, but he didn't want to start toying with them, even if there was still power to shift the architecture. Without knowing what he was doing, there was more than a fair chance he would just trap himself—if he wasn't crushed in the process.

That was when he heard it—a loud clicking. Daud knew the sound—most recently from his time aboard the whaling ship that had brought him here. It was the sound of a gear wheel, the teeth spinning through a lever. And it sounded like it was coming from behind him—

He turned and jumped through a doorway, just as the floor beneath him dropped away by more than a foot before lifting back up and rotating, the entire base of the room turning on a huge axle. Daud watched as the walls opened out and the ceiling lifted, the gaps in the structure exposing gears and motors as the room was rearranged.

There was a clank. Daud saw one of the levers on the far side of the room flip, apparently by itself.

Another clank—this time from in front of him. Daud turned, looking down the corridor. At the end, the open door led through to another large room, and in the middle of that room—in line with the open door—was another lever. It moved again, entirely of its own accord, and the room ahead began to reconfigure.

The corridor in which he was standing began to disappear, the walls on either side lifting an inch and then sliding together. In just a few seconds, Daud would be crushed.

Ahead, the door was still open, but a steel panel was sliding up as the next room was lifted into the air. Glancing over his shoulder, Daud saw the room he had just left had gone, the corridor now a dead end.

As the walls of the corridor brushed Daud's shoulders, he turned and sprinted for the rapidly closing gap at the top of the rising steel panel. He reached out and transversed forward, willing himself to slide through the gap even as he moved so he wasn't cut in two.

He made it, skidding across the floor of the next room, the heavy rug piling up in front of him as his body pushed against it.

The clanking stopped, and the house was silent.

Daud looked around. He was in a library, the room devoid of furniture but lined with bookcases, the shelves tightly packed with leather-bound volumes. The Mark of the Outsider burned on his hand, but he had managed to draw on its power well enough, even if it felt harder to do. Taking a breath, he stood up.

The floor dropped away, turning on a pivot. Daud cried out in surprise and found himself falling. Below him was a steel chamber, the walls lined with geared mechanisms—and directly underneath, a large motor with spinning flywheels.

Daud transversed downwards, angling himself to land beside the motor, out of the way of the rotating wheels. He hit the floor with a thud, the energy of the impact surprising him. He pushed himself up, shaking his head.

The room moved again. Daud spun around, saw a larger control panel—the controls on it moving of their own accord—and made for it, only for the wall to which it was attached to shoot upwards as the reconfiguration continued.

Here, somewhere in the heart of the machine-house, Daud could see into multiple levels and rooms as everything moved around him, the entire house changing shape. If he was going to get out, he had to move quickly.

Looking up, he judged a gap between two rooms as their walls swung away from each other. He reached forward and transversed, finding himself in another wood-paneled chamber. But again, as with the steel box below, he slammed into the wall, the force of the impact knocking him off his feet.

The room shifted, pulling apart at the seams. Daud turned, picked his spot and moved again.

And found himself in a dead end.

He turned. The wall behind him was moving away, exposing another gap in the structure on the left.

He focused. He transversed—but the wall moved *toward* him, as though his power had tethered it and was pulling it in.

The wall hit him, knocking him back. He fell against the panel behind him.

He turned. Another gap, another chance.

He transversed.

And he cracked his nose against the wood, his power once again not having moved him anywhere, but brought the wall *to* him.

It was impossible. That wasn't how his powers worked, he knew that. Maybe it was something to do with his sickness, his connection to the Void unpredictable and slipping out of his control.

He thought back to his dream. Was the Outsider watching him? Playing with him? Turning the Mark on his hand against him?

The walls closed in. Daud spun on his heel as the light faded. There was nothing around him but wood and steel.

He yelled in anger, his voice deafening in the tiny box that continued to shrink. He curled in on himself, the walls pressing ever closer.

He was trapped.

31

"The most elegant approach to warfare is to never fight at all. If you can subdue the enemy without a single strike, then you shall know the purity of victory."

—A BETTER WAY TO DIE
Surviving fragment of an assassin's treatise,
author unknown

Daud stood at the top of the sweeping flight of shallow stairs that led up to the grand entrance of Kirin Jindosh's hillside mansion. The door behind him was open.

He stood with his back as straight as a rod, his arms stretched out at his sides. He shuddered, like he was touching the live terminal of a whale oil battery. His chin was up, his eyes open, staring into the milky-blue haze that connected him to the dead man standing in front of him.

Challis's body mirrored Daud's, his back straighter

than it had been in years, his skeletal arms rigid as they poked out from his tattered cloak. His body, like Daud's, shook, trembling with arcane energy as it poured between them. His face was missing from forehead to chin—in its place was an oval of blueish glass, an Oraculum lens, jammed into his skull, the bottom wedged against the witch servant's broken jaw, the top scooped under the flap of scalp that remained on the dead man's head.

Smoke-like tendrils of energy coursed from the Oraculum lens, pouring into Daud's staring eyes.

Caitlin peered as close as she dared at Daud. She almost wanted to reach out and poke him with a finger, to see if he would just fall over. He probably would—but she didn't want to interrupt the spell. To be able to mesmerize a victim like this, holding them as though in a clenched fist… this was a rare spell indeed for a witch.

Lucinda stepped out from behind Challis, joining her sister.

"It worked!" said Caitlin. "The trap worked!" She paused, one finger pulling playfully on her lower lip. "I wonder where he thinks he is?"

Lucinda looked into Daud's face, her already bleached skin looking almost translucent in the blue glow of power. The morning air was warming, but already she was soaked with sweat. It ran out of her hair, down her face, dripping from her fingers.

"Inside the house," said Lucinda. "Forever running, trying to free himself as the walls close in around him. The ultimate nightmare."

Caitlin clapped and danced on her toes. "But it worked! We have him! We have him!"

Lucinda nodded, a smile breaking across her tired features, the effort to sustain the unusual witchcraft—a mix of true magic and natural philosophy, the last remnants of power inherited from her mistress, Breanna Ashworth, channeled through the Oraculum lens and the dead mind of her servant, Challis—now showing.

"We have him," said Lucinda. "Daud is finally ours."

EPILOGUE

The world turns, and the Outsider watches, and waits.

The Outsider is patient.

But a change is coming. The Outsider knows it—he has seen it. And he is ready for it.

So the world turns, and the Outsider waits, and he watches.

He sees:

In Karnaca, the Duke fell and in his place rose up a man of the people. Paolo had come into the world with nothing and knew the lives of the least privileged.

Sometimes power shouts, and sometimes it whispers.

He sees:

In Dunwall, without ever realizing it, Delilah passed into an imagined world where her father's promises were fulfilled and her subjects would love her forever, as she sailed the ocean with a great fleet and trekked across the Pandyssian wastes.

While in the true capital, Emily the Just—Emily the

Clever—ruled for decades over a prosperous, mended empire with Corvo Attano by her side.

He sees:

In his day, Anton Sokolov fired the engines of industry, hurtling the Empire into a more sophisticated age. He dallied with nobles, wayward artists, and great inventors alike, drinking in all that life could offer. Leaving Dunwall for the last time, he headed to the cold north, contented at last, on a final voyage to take him home…

He sees:

Her.

There are things that never change, no matter how hard you try, questions you must answer. As Meagan Foster faded from the world, Billie Lurk stepped from her shadow, setting out to discover her truest self, and seeking the closest thing she'd ever known to family.

The world turns and the Outsider watches.

And he waits.

And he is ready for what is to come.

"My lords and ladies, gentlemen and scoundrels alike!"

The chamber is large and rectangular, the ceiling high, the walls covered in acres of patterned tiles now stained and cracked, if they have even remained on the walls at all. The floor is tiled too, as though the whole chamber was designed to be wet. The hard surfaces reflect the voice of the fight announcer loudly as he paces the boxing ring, arms raised as he addresses those assembled. The crowd is sparse, but they are all here for a singular purpose.

They are all here to fight.

"You know the rules. You are here of your own free will. The choice you make is yours and yours alone. Don't go crying to Jeanette if things don't go how you want them."

Some of the assembled snicker. Others remain silent, focused on loosening their muscles, adjusting the bandage wraps around their fists.

The ring in which the announcer stands is a makeshift thing, a high stage of wood built over the back half of the deep rectangular depression that otherwise dominates the chamber—an old swimming pool, the sides stained, the top covered with a heavy mesh grille. The fight announcer walks to the edge of the boxing ring and looks down at the man strapped to the chair that is bolted to the bottom of the empty pool.

The man is motionless, his head slumped forward on his chest. On the walls around the chair are fastened mechanical devices that hum and spit and the air around the man shimmers and cracks with power.

The announcer grins. Leaning on the ropes, he signals to the other end of the chamber. By the edge of the pool is a stand and on the stand is a box. Cables drop off the back of the box and fall down into the pool, spidering across the cracked walls to the arcane devices.

There is a woman by the box. Like the others in the chamber, her hair is short, her skin is scarred, and below her collarbone she displays a tattoo—a hollow triangle and a cross, the brand like an arrowhead on her flesh.

Like the others in the chamber, she is a member of the Eyeless.

At the announcer's signal, the woman pulls a key from her belt. She unlocks the front panel of the control box, swings it open, then pulls down on the lever within. Immediately the hum of power ceases, and the yellowish sparking from the empty pool dies away.

The assembled brace themselves, backing away from the mesh, as the man in the chair snaps his head up, casting his gaze around them.

The announcer gestures to the cage.

"Is there anyone here tonight brave enough to fight the Black Magic Brute?"

The man in the pool rises from his chair. He snarls and flexes his muscles, the tendons in his neck sticking out like cables as he balls his fists.

As the announcer repeats the challenge again, Daud grinds his teeth and stares up at the gang.

Another night at the underground boxing ring, another night where he must fight for his life.

Daud lets the anger grow inside him, fueling him. He

will survive. He knows it. He must survive.

Because he still has a mission to accomplish.

The Outsider must die.

The Outsider *will* die.

And then the first fight begins.

ABOUT THE AUTHOR

Adam Christopher is a novelist, comic book writer, and award-winning editor. The author of *Seven Wonders*, *The Age Atomic*, and *Hang Wire*, and co-writer of *The Shield* for Dark Circle Comics, Adam has also written novels based on the hit CBS television show *Elementary* for Titan Books. His debut novel, *Empire State*, was *SciFiNow*'s Book of the Year and a *Financial Times* Book of the Year for 2012. Born in New Zealand, Adam has lived in Great Britain since 2006.

Find him online at www.adamchristopher.ac and on Twitter as @ghostfinder.

For more fantastic fiction, author events,
competitions, limited editions and more

VISIT OUR WEBSITE
titanbooks.com

LIKE US ON FACEBOOK
facebook.com/titanbooks

FOLLOW US ON TWITTER
@TitanBooks

EMAIL US
readerfeedback@titanemail.com